Determined

A Second Chance Romantic Suspense

Marsha R West

Published by MRW Press LLC, 2024.

COPYRIGHT

Table of Contents

Dedication

I attend Ridglea Presbyterian Church where we have a Matthew 25 Action Team, a group of folks who try to live out the meaning of Jesus' words in that scripture. "As you do it unto the least of these, you do it unto me." We've studied issues around poverty and racism. Part of that study included learning about homelessness from various agencies in Fort Worth. There is the overarching Homeless Coalition which is home to lots of organizations including The Presbyterian Night Shelter and DRC and which provide housing for the recently homeless. In recent years, there has been a movement to house people first before insisting they get training or find a job or get off drugs. Those are all hard to do, especially if you don't have an address. The people I've met at Quail Trail, one of the new communities, are just folks like everyone else. They've fallen on hard times, but they could be any of us. Of course, Determined is just a work of fiction, but I hope it will encourage others to get involved in helping the less fortunate.

I dedicate this book to all those who work to improve the lives of the homeless wherever they are, helping their clients become rehomed.

Marsha

Chapter One

On a beautiful Tuesday, the first of March, Holly Grant pulled to the side of the road and put on her hazard lights to safely check the map on her phone. Whizzing down the Chisolm Trail Parkway, she'd zoned out on her way to her destination, a piece of property in southwest Fort Worth she wanted to buy. She didn't remember driving this far the last time she checked out the property. A quick glance at her map assured her of what she feared. She'd missed the turnoff. Good grief. Hard to believe she'd done this for the second time. She should've just braved the traffic on Bryant Irvin. Okay, she'd keep going forward and take the next exit and head back. What a pain.

Carefully, she eased back into the traffic and exited as soon as she could, traveling on the bridge across the highway and going in the opposite direction. A glance at her phone in the holder showed her the next turn to make. When she reached Bryant Irvin, she turned and traveled south. New homes were going up on the right and left. Amazing how many people kept moving into the Fort Worth area.

Her heart took a leap when she spotted the for-sale sign on the west side of the road proclaiming her destination. After pulling off the road, she shut off the ignition, got out, closed, and locked the door. She wore tailored khaki pants, a light blue blouse, and comfortable, closed-toe walking shoes because she never knew what property she might need to look at in her development business. To get a closer look, she wandered over the property she'd had her eye on for several years. The property had many large oak trees surrounding a small pond in the far back center of the property with an open meadow in the front. Lots of nature right here in the middle of town. Well, the south end of town.

This would make a great place for the tiny house development for people who were coming out of homelessness. The hospitals in southwest Fort Worth weren't far, and the residents, after a short walk to catch the bus, could reach a large shopping center. The location being on the bus route had been important in the selection process. A nice housing development not unlike her own with a white brick wall stood across the road from the property. Perhaps those who lived in that development would like to volunteer at the tiny home community.

Several people and groups had tried to purchase the land, but the sale ultimately fell through, or once they purchased the property, the new owners became dissatisfied and let it go. Recently, this property had re-entered the market. Holly needed to talk with her sisters again. They had discussed various options for the trust fund their parents had set up for them, and after research, they'd decided a tiny home community for people coming out of homelessness would be perfect. This piece of property would work well for the community. Using her phone, she snapped a few pictures and sent them to her sisters with the question: *Are you still interested? Can you spare thirty minutes for a meeting?*

Quickly Lee responded: *YES! I'm already putting ideas together for decorating the houses. Where?*

Then Kay: *LOL. And I started tinkering with ideas for a sign for the front gate. Guess we're definitely in, Holly.*

Holly: *Great. Meet at my place in an hour?*

Both sisters sent smiley faces. Holly's heart warmed at how lucky she was to have Lee and Kay as sisters. Their parents expected Lee who was fifty-seven and the oldest, to be a boy, and her parents planned to name him Leland, their mother's maiden name. When she turned out to be a she, they decided to stick with the name and to call her Lee.

Kay, the baby at fifty, had shortened her name from the longer Kaitland. And of course, Holly, who had just turned fifty-five, had insisted as soon as she began school to use Holly instead of Hollister, another family name. Family had been important to their parents, and the sisters tried to carry on that tradition.

Holly climbed back into her car and steered north toward her condo located off Camp Bowie Blvd. The Oaks, as the complex was called, brimmed with live oaks and red oaks, small ponds, springs, and plenty of greenery. Two large cottonwoods stood by one of the ponds. While the cotton puffs they shed were something of a pain, Holly loved the sound the wind made rustling the leaves, almost like rain. The area was a surprising joy in the middle of town, not unlike what she and her sibs wanted to create for those who were less fortunate.

The drive home took a short fifteen minutes. Holly activated the security gate and drove into the compound as she considered where she'd chosen to live. Approximately twenty mostly stucco houses with red tile roofs spread out about the green spaces. A sidewalk wound through the grounds with small bridges spanning the water features. Some of them were wide enough for benches so people could sit and enjoy the outdoors. Her home was toward the rear and backed up to the golf course that ran along behind the entire complex. Besides the stucco, her house had stone accents and a stone chimney. At just under two thousand square feet, her home fell into the group of smaller homes in the complex.

She used the keyless lock to enter her three-bedroom house with its open concept. Lee and Kay would arrive soon, and they'd probably want to sit out on the patio to enjoy the spring day. Bright blue skies, a few white puffy clouds, a soft breeze, and the scent of flowers made a person want to stay outside to enjoy nature. Before long, the heat of a dreaded Texas summer, not Holly's favorite season, would set in. The gated community suited her. The walls and gates didn't guarantee safety because if bad people wanted to get you, they could. She'd learned that the hard way. But she wouldn't let those people keep her from living the life she chose. And today she chose to sit on the patio with her sisters.

Holly poured tall glasses of iced tea, set out the sugar and lemons on a turquoise tray, and carried everything out to the patio. She set the tray in the middle of the wrought-iron table. She was returning to the kitchen for napkins, cheese, crackers, and grapes as the door opened and her tall, slender older sister Lee entered followed by shorter and youngest sister Kay. Shortly after moving into The Oaks, Holly had given both sisters the code to get in the gate and into her home. That action made coming and going more convenient for everyone.

They exchanged hugs, which they always did regardless of how recently they'd seen each other. "Come on out to the patio. I've got us set up there."

"Ahhhh. I never get over how lovely your place is, Holly. And the season doesn't even matter. The peacefulness and serenity with the trees and the trickling sounds from the little stream feed my spirit." Lee settled into one of the chairs with turquoise and hot pink flowers scattered across the covers and stretched out her long legs encased in designer jeans. Her interior decorator business kept her busy running here and there. Things were less hectic now that her son and daughter had graduated college, and both had solid careers. Brad had moved to Dallas where he worked at a law firm, and Leeann, while she'd gone into her mom's business of interior design, couldn't leave Austin after college. The town affected people like that. Austin got into young people's blood, and they never wanted to leave.

"This view topped my list of reasons for buying this property."

"And I imagine the security, too." Kay took the chair on the other side of Holly. She was the real artist of the sisters, painting beautiful landscapes that she sold out of an art studio in downtown Fort Worth. She worked on her creations in a special room in her house with plenty of northern light. Her daughter, Sarah, attended Texas Christian University and studied art with an eye to following in her mother's footsteps. Kay's artistic nature bloomed in her clothes as you'd most often catch her in colorful and flowy skirts and blouses except when she had a paintbrush in her hand. Then you'd find her in jeans and a brightly colored t-shirt covered by a large apron.

Holly chose to ignore Kay's comment about security, though that had also been a reason for her selection of the home. She didn't want to be reminded of the business with her ex-husband. She shoved those memories behind her.

"Okay, girls. If we're going through with this, we need to move quickly. It's been on the market several times, and before I could jump in and get it, someone else has always stepped in and snagged the property."

"And those deals have fallen through? What's with that?" Lee added two spoons of sugar to her tea and squeezed a slice of lemon into the glass. Holly didn't understand how her sister could be so thin and eat so much, especially sweets. My goodness. They used to have to hide the Girl Scout cookies from her when the sisters sold those luscious morsels. But she'd gotten some of her father's height and stood five six. Kay only reached five two like their mother. While Holly, the middle daughter fell in the middle height range at five four.

"Did you ever find out why that was? Weren't you planning to check on that?" Kay ate a bite of cheese and crackers. Her eyes closed and she sighed. "Thanks, sis. I needed this pick-me-up. Missed lunch today."

"So, you've started a new painting?" Holly knew when Kay got going, she forgot to eat.

Kay nodded and finished the cheese and cracker and reached for more, adding several ripe green grapes to her plate.

"Good for you. You were having trouble figuring out what to do next." Holly nodded at Lee. "But we had faith. We knew you'd do it. And to answer your question, Kay, I did check around. Seems like whenever someone buys the land, odd stuff happens to the purchasers or when they got to the point where they had workers on the property, lots of unexplained accidents happened. Stories flew around like they will. The word *haunted*"—Holly finger quoted—"was bandied around. You know, crazy stuff."

"And that's why the property is back on the market again?"

Holly nodded.

The ice cubes rattled in Lee's glass as she lifted it to take a sip. "Mmm. Nothing beats your iced tea in the afternoon. Refreshing."

"Glad you like the tea. What's your decision? Are you still in?"

Lee's gaze slid to Kay's and back to Holly. "I ain't afraid of no ghosts!" She rose and held out her hand.

Holly glanced at Kay, who burst out laughing. "Boy, isn't that a blast from the past." She rose and put her hand on top of her sister's. "Yes, let's do this. It's an important issue, and we would make mom and dad proud of us."

Holly rose and plopped her hand on top of her sisters', and then they pumped the air. "We're doing this."

They settled back in their chairs. "Have you thought of a name for the project?" Lee asked.

"I haven't settled on anything because y'all need to have your say. But I wondered if we could come up with something with *Grant* in the name?"

"Because we're using money from the endowment mom and dad set up?" Kay popped two more grapes in her mouth.

"I like that," Lee nodded. "Grant Park or Grant Meadows?"

"I like the alliteration of Grant Gardens," Kay offered.

"Oh yes, I love Grant Gardens." Holly smiled at her sisters. "That perfectly describes the area. Are y'all good with that? Do we need to kick around more options? Having a real name makes filling out all the paperwork easier."

When both Lee and Kay agreed, Holly picked up her iced tea. "Let's drink to the project forever after called Grant Gardens." The sisters joined in. "To Grant Gardens and to Mom and Dad for providing the needed resources." Their glasses clinked, the ice cubes rattled, and Holly beamed at her sisters, thrilled they were moving on the project.

After her sisters left, Holly wasted no time contacting her attorney, Daniel Morgan. He specialized in real estate and handled all the documents for her buying and selling. She tapped his name. When he answered, she said, "Hey, Dan. Can you talk? If not, tell me when to call." Holly clasped her cell in her hand and paced the large open concept living area of her garden home.

"I always have time for you, Holly. What'cha got?"

"The property I want on South Bryant Irvin has come available again."

"And you're going after it?"

"Yep. Lee, Kay and I are going ahead with the plans to build tiny homes for those who've been continuously homeless for a year. That's the requirement for people to get permanent supportive housing assistance set by the U.S. Department of Housing and Urban Development."

"I've heard you talk about that idea before, and I'm glad you're going forward. Who's the current owner?"

"Bud Henderson. Will you go with me to meet with him?"

"Of course. Can you set up a meeting for Monday or Tuesday of next week? That will give me a chance to do research regarding zoning to see if we need to make plans to meet with the city planning and zoning commission."

"You seem pretty sure I can get the property to take those steps."

Laughter filtered through her cell. "Let's say I know how determined you are when you set your mind to something, and if you've got your sisters on board...well, look out."

Holly couldn't stop laughing. Finally, she sputtered out, "Should I take that as a compliment?"

"Absolutely." His deep chuckle made Holly smile.

"And I'll let you know what I get set up with Henderson. Do you want to grab supper this evening?" Holly enjoyed time with Dan. They'd been good friends for a long time, nothing romantic, but close friends. He and his wife divorced years ago, when she'd taken up with another man. They'd never had children, and Dan never remarried. People often told him he should play Santa Claus. Oh, he didn't have a pot belly, but his beard and hair had turned snowy white at an early age.

"I'd love to, Holly, but I've got a project I have to get out today. And I'm staying until I send it, no matter how late."

"If you didn't spend so much time helping out others, you'd have more time for your business."

Dan chuckled. "Well, yeah, but I wouldn't be as nice a guy, and you wouldn't trust me with your business and friendship now, would you?"

"You got me there. Don't forget to eat something."

"Yes, ma'am." His laughter rang out before he disconnected.

Holly smiled. She was lucky in her friends. She'd have been lost without Dan's support when everything crashed with her ex. No. No. Not going there. A shudder shook her at the idea, and she shoved those memories deep down in her soul.

Looked like she'd be on her own for supper. Before she fixed a bite, she'd email Bud to set up a time for Bud and Dan and her to sit down and hash out a few things.

She'd turned one of the bedrooms into her office. Before she'd moved into The Oaks, her desk had been in the main living area of her home. Not great. Whenever she asked anyone to stop by, she had to hurry and clean up the papers. She did a lot on the computer, but still she had paper clutter. Having a separate space for her office worked way better.

After sending the message and giving Bud the option of Monday or Tuesday, she opened the refrigerator to see what her prospects were for supper. "Mmm." Leftover baked chicken with frozen green peas. Perfect. And she'd splurge on one of those pieces of frozen Texas toast. A chuckle escaped as she thought of the TV commercial for a fast-food place with a character saying those words in such an exaggerated manner, she always laughed. Nothing as good as Texas toast.

She'd finished eating when her phone pinged indicating she'd received an email. Oh good, Bud could meet on Monday at five p.m. She checked with Dan and then confirmed the date and time with Bud. Progress, finally some progress. A long way to go with all kinds of technicalities to sort through. Nevertheless, excitement zinged through her veins as she considered the project they wanted to do to honor her parents and help out a bunch of people who'd fallen on hard times.

Chapter Two

A little before five p.m. on Monday, March 7, Holly parked in the lot near the La Madeline on Camp Bowie. She opened the door and breathed deeply of the lovely fresh pastry smells and roasting chicken. Yum, wonder if she and Dan could eat supper here after their meeting. She made her way through the line, picking up an iced tea. After paying, she wandered through to the small room in the back, which wasn't usually busy. They would be more private. Yes, empty, and she'd arrived before either Bud or Dan. She texted to tell them where they could find her. While she waited, she surfed through Facebook posts until the others joined her. She was deep in Wordle and jerked at Dan's words.

"Hey, lady. How're you doing?" Dan entered the small room carrying a large cup of coffee, which he drank in any sort of weather, and joined her at the table. He wore light gray colored slacks, a white shirt, and a dark gray sport coat.

"Waiting for you. What's the word? If the price is right, can we proceed?" Holly tapped her nails on the table filled with nervous anticipation.

"We're in good shape." He settled into a chair next to Holly. "The property had been zoned residential by a previous owner, and Bud hadn't asked to make a change. We may have to get an adjustment for the size of the homes, but I'm sure we can pull that off. If this goes through with Bud, I'll start working my traps with the board of adjustment members and the city council."

One of the things that made Dan such a good businessperson and a person she loved to work with was how many people he knew and had good relationships with. Because of those relationships, business flowed more efficiently. She nodded. "Fingers crossed, that we can work a deal."

Raising her tea glass, she caught sight of a tall slender man dressed in jeans, boots and a wind breaker entering the small room. Recognizing Bud from several industry meetings, Holly rose and extended her hand to the older gentleman.

"Hey, Bud. Thank you for making time for us. Do you know Dan Morgan?"

"Sure. We've run into each other at different city functions." After shaking hands all around, Bud slid into the chair on the other side of the table from where Holly and Dan sat.

"You're interested in buying that property off South Bryant Irvin?" Bud raised his tea glass and took a big gulp.

Apparently, Bud didn't believe in nice chit-chat. She could handle that. "Depends. What are you asking?"

Bud snapped out a number that surprised Holly, much lower than she'd expected.

"How soon can we make a deal?"

Holly met Dan's gaze. He had a slight frown between his eyes. Probably wondering why Henderson asked such a low amount. Dan gave a slight nod.

"Okay, I'd say we can proceed fairly quickly if that's your asking price."

"Listen, Holly, I've heard you're a straight shooter, so I want to be honest with you. Ever since I bought this property, weird stuff has happened."

"What kind of weird stuff?" Dan leaned forward with his elbows on the table as if afraid he'd miss Bud's answer.

"We had a fire." He ticked off his fingers. "We found a couple of dead cats. And then a dead cow."

"Had you put cows on the property?" Dan asked.

"Nope." Bud shook his head. "The cats were bad, but when the cow turned up dead, I wanted out. The police couldn't find out anything. I should've listened to the rumors before I plopped down any money. I'm taking a loss on this, but I want to get out from under. Something's not right about the property." He shook his head before sipping his tea.

"What do you say, Holly?" Dan looked over his coffee cup at her.

She met the gazes of both men then reached out her hand toward Bud. "I say we've got a deal."

A smile broke across his face in relief, as he met her grip. "That's great. I worried after I told you, you'd back away, but in good conscience, I had to tell you."

"I'll put together the contract and email the document to both of you by the end of the week. How will that work?" Dan set down his coffee cup.

"I'll have my attorney look over the documents, but I expect we can have a done deal in a short time. Can't be too soon for me." He rose, shook hands with Dan and then turned to Holly, taking her hand in both of his. "I sure wish you well with this purchase, Holly. But be careful, okay?"

"I will do that, Bud. Thank you."

Bud nodded to them both and left the room as if someone were chasing him.

Holly dropped into her chair, relief flooding through her veins. "Well, what a surprise. I can hardly believe we're getting such a great deal on the property. My sisters will be thrilled." She pumped both arms in the air.

"What did you think about his warning and the story of the dead animals?" Dan raised his cup.

"I'm guessing we have a few troubled teens on our hands. I'm glad he reported the incidents to the police. People who harm animals frequently end up hurting people."

"If you're worried, you could hire security to keep an eye on the property."

"That might be a good idea, but let's wait. This could be a weird set of circumstances, or maybe Bud has enemies."

"My first research into the owner didn't reveal any problems, but I'll dig further back into the past and make sure it's not an ancient burial ground." Dan made a note on his phone.

"Well, that would be awful." Holly worried her lower lip with her teeth. "Hope that's not the case. As to the extra security, if something else happens after the transaction is complete, then yes, we'll talk about security. I won't take a chance with people's lives."

"If you have trouble, once work begins, I can get you a security guy out there. We can set him up in a trailer."

"Good to know. We'll hire him full-time if we have to. That will shut down any problems. We could just be borrowing trouble, and everything will be okay."

"I'll email the contract to you and your sisters when I've completed the first draft. Should be fairly straightforward." He raised his cup for a last sip of coffee.

"Thank you, Dan." She lifted her tea glass and tapped his cup. "I'm excited about this new venture."

"Let's celebrate then. We can eat supper here and sip a glass of wine. Sound good?"

"Yes, but I need to text Lee and Kay about the progress." She tapped out a message to her sisters and then rose. "All the food here is sooo good. The aromas made me hungry as soon as I entered. I'm glad we can take time for a bite."

Dan followed her through the cafeteria style line. He chose the quarter chicken and roasted potatoes and salad. Holly ordered the chicken Friand, chicken in a lovely puff pastry smothered in a creamy mushroom sauce and the field green salad. Dan insisted on paying for their meal, and they returned to the table in the back room. They enjoyed their meal and wine, but then Holly parted ways with Dan.

"Thanks for dinner, Dan. My treat next time."

"You're on." Dan held the door for her, and they both walked to their cars. Holly headed to her house, which was only five minutes away. She quickly made her way through the gates of the complex and steered along the driveway to her two-car garage. After entering the house through the kitchen, she walked straight through to her office, set her purse on her desk, and put her car keys on the wall rack.

Some houses had a mud room connecting the garage to the rest of the house where upon entering, the owner left purses, boots, and jackets. Since she entered from her garage right into her kitchen, she didn't have that, and soon after settling in, decided the best place to drop her stuff was her office. Being a bit scattered, Holly found her life ran more smoothly when she had a place for everything, and she faithfully put things back in their place. A bit anal perhaps, but her life worked better when she stuck with the plan.

After pouring a glass of her favorite south Texas wine, she settled in the main living area in a comfy rocker recliner. She had to consider what steps to take next with this project. She'd already preliminarily reached out to the president of the board of the Fort Worth Homeless Coalition. Dan served on that board and had suggested she make that contact. The president had been excited about the possibility of other options for their clients. As soon as they completed the sale, she'd contact him again.

Her glance fell on a picture of her parents that sat on the end table next to her chair. She lifted it. "We're doing this, guys. Lee, Kay, and I are building tiny homes for people so they will no longer be homeless. We hope to significantly improve the quality of their lives, getting them off the streets and out of shelters. I hope you'll be proud of what we're doing with your legacy. In honor of Aunt Lee." She rested her head against the back of the chair as a couple of tears trickled from her eyes.

At the end of March, Holly parked out on the edge of the property in southwest Fort Worth to wait for her sisters' arrival. She opened the trunk of her SUV where she'd stashed a bottle of champagne and plastic glasses in a basket along with a hammer and a sign. A gust of wind lifted the loose-fitting beige linen jacket she wore over black slacks.

"Hey, sis." Lee, dressed in navy slacks topped with a long-sleeved bright yellow, white and navy striped shirt climbed out of her even larger SUV and gave Holly a hug. "Where's Kay?"

"Well, you know our sister. She's late, but she'll get here."

Just then, Kay's small electric car pulled silently to the side of the road, and their younger sister climbed out. Her skirt in shades of purple and lavender swirled around her short legs. She maintained her legs looked longer in the longer skirts. No one but Kay would pair the skirt with the orange blouse, but she pulled off the combination. "Sorry, y'all. I forgot to set the alert on my phone and got lost in my painting." They exchanged hugs all around.

"It's okay, sweetie. Glad you're being creative." For a time after her divorce, Kay didn't pick up a brush. Her ex's infidelity killed her creativity. Holly and Lee breathed sighs of relief when Kay finally pulled out a canvas and her paints, and a twinkle returned to her blue eyes, the same color all the sisters shared.

"So did I miss anything?"

"Of course not. We waited." Holly pulled out the hammer and sign from the trunk. "First this. You two hold the sign, and I'll hammer."

Her sisters' grins matched Holly's when they held the SOLD sign in front of the For Sale sign. Holly placed a nail and swung her hammer. Three good taps, and then she repeated that with a second nail.

"Wait. Let's take a selfie." Kay grabbed her phone and handed it to Lee. "You've got longer arms."

"Okay. Let's do this. Say yea!" Lee snapped the selfie with the girls standing beside the sold sign. All three cheered and walked back to Holly's car. "Lee, can you open the champagne? I've never been good at that." Holly handed the bottle to her sister.

"Happy to." Lee handed Kay's phone to her and with little effort, popped the cork, and then filled Kay's glass and the two in Holly's hands.

The three women held up the plastic glasses.

"To Mom and Dad for making this possible," Holly said.

"To all those lovely people we'll provide homes for and, hopefully, help set their lives in a better direction." Lee raised her glass.

"And to us for getting to do this together. I love y'all." Kay wiped the tear about to spill from her eye before raising her glass.

"Amen to all of those." Holly raised her glass to her sisters'. The dull clicking sound made them laugh. "Not as nice as crystal but much more practical."

Chapter Three

Barrett Armstrong raised the binoculars again and peered at the three women appearing to be having a party on his property. The upstairs balcony on the back of his house provided a great space to observe from, and he frequently sat there using his binoculars to keep an eye on who came and went into his High Trails housing addition. He and his wife had been one of the earliest families to purchase a new-build in the development and move in. Unfortunately, Ellie hadn't been around long to enjoy their new community with its pool, walking trails, sidewalks, and composting area. She'd been into the whole environmental thing.

Rising from his favorite chair for a better look, he peered at the group across the street parked on his property. Who did they think they were? Looking through the glasses again, his blood pressure rose as they tacked something over the For Sale Sign. SOLD jumped out at him. *SOLD? No.* That's not possible. The property had belonged to his family for many years.

His damn father had a gambling problem and lost the property across the road, but the land would always be Armstrong land. Everyone knew that. His grandfather and great grandfather owned the property. Besides that, his father had been cheated and shouldn't have lost.

Over the years Barrett had done his best to keep anyone else from developing anything on the land. Oh, he let, and even encouraged, his neighbors to go over and have picnics there and to enjoy nature. That's what Ellie would expect. As the president of the neighborhood association, he had a lot of power. Everyone listened to him. He made sure they did.

Well, he'd kept Bud Henderson and the others before him from doing anything with the property. He'd stop these women. He'd check the records and see who they were. Then he'd act. Before you knew it, they'd bail out too, like everyone else had. He kept what was his.

Dan hung up the phone in his office in a downtown high-rise building on the last day of March. He was a partner in a large firm and specialized in matters dealing with real estate and oil and gas. As one business ebbed and flowed, he fell back on the other. He'd been lucky that neither had gone bust at the same time, and he'd done well for himself.

"Hey, Dan. You got a minute?"

"Sure. Come on in. Sit. What's up, Jon?"

Jonathan Baxter, Dan's best friend and law partner, settled into the leather chair in front of the desk. He'd taken off his suit jacket and rolled up his shirt sleeves. "I've got good news you should be happy to hear."

"Yeah?"

"I got your issue on the agenda for the next board of adjustment meeting. I've informally mentioned your tiny house project to a couple of folks, and I sense they will be inclined to go along with your request."

"That is good news. Thanks, Jon."

"Don't celebrate yet. I'm counting on you bringing your A-game to the meeting and selling the entire board on the importance of the project."

"I can do that. Holly Grant will come, too. Her passion will for sure light a fire under the board members. I'll ask the president of the board of the Homeless Coalition to come and add his two cents about the shortage of locations and facilities for people to live."

"I don't doubt you can do this. Listen, you remember Janey has a program at TCU at seven thirty this evening, right?"

At thirty-five, Jon had his one and only child, Janey, who hung the moon for him. She was twenty now and in the dance department at TCU. Jon's wife died when Janey was in middle school, and not having kids himself, Dan acted as an uncle for her and had gone with Jon to lots of Janey's activities.

"Yes. I've even got the reminder set on my calendar to make sure I don't forget to leave here."

Jon laughed. "Glad to hear that. Don't want you missing this like you did that wedding a couple of years back."

Dan shook his head. "Don't guess I'll ever live that down. I had two hours, and then the next time I looked up those two hours had disappeared. At least I showed up for the reception. Ever since that faux pas, if it's important, I put the alert on the event."

"Janey has left our tickets at Will Call. I'll get there before you, but I'll wait for you in the lobby."

"You live down the street from the school. Easy for you to get there on time."

"True. The board of adjustment will take up this issue on Tuesday, April 12. Can you get your presentation ready by then?"

"Sure. I'll get to work right now. Thanks for getting us on the agenda, and I'll see you at TCU."

"You're welcome. See you tonight." Jon left Dan's office. They had been friends since their law school days. A weird fluke landed them both in the same firm. They'd stood up for each other at their weddings. Jon helped him keep his act together when his wife cheated on him and then split. Dan didn't entirely blame her. He spent a lot of hours at work. And he still did, except for hanging with Jon and Janey and serving on the board of the Homeless Coalition and making himself go to the gym to exercise.

Well, he better get crackin' and make sure Holly and the president of the Homeless Coalition could make the board of adjustment meeting.

"Thanks for meeting me for breakfast, Lee." On the first day of April, Holly and her sister walked into First Watch, one of their favorite breakfast places, not far from where Holly lived.

"Sure. Never turn down breakfast out. Is Kay coming?"

"Two?" the staff person asked.

"There'll be three of us, and can we have one of those tables in the back corner?" Holly tipped her head toward the rear of the restaurant.

"Of course. Follow me." The staff person led them to a corner table where no one was sitting within earshot.

"Thanks." Lee settled herself on one side of the table, and Holly sat on the other.

A wait person came up and took their coffee orders, including one for Kay, who arrived as their coffees did.

She hugged each sister around the neck. "Sorry. Sorry. Had an early call with my agent. She would not stop talking. And Happy April Fool's Day." Kay settled next to Holly. "So, what's up?"

"I have no pranks." Holly laughed at her younger sister. "Let's order, then I'll explain." Holly ordered her regular egg white omelet. Lee ordered the eggs, bacon, and potatoes, and Kay ordered Belgian waffles.

As soon as the server stepped away, Kay asked again, "So talk. What's up?"

"I want y'all to come with me to a meeting of the board of adjustment Tuesday, April 12. Dan will make a presentation about the need for the adjusting the size of the homes allowed on the property."

"I don't want to talk. You're not asking me to talk, are you?" Being the introvert of the three sisters, Kay was most happy when she lost herself in her painting.

"No, sweetie. I'll do that. But I want to be able to refer to y'all and ask you to stand. You can do that, right?"

Kay looked at Lee who nodded at her. "You can do that, Kay."

"Okay. I can do that. I'll do whatever I can because we need them to approve the change to do the project, right?"

"Yep." Lee sipped her coffee. "You and Dan will talk. Will that do it?"

The server arrived with their food, and after he left, Holly answered her sister. "Dan will introduce me, and he's also arranged for Bentley Stevenson, the president of the Homeless Coalition, to speak."

"Dan is on that board, right?" Lee spread jam all over her second piece of toast.

"Yes, but he felt the president would carry more clout than he as a board member. And since he's representing us, it wouldn't be appropriate for him to speak for the board. Before that meeting, Dan and I will meet with the neighborhood association board for the housing addition across the road from our property."

"Oh, that's a good idea." Kay poured syrup on the second half of her waffle.

"Yes, Dan's partner, Jonathan Baxter, suggested it. He told Dan that is the question someone on the board of adjustment asks when someone asks for a variance."

"Well, Grant Gardens is across the road from that housing addition, right? Not right next door. I can't see why what they think should matter." Kay stuffed the last of her waffle in her mouth. "Oh, so good. From the first bite to the last. I love these." And licked her lips in an unladylike manner.

"You ate like you were starving."

"Yeah, I was. I worked through supper and fell into bed around three. I'm amazed I heard the alarm."

"I guess that means your project is going well. But, Kay, you have to make sure to eat. We don't want you getting sick," Lee said in her best big sister voice.

Holly smiled. Lee used her in-charge tone when she felt she needed to fill the mom role to either of them.

"I made up for skipping a meal or two with breakfast. Thanks for worrying, but I'm fine."

"Neither of you needs to speak at the board of adjustment meeting. You're welcome to come to the neighborhood association meeting if you'd like, but hopefully Dan and I can convince the neighborhood association not to fight us. Their meeting is Wednesday, April 6, at 6 p.m.

"I'm good leaving the neighbors to you and Dan." Kay sipped the last of her coffee. "I'm not sure I'd be patient with any objections they'd make. I mean, holy cow, we're building houses for people who've been homeless! What kinds of folks object to that?"

Holly smiled at her more emotional sister. "I'm afraid you can find people who never want a community like this in their backyard."

Lee winked at Holly and added, "You're right, Kay. You stay home and paint. I can go along with Holly and Dan to be their reinforcements if they need any."

"Thanks for the offer, Lee. I'll check with Dan to see what he's found out about the group and whether he feels we're better with fewer or more of us."

"Good deal. Let me know when you decide. I'll keep the time open on my calendar."

"Have you talked with your kids about our project?" Holly picked up the small coffee pot on the table and refilled everyone's cup.

"Sarah is very excited about it. I've talked with her about sign ideas." Kay added cream to her coffee.

"I've talked with both Brad and Leeann. Brad offered free legal services, but I explained that we were working with Dan, your regular lawyer. He understood. Told me to have Dan give him a call if he needed any assistance. Leeann is thrilled. She said Austin has several places like what we're talking about doing."

"Good to hear that. I think there's a tiny house development nearby I want us to check out sometime. If that doesn't work out, we can take a girls' trip to Austin."

"We could just take a long weekend girls' trip to Austin in any case. We can take Sarah and meet up with Leeann." Kay swallowed the last of her coffee.

"Sounds great, but I feel sort of sorry for leaving out Brad." Lee's mouth turned down.

"When we get through with all this, we can take a family trip somewhere and include Brad. Don't want to leave out our nephew." Holly patted Lee's hand.

"That's a great idea, Holly. Let's try to get something scheduled." Kay picked up the ticket the waiter had left. "This one's on me."

Chapter Four

Holly took care with her outfit for the meeting with the neighborhood association. Studying her reflection in the mirror, she decided the black skirted suit sent the right hint of seriousness while the turquoise silk top added a touch of fun. Adding short black boots kept the outfit from being too dressy. Her phone beeped, and she read Dan's text. He'd stopped on the outside of the gate. She clicked the device to open the gate, picked up her purse, set the alarm, and stepped out onto the small porch.

Dan's large SUV pulled up in front of her house. He hopped out and came around to open the door for her. "I'm sorry. I didn't have time to get my sedan. I know you have trouble climbing in. Let me help you." His hands slid around her waist and hoisted her easily into the seat.

"Oh, my. Thank you." Holly fanned her face as he stepped around the front of the vehicle. She and Dan had been friends for years, but his hands on her waist now and how easily he lifted her into the SUV...well, she found herself a bit breathless. What was that about?

Dan slammed his door and pointed the car in the direction of the gate. "Before I forget, you look fantastic. Love the turquoise or aqua or whatever color you call it."

"Thank you. You've used several terms that work. This blouse I'd call turquoise, but you've seen me in teal, and something I call blue-green."

"Okay." Dan chuckled. "I didn't expect a color lesson from you. From Kay, yes, but you're a more feet-on-the-ground, practical kind of person."

"Thank you, I think?" Holly laughed.

"In my experience we shouldn't have to stay for their whole meeting. Why don't we grab supper afterwards? How about Aventino's?"

Holly shot a glance at Dan who'd focused his attention on making sure they got safely out onto the road, busy with going-home traffic. "Uh, sure. That would be lovely. Aventino's is one of our favorites. It's fun knowing the owners." Aventino's was a special kind of place to eat a quiet dinner with a special someone. She and Dan didn't have that kind of relationship. She didn't have that kind of relationship with anyone. Not since Joe Bryant.

She and Joe met in high school, dated, and fell in love. They went to the same college and after two years decided to get married. Her family wasn't too thrilled. They wanted her to finish school first. But she'd been hell bent to have that fancy full-blown wedding with six bridesmaids and the country club reception. Many of her sorority sisters got married young. That's what young people did back then. People didn't live together as much as now. The relationship began to fall apart almost from the very beginning. They argued over money, his friends, her friends. Joe thought any guy who spoke to her wanted to get in her pants. His insane jealousy had no basis in fact. She'd never been able to convince him otherwise.

"Holly."

"What?"

"Where'd you go? I called your name three times. We don't have to go to Aventino's after if you'd rather not."

"Oh. Sorry. Guess I drifted off for a moment. Aventino's will be lovely." Dear heavens, had she looked like she'd lost her mind? She feared that in certain matters she had. Despite two years of counseling, and the passage of almost thirty years, those memories flooded back with too much detail, and the emotions took possession of her. "Let's get this meeting with the homeowners over. Then maybe we can have a celebration."

After a twenty-minute drive, Dan turned into the High Trails development and parked in front of their club room. They parked and climbed out of the SUV. He held the door open for Holly, and she stepped into the large room with chairs set up theatre style facing the front. She rubbed her hands along her thighs. Nerves made her palms sweat. Unusual for her. Calm and cool were how people often described her. But this was personal, and she badly wanted to report back to her sisters that these people would be supportive of their project. Grant Gardens meant everything to all three of them.

A tall, gray-haired gentleman who Holly guessed to be in his mid-sixties made his way from the front of the room toward them where a microphone, speaker's stand and U.S. flag stood.

"I'm Barrett Anderson, president of our neighborhood association. You must be the person who bought the land across the road."

Holly extended her hand. "Yes, I'm Holly Grant, and this is Dan Morgan, my attorney."

Anderson clasped her hand and squeezed harder than seemed necessary. "Not sure why you needed your attorney, Ms. Grant." He turned to Dan and extended his hand. "Nothing personal, you know."

"No offense taken, Mr. Anderson. Besides being a lawyer, I'm Ms. Grant's friend, and I'm here more in that capacity today."

"Okay, well, follow me up to the front. We're about to begin. You can sit here." He gestured to the chairs in the front row.

Holly cut Dan a quick glance. How would this meeting go?

The president moved to the microphone and cleared his throat before speaking. "May I have everyone's attention? Please take your seats." He paused while about twenty-five people settled down. "Sue Pittman, please come forward to lead us in the Pledge of Allegiance."

A short, slightly built woman with white hair took her place at the mic. Everyone stood, and she led the group in the pledge.

Anderson stepped to the mic. "The minutes of the last meeting were in our monthly newsletter. Anyone have any corrections?" He paused for a moment. "Hearing none, they're approved as printed. We have a couple of things on the agenda, but we'll start with our guests. Ms. Grant, you want to come up and tell us what you're working on?"

"Yes." She rose and walked to the mic. "First, let me thank you for giving me time this evening, Mr. Anderson." She turned to the gathering of folks. Looking at the group, she made eye contact with many individuals. "Let me start by telling you a bit about me. My sisters and I grew up in Fort Worth, and we all three still live here. Our parents were fortunate to do well in oil and gas. Unfortunately, they've both passed, but they left us an endowment with the idea we do something for others with the money. Our mother served on several boards. Two were especially close to her heart—Safe House and the Homeless Shelter. In that position she met many people who found themselves in circumstances where they had no place to live."

Holly paused and let what she'd said sink in. "These people are not bad people. But they have hit a run of bad luck and find themselves needing a bit of help. Haven't we all found ourselves in that position at one time or another? Maybe not as dire as needing a home but needing a boost?"

Her heart swelled at the few nods and smiles she noted from a couple of the women.

"My sisters and I bought the property across the road from y'all and want to put in a tiny house development for people whose circumstances have resulted in them not having a permanent home. We're not talking about the chronically homeless. Other strategies are used for helping those folks. The area is already zoned for houses, and we'll be attending the next board of adjustment meeting to get a waiver on the size of the homes we'd like to put there. We'd really appreciate the support of your organization for this endeavor. Do you have any questions?"

The woman who'd led the pledge raised her hand, and Armstrong called on her. "What do you have to say, Sue?"

She stood. "I say this is a lovely idea. I've watched shows on the HGTV Channel where they build amazing tiny homes. They look cute and cozy to me." She sat down.

Armstrong scowled at her and then asked, "Anyone else?"

A tall, man with a bit of a pot belly raised his hand. "Yes, Kurt. What do you want to say?

"I'm Kurt Donaldson, the vice president of our association. My church is involved in helping the homeless, and this sounds like a great idea to me. Our association could find ways to help out the residents sometimes."

"Thank you, Mr. Donaldson. I'm pleased to hear that." Holly nodded her head toward the man.

"I'd like to talk." A tall, angular woman with glaringly red hair in an Annie cut stood.

"What do you want to say, Maxine?"

The woman strode to the mic, not content to speak from her place as had the others. "This is a dreadful idea to have *those people* living close to us. They're all druggies and criminals. They could steal from us and will bring down our property values." She glared at Holly. "Find any place other than here for them. We've used that area as an extra park. Now we won't be able to do that."

"That's enough about that, Maxine. Thanks for your comments. You can sit down now." Anderson shushed the woman.

Hmm. What did she mean they'd been using the property? Holly would have to talk to Dan about that. She wanted to ask Maxine where she thought the tiny houses should be. In a food desert in a poor part of town? Holly clenched and released her hands. Not good form to go off on the woman. She needed to get as many people as possible on their side.

"For the record, I'm on Maxine's side."

"Thanks, Roger. We'll all have a chance to discuss this after our guests leave." He turned to Holly. "Ms. Grant, do you have anything else you want to say?"

"I ask you to consider what you'd want if you found yourself in these circumstances. We're all fortunate to live in lovely homes, but what if we didn't? Wouldn't we want someone to reach out and help? Your support of Grant Gardens would be appreciated." Again, she made eye contact with many of those present, especially those who spoke. Then she turned to Anderson. "I hope your organization will decide to support us with the board of adjustment." She held out her hand to Anderson. "Thank you for your time." He again squeezed her hand harder than needed.

Polite applause followed her from the front of the room and outside. She and Dan climbed in his SUV, and they drove away without speaking.

After a time, she let out a long sigh. "Not as bad as it might've been."

Dan laughed. "Not at all. I've seen way worse. And you did well. I see support from one group and from others not so much. Be interesting to see if the association decides to take a stand. If they don't take a total position against us with the board of adjustment, we should be okay."

"Good. Guess we'll have to wait and see. But boy, that's hard."

"So, are you ready for dinner now?"

Holly nodded. "Yes, and a large glass of wine if you don't mind." She laughed.

"Hey, Barrett. Wait up."

Barrett Anderson stopped walking and turned toward Roger and Maxine hurrying to catch up to him. "Sure."

"I want to talk with you more about what this woman wants to do. I have a bad feeling about the project, and I want us to fight the concept." Roger rubbed his chin.

"I'm with you, Roger. Those people will increase the possibility of crime. We moved out here to get away from all of that." Maxine stabbed her finger with each point she made.

Barrett eyed them. "Would you like to come back to my place for coffee or a drink?

"Sounds good," Roger said.

"I especially like the idea of a drink, Barrett."

He laughed. "You're on, Maxine." Interesting conversation. Barrett had appreciated hearing their negative comments about the project during the meeting. But now they wanted to talk more about their concerns. Yes, very interesting. Could he use them in his campaign against the tiny houses?

He lived three houses from the club room, and in moments, they entered his house. Everything was on the first floor except the game room and the balcony off the back. Being among the first in the division, he and his wife had walked through each house as companies built them, commenting on what they liked and didn't. Barrett had organized the people into the neighborhood association and had served as its president since its inception. He enjoyed the power and attention he had as president. When they had their annual meeting, they asked their councilman to be there, and he made a point to attend. Barrett sat with him and introduced him. Yeah, he played an important role.

After fixing a Bourbon for him and his guests, he settled everyone in the living room.

Roger took a healthy swig before setting his drink on the glass coffee table. "So, I don't like the idea of those people living across the road from us. Looks like we three may be on the same side."

"I'd hoped to get a no vote from the association after they heard the presentation, but that's not how the vote went. If that had happened, I could've gone to the board of adjustment meeting and spoken against the project representing all of us."

"Well, I can go, can't I? Speaking for myself?"

"Yes, Maxine, you can. Any of us can. We won't carry the same weight as if I spoke for the association. A case of bad luck we lost that vote."

"I can drive us, Maxine. The board needs to know everyone doesn't support the plan. Let's try to at least delay the project if not stop it completely." Roger lifted his glass and took another sip.

"Thanks. I hate driving at night anymore." Maxine sipped her Bourbon.

"You'll have only three minutes to speak. They will time you. Make sure you plan what you want to say. They will cut you off if you try to go over, and you'll lose any points with the board members if you push their time limits."

"Will you speak, Barrett?"

"Yes, I will. My comments should carry special weight as president of the neighborhood association. I can word my remarks to give the impression I'm officially speaking for the group even when I'm not."

"What are our chances of getting away with that?" Roger finished up his drink.

"Unless someone else attends the meeting, who's to tell the membership?" He chuckled and finished off his drink. "I appreciate your support on this. We don't want a group of homeless people living across the road from us. Our property values would drop like a bomb. If we stick together, we should be able to stop the project. Nothing else has gone in there even though several people have purchased the property."

"That's true. We appreciate all you do for us, Barrett. Thanks for the drink. Let me know when you'll pick me up for the meeting, Roger. See you later." Maxine set her drink on the coffee table and headed for the door.

"I'm taking off, too. Thanks for the Bourbon. It's good. We'll talk before the meeting."

Barrett closed the door behind his guests. Yes, they would stop this project like all the others. If they couldn't count on the board of adjustment squashing the project...well, then he had other ways of discouraging the new owners.

L ater, as Dan and Holly finished the meal, Holly reached across the table and took his hand. "Your support of me, us, and this project means everything to me."

"Of course." Dan covered her hand with his other. "We're in this together."

"Can I get you any dessert?" Ericka, the owner and their friend, stopped by the table.

Holly and Dan both dropped their hands and jerked back. Not like they were doing anything wrong, but Holly didn't want others to get the wrong impression. But what would that wrong impression be with respect to her and Dan's relationship?

"Gosh, no. I overindulged in the pasta and bread. As usual, Ericka, the meal was scrumptious."

"What about you, Dan?" She rested her hand on his shoulder. "Can I twist your arm?"

"No way." He patted his flat stomach. "I gotta watch my girlish figure."

Ericka laughed. "Well, I'm glad you enjoyed the meal. Were you celebrating anything?" She looked between the two of them, her eyebrows raised in question.

"Not really," Dan answered. "Hopefully we will be soon."

"Okay. Well, please come back when you do have something to celebrate or before." She laughed. "Really good to see you two this evening."

"Thanks, Ericka." After taking care of the bill, Dan held her chair, and they walked to the door and headed to his SUV. They were quiet on the ride back to her place.

Holly clicked the gate opener she'd brought with her, and he pulled around to the back of the complex where her house was. He came around to help her out and held her hand as they ambled up to the door. She unlocked the door and turned to him.

"Thanks for everything you're doing, Dan, and for dinner this evening. We did need to celebrate. My mother said don't forget to celebrate all the little stops along the way."

"I agree. Hopefully, we'll celebrate again after the board of adjustment meeting."

"Absolutely. Fingers crossed."

Dan leaned in and kissed her on the cheek. "You're doing a good thing, Holly. Happy to be a small part of this endeavor. Lock up."

"Of course. Goodnight, Dan."

He walked back to his car, and she went inside. She flipped the lock, then her hand touched her face where Dan had kissed her. He'd never kissed her before. Oh, he'd hugged her on several occasions, but tonight he kissed her. Only on the cheek. Only. Did she want something more from Dan? Surely not. She'd been off men ever since the mess with her ex. But Dan was different. Nothing at all like Joe Bryant. No. Dan Morgan epitomized everything her ex hadn't been. She trusted Dan. Trusted him to be honest with her. Trusted him not to hurt her and trusted him to always have her back. He'd proved himself more times in the past than she could remember. Finding the right lawyer to defend her put him high on the list. Her situation would be unimaginably different if Dan hadn't found the right person. Holly shuddered as she contemplated where she might be now.

Chapter Five

It took more than thirty minutes for Holly to drive her sisters from her home to the tiny-home development on the northwest side of Fort Worth. All three of them had done online searches, learning all they could about tiny homes, but they hadn't looked at one in person.

"It's wonderful you found this community close to us, Holly. I'd have been willing to drive farther, but thirty minutes is easy. Especially with you driving, and me riding." Kay laughed from the back seat.

"Looking at pictures is one thing, but in person is way better. Certainly, a trip to Austin to see Leeann and the villages she talked about would be fun, but this is much more convenient." Lee glanced out the passenger side window.

"I agree an overnight trip would've been fun for all of us, but this is way more practical time wise. We're here." Holly slowed her SUV and turned into the gravel road in front of the tiny-home village.

Tiny homes of various designs sat around what looked to be a central meeting space—a long low rectangular shaped building. "What do you think? I'm guessing fifteen to twenty structures?" Holly cut the ignition, climbed out, and shut the door. Her sisters followed.

"This is cool." Kay slipped an arm through Lee's. "I mean really cool."

Lee and Holly laughed at their baby sister's excitement.

Holly stepped on the porch and opened the front door. "Hello?" No one responded. Sofas and chairs faced a large fireplace against the wall on the left. Doors led to restrooms on the back wall. "Hello?" She raised her voice.

"Be right there."

In moments, a tall, burly man in jeans and a red and gray plaid shirt pushed open a door from what might have led to an office. "Sorry about that. I couldn't get off the phone. I'm Jim Wheeler, the property manager, how can I help you?"

Holly stepped forward with her arm extended. "I'm Holly Grant, and these are my sisters, Lee Kennedy and Kay Clayton. We're looking at developing a tiny-home community in the far southwest of town for people who've been homeless. While we've done a lot of online research, we haven't seen a community in person. Would you mind if we looked around? And we'd like to pick your brain a bit since you have experience, if you don't mind."

"Happy to, Ms. Grant."

"Call me Holly. We appreciate your time, Jim. Do you have any houses that are empty we could look at?"

"You can go in the only two we've got empty right now, but you can look around at the others from the outside. Let me get the keys." Jim went back to his office, and Holly grinned at her sisters.

"Here we go. Follow me. The first one is close, the other is about a quarter of a mile back." Jim glanced at each of the women's feet. "Can you make that hike?"

Holly glanced down at the flats they all three wore. "Yes. We'll be fine. Thanks."

Jim held open the door, and Holly and her sisters slipped through. The tiny homes lined up in three semi-circles behind the community building. He led them toward a structure on the far right of the first line.

Holly gazed at the country cottage appearance of the tiny home. The pitched roof had scalloped wood trim and a small front porch. A box of flowers hung in the front window. "Oh, this is quite charming."

"How many square feet is this one, Jim? Lee asked.

"At four hundred square feet, this one is one of our smaller versions. Our homes range in size from three hundred to eight hundred square feet." Let me unlock it, and y'all can take a look. I'll wait out here. The three of you should be okay, but if I go in, y'all will be crowded."

"Thank you, Jim. Let's go, girls." Holly held open the door for Lee and Kay to enter. She followed them in.

"Wow." Kay gazed around at the main room which held a two-seater sofa and a TV on the opposite wall.

Holly pushed past her sisters into the kitchen with a small fridge, a two-burner cooktop stove, an oven, and sink. Open shelves forced the tenant to keep things neat. "I'm amazed they got a dishwasher in here."

"Oh, look at this." Lee lifted a table which fell into place next to the counter. I love how the table folds down and then out of the way when you don't need it." She lowered the piece back into place.

"What's in here?" Kay walked toward a door, which she slid open. "The bathroom. A shower stall, a couple of shelves for storage, a potty and a small sink. Nicely done with everything you need."

Holly glanced at the stairs that doubled as storage boxes on one side of the structure. "Shall we? The bedroom must be up here."

"You'll have to check. You're the only one in pants. While I'm the youngest, I'm not sure I want to try to negotiate those stairs in my long skirt." Kay declined.

"Yeah, you go, Holly. And take pictures." Lee spread her hand down her slim skirt. She'd been to a luncheon meeting and didn't wear her usual slacks. "Guess we didn't dress for this event, sis." Lee smiled at Kay.

"But this is how I dress for everything—that doesn't include a bunch of climbing."

"Y'all stay here. I'll research the layout." Holly started up the stairs, using the handles that were on the side wall to help her balance. "I love how they used the stairs for storage. Oh, this is nice. Looks like a queen bed. At five four, I'm on the shorter side of average. There's plenty of space for me to stand. Not much closet space." She snapped pictures. "There's a five-drawer unit against the wall, but not sure where you'd put hanging stuff. Great view of the sky through the skylight. Nice touch. Okay, I'm coming back down."

Holly gulped. "Oh my, this is scarier than going up. I have to step down on my own before I find a handle. This wouldn't work for an older person or someone not in great health." As she got lower, Lee reached a hand to steady her. "Thanks."

Holly led them outside. "This is nice, Jim. We'd like to see the other one you have available. Is the bedroom upstairs in the next unit?"

"Follow me. We'll walk to the back row on the other side. This tiny house is larger than the first and, the bedroom is on the ground floor."

"I love all your trees. Were they here when you built the units, or did you bring them in?" Lee asked as they passed under the shade of what looked like an old red oak tree.

"The trees were here. We tried extra hard not to take any out and were lucky. We only lost a couple." Jim ambled toward the back of the complex.

"And did you hire a company to build each of these or did the people who bought here hire someone and build their own?" Kay brought up the rear of the group.

"A bit of both. We initially hired a company to build ten of the units in a variety of styles and sizes. As people came out here and found people living in this simpler, easier way, some folks bought the house designs we had, and others wanted to do their own thing. Here we are."

Jim stopped in front of a unit with a pitched roof.

"I thought you said the bedroom was on the ground floor," Holly asked. "This looks like the other unit. Not as sweetly country as the other, but about the same size."

"It's six hundred square feet, and it's all on one level. Come around here, you'll get a better sense of the size."

Holly and her sisters followed Jim to the side of the unit.

"Oh, my gosh, yes. This one looks huge next to that first one," Kay agreed.

"It's two hundred square feet more, and all on the ground floor. Let me unlock this and you can go on in." He stood back to let them enter. "I'll wait out here."

Holly went first. "Oh, I like this. Much more modern and not as cutesy-cozy as the other unit. What do you say, gals?"

"I love that the bedroom must be on the ground floor." Lee made straight for the room at the back. "Oh, yes, this is much better. There is even a closet for hanging items and more storage. I know the people we're creating the units for have been homeless and I'm guessing don't have many possessions, but still, we hope their situation will improve, so storage is important. This is much more practical. Take a look." Lee came out into the kitchen area to allow Holly and Kay to enter and check out the bedroom.

"You're right, Lee. I could live in this space."

Kay's laughter exploded. "Not without getting rid of a whole bunch of stuff."

"Well, yes, but I could do it. Not sure I could've managed in the smaller sample. However, I liked the country chic style of the other over this more modern style, which seems a bit cold to me."

"I hear you saying we need to have a variety of styles as long as they are roughly the same space. If we have houses with vast differences in size, that could make for jealousies," Lee said.

"What if a family is made up of two people? You know a mom and her teenage child or a husband and wife or a woman and her mom?" Kay wondered out loud.

"Y'all both make good points. Let's stick with the six hundred square feet set up as a one bedroom except we have a few that are eight hundred square feet with two beds," Holly concluded.

"I love how they manage to cram in as many cool conveniences as they have in these small spaces," Lee said. "Maybe after we get Grant Gardens set up and going, you should set up a company to build tiny homes. I bet we could find lots of people who'd love to get into this kind of simplicity."

"That's a possibility, Lee. But first, let's get Grant Gardens off and running, okay? If you've seen everything you want to, let's go pick Jim's brain for more info."

When her sisters nodded, Holly led the trio outside to find Jim sitting in a chair under the awning of the tiny house's front porch. He stood when they came out.

"What's your opinion of the place? Pretty neat set up, huh?"

"Absolutely, Jim. You've done a good job here. Can you spare us a little more time for questions?" Holly asked.

"Right now, you mean?"

"Yes," Holly nodded.

Jim glanced at his watch. "I'm expecting a phone call in five minutes."

"We're flexible. I know we'd like to walk around and take a few pictures if you don't mind. How about in say fifteen or twenty minutes?"

"That will work for me. See you back at the center in a while." Jim set off toward the front of the complex.

"He seems to be a good guy." Lee stood watching after the man. "This development is kept up well. I don't see anything that looks run down. Trash cans are put out of sight, and I see flowers peeking their way above ground."

"Let's start on the back row and take a picture of each tiny house that is different and take notes of anything we especially like." Holly's sisters fell into step with her. After about fifteen minutes, they made their way to the Center and inside.

"Hey, Jim. We're back." Holly raised her voice.

"Be right there." Jim's voice came from the depths of his office.

Holly and her sisters settled into the overstuffed chairs gathered around a large screen TV and the fireplace.

"This is also a nice touch." Kay sighed as she propped her feet on a hassock. Because she was so short her feet seldom touched the floor. "Do we have plans for a fireplace in the gathering room for the residents?"

"As a matter of fact, we do. I need to get you the most up-to-date plans for our center. We've got washers and dryers for the residents, too."

"That second tiny house we went in had a washer-dryer combo like you find in a lot of apartments in Europe." Lee crossed one long leg over the other, swinging it gently back and forth.

"Sorry to keep you waiting, ladies. What more do you want to ask?" Jim settled on the heavy wooden coffee table, strong enough to easily hold him. His gaze lit on each in turn.

"Do you have a neighborhood association? We noticed how everything is nicely kept up." Holly asked from her real estate perspective.

"Actually, we do, with officers and everything. Everyone feels a responsibility for keeping the area nice. I've had few problems with any of the residents. Knock on wood." Jim literally knocked on the coffee table. "I've probably jinxed myself." He laughed as did Holly and her sisters.

"For the units you built yourself, did you hire an interior designer? The two homes we saw were vastly different in style." Lee asked from her own perspective.

"Yes. Even for the units we weren't building, we provided guidelines. Like the height of the roof. People had to make sure not to block their neighbor's view. The houses on the back row didn't have to follow that guideline, but the people moved here to downsize into their tiny homes. They weren't into ostentatious bigness to outdo anyone else."

Jim's cell beeped. He glanced at it. "I'm sorry, I've got to get this. Y'all come back anytime." He rose and headed for his office.

"In my opinion, this has been time well spent. What do y'all think?" Holly glanced at each of her sisters as they rose.

"Absolutely. I have such a better picture of what we're trying to do." Kay held the door of the center for her sisters. "I mean, I knew, but still, this is cool to see such a variety of tiny homes in real life and in one place."

"Thanks. You know how I love to watch HGTV. When they had the tiny homes series, I recorded all the episodes and watched and rewatched them. Still, this is much better." Lee walked toward Holly's SUV.

"It sure helps to see examples in person, I agree. And I'm even more excited about our project." Holly unlocked her SUV, and they all climbed in.

"When is the board of adjustment meeting, Holly?" Lee pulled out her cell. "I can't find where I put the date on my calendar. Do you have time to attend, Kay?"

"Yes, I do, though I'm dreading having to go. The date is next week, Tuesday, April 12."

"I've told you not to worry about the meeting, Kay. You don't have to speak, but I want you to stand when I point to you."

"Okay, okay. I want to do my part. Did you get the meeting on your calendar, Lee?"

"Yes, ma'am. Thanks, I'll swing by and get you. I'm sure Holly will ride with Dan."

Holly drove back to her place where her sisters had left their cars. Her stomach knotted at the possibility the board wouldn't grant their request for a waiver. Well, no sense borrowing trouble. She'd work on her presentation. Having the president of the Homeless Coalition there would be great. It was good Dan had been able to get him to come. She had to believe together they could touch members' hearts.

Chapter Six

*H*e yelled at her as he jammed the point of a shotgun under his chin and threatened to kill himself if she didn't promise not to talk to a guy they both knew from school. She'd given her husband no reason to believe she cheated on him. And nothing she said convinced him. God, she hated when he got like this, but never had he threatened to kill himself. Her mind kept flashing forward to what would happen if he actually pulled the trigger. The blood, the police, the utter desolation of having someone you love taking his life and right in front of you.

Holly woke with a start, her heart galloping in her chest, the sheets strangling her. Damn, she hadn't had that dream in several years. Must be the stress over the board of adjustment meeting this evening. She struggled out of the tangled sheets and pushed up against the headboard. The dream always left her drained and wiped out a good night's sleep.

Her gaze swept to the clock on the bedside table. 5:30 a.m. Too late to go back to sleep. And did she want to chance having the other dream, the real nightmare? No, she did not. Throwing back the covers, she struggled out of the bed and staggered to the kitchen to start coffee brewing. She'd need several cups of the high-octane liquid to get her going today.

With her second cup in her hand, she walked to the study and settled in front of her computer. Not making use of this extra time to proof her comments for tonight would be stupid. And no one had ever called her stupid. The presentation must be spot on. Having heard both Dan and Bentley Stevenson, the president of the board of the Homeless Coalition, speak on the subject, she had no worries about either of them bringing their A-game.

After making a few more tweaks, she finally clicked Print and settled the two double-spaced pages into a folder to carry with her to the meeting. She wandered into the bathroom for a hot shower, guaranteed to blow away the lingering entanglements of the dreadful dream. At least she hadn't dreamed the other one. If she had, she might have had to cancel tonight. And she absolutely could not cancel. She had to be there and convince the board to grant their waiver.

Late afternoon, she ate a light supper of leftover minestrone soup. She'd picked up a double batch yesterday from one of her favorite restaurants. Glancing out the patio doors, she was surprised to see how dark it had gotten and how strongly the wind blew. The trees whipped around.

At the moment her nerves began to tighten, her cell pinged with the ominous warning that came too often with a Texas spring. Severe thunderstorm warnings. Gosh, she hated to leave the house with the possibility of storms. She clicked on the TV, and yes, the meteorologists had taken over the whole news show. A level-three warning covered all of Fort Worth and surrounding counties. The cap hadn't held. Very bad news. In Texas, people prayed for the atmospheric cap, a warm stable layer of air, to remain in place lowering the possibilities of severe thunderstorms.

Holly hoped the city would cancel the board of adjustment meeting. Severe storms had spared Fort Worth so far this spring. Others hadn't been so lucky. Holly texted Dan.

Hey, is our meeting still a go?

In moments, Dan responded. *Haven't heard it's canceled. That's a possibility. Storm looks to be serious. Do you still want to go?*

Yes. Hate to get out in it, but if they're meeting, we have to be there. I'll tell Kay and Lee to stay home.

Not a bad idea. I'll pick you up if they don't cancel.

Thanks. Keep in touch.

Holly disconnected and texted her sisters.

Do you know we've got a bad storm coming? I don't want you to get out tonight. Hoping they'll reschedule the meeting.

Kay responded: *Are you sure you have to go? Sarah got a storm warning from TCU telling everyone to take precautions. I don't like you driving in a storm.*

Dan will pick me up.

Good. Keep us posted. Hope they reschedule, Lee texted.

Will do. Y'all be safe.

After disconnecting with her sisters, Holly went around doing her usual preparations for storms. First, she changed out of the suit she'd planned to wear to the board meeting and into jeans, a t-shirt, and tennis shoes. Then she walked outside and removed the seat cushions from the chairs and the swing and brought them inside. She brought in several of the lighter potted plants and set them in the dining area. Three pots were too heavy for her to carry. They'd have to manage on their own. She shoved all the patio furniture up against the house to help prevent the wind from blowing pieces into other people's property. If she didn't get hail, they'd probably be okay. Fingers crossed. Just as she got back inside, the deluge struck. Rain pelted down in a gully washer. They'd already had quite a bit of rain this spring. But come July, they'd be grateful.

She turned off and unplugged her computer, gathered up all the other electronics and the cords, stuffed them in a special bag, and put them in her safe place, which happened to be a pantry in the kitchen surrounded by her house. Her bathrooms were all on outside walls, so she never used them as a safe room. Then she gathered medications and her skin care products. She chuckled at herself. If the house had serious damage, makeup would probably be low on her list of priorities. She checked her big flashlights. Yes, they all worked. She put one in the pantry and kept the other one handy. The clock read midafternoon, but the dark clouds made it seem much later. Wind howled.

Holly locked the sliding glass door and pulled the drapes across, as if they would protect anything. The TV weatherman caught her attention. He showed pictures of golf-ball size hail that had fallen west of her location. Gosh, this could be bad. She gulped and ran to the kitchen. She needed a travel iced tea to have with her in the pantry.

She finished preparing her cup as the weather sirens screeched. The ominous sound accelerated her heartbeat and made her palms grow damp. This looked like they could be in for something serious. But the sirens didn't always mean a tornado anymore. They also sounded for severe thunderstorms with winds from forty to eighty miles an hour. But that much wind, even straight lines, could do terrific damage. Her house constructed of brick and stucco should withstand high winds, but still....

Holly jumped when lightning flashed, and thunder crashed simultaneously. Her TV and lights all went off. She pulled back a bit of the drapes at the sliding glass window but stepped back quickly after seeing debris flying by along with golf-ball-size hail pelting her patio. She raised her hands to her ears to shield them from the deafening sound of the hail on her roof. She shook all over. Okay, this was bad. The sirens that had died down earlier now again squealed their warning sound.

Time to head to the pantry. Better safe than sorry. Trite but true. She hurried into the pantry and pulled the door behind her, settling on the small stool she kept there to help her get things off the higher shelves. Her cell pinged with messages. One from Dan saying the meeting would be rescheduled. He was in his downtown high-rise office building but had moved from his eighteenth floor to the basement.

Holly checked in with her sisters. Lee said she only had a little light rain. Pea-sized hail hit Kay's house but didn't do any damage. Nevertheless, she'd taken shelter in her central bathroom. Holly sipped her iced tea as the howling of the wind bellowed like a train. Dear God, could this be a tornado? Would her house withstand a direct hit?

She missed having her dog. Charley had been a great companion especially on days like this. Being deaf, he wasn't bothered by storms, and he comforted Holly. She'd lost him six months ago, and the sadness lingered. The howling of the wind sent chills down her arms. She didn't scare easily, but she admitted she was scared now. A loud crash made her jump. Was that glass breaking? What in the world? Should she creep out to look? Maybe not yet.

The sirens at last grew quiet, and the wind didn't howl as loudly as before. Guess she'd better investigate. She pushed open the pantry door and peeked around. The kitchen looked intact. Good. She eased into the main living area.

"Oh my God."

Broken glass surrounded a tree that had crashed through the patio doors and lay in the middle of the living room. Holly looked outside. The drapes had come down with the entrance of the tree, which apparently pulled out of the soaked ground, and the force of the wind drove it into her house.

As she stared outside, glimmers of sun streaked across the patio. And just as fast as the rain, winds and hail had arrived, the storm moved on. The rain trickled into nothingness, which was a blessing because the broken patio doors would be no help in keeping out the rain. Her pretty curtains, ruined now, wouldn't be of any help either. Holly grabbed her cell and snapped pictures. She'd need it for insurance. Her sisters and Dan would want to see the size of the hailstones.

Her cell blew up. Dan and her sisters. She snapped a few more pictures before doing a group text with them.

Think I was lucky. How are y'all?

They all responded they were fine. They sustained no damage, and they didn't lose power. Sarah was fine at TCU. Storms were fickle the way they hit and missed folks.

A tree blew through my patio doors, and they are smashed.

I'm on my way over there. I'll bring a tarp to cover your patio doors. Not sure how long I'll be. Depends on what the roads are like.

Just like Dan to be prepared for everything.

Someone knocked on her front door.

Holly walked on shaky legs. Reaction had set in. Her hands trembled as she reached to open the door.

"Hey, George." A man in his early sixties, who lived in the next house over with his wife, stood on the front porch. George Sanderson acted the part of the mayor of their small community. "You and Melva okay?"

"Yes, but that lightning bolt sounded like we had a direct hit right between our two homes. We lost power. Did you?"

"Yes, come see what happened." Holly led George into the main living area.

"Wow." He stood with his hands on his hips. "That is something else. But you're okay?"

"Yes, thanks, except for being on edge. The wind blasted the tree through the patio door."

"What are you planning to do?"

"Dan is on his way here with a tarp we'll put up. I've taken pictures, and I'll call the insurance company."

"You let me know if you need any help when Dan gets here."

"Thanks, George. I'll call if he needs help. Y'all will be okay without power? Darkness is fast approaching."

He almost reached the front door when he turned. "We've got a small generator that keeps the refrigerator working. And it's not too cold or too hot. We'll be fine. No telling how long the power will be out. I'm going to get a bigger generator before summer. I'd hate to lose power when the temperature hits a hundred and two."

"Guess we all need to consider that option, George. Thanks for stopping by."

"I'm off to check on everyone else."

Holly closed the door and wandered back into the living area, snapping a few more pictures. She stepped carefully through the broken glass to get a better look from outside. Tree limbs were strewn across the lawn outside her patio. Hailstones covered the patio and hadn't melted yet. She quickly snapped a few more pictures. Because the roof seemed okay now didn't mean she'd have no problems later. Always better to be prepared with documentation.

Hard to imagine the strength of the storm that tore through her small community. The light breeze and sweet smell of the recent rain brought comfort. Several of her neighbors walked around in the common areas. Holly waved and made small talk before going back inside.

She removed work gloves from the bottom junk drawer in the kitchen, brought in a large empty box from the garage then began the arduous task of picking up the pieces of glass. It would take time to pick up all the glass and debris while being careful not to cut herself. She'd gotten about half the pieces put in the box when her cell beeped with Dan's ring. She answered, "Are you here already?"

"Yep. Just now parked by your house."

"How'd you get through the gate?"

"It stood open."

"Well, that's weird."

"Yeah. I thought so. I'm disconnecting, so I can see for myself how bad your place is."

And in one minute he walked up her front steps. Holly stood on the porch. Without considering the outcome, she threw her arms around him. A solid source of strength. His hands rubbing up and down her back comforted her.

"I've got you. You're fine."

Holly dropped her hold and stepped back, flustered. "I guess I was more scared than I realized. Thanks for coming."

"Of course. Now let's take a look at that tree." He held her hand and led her back inside.

They stopped in the living area. "See." Holly gestured with her other hand.

After one look, Dan pulled her in for an even bigger hug, then released her. "Your pictures didn't do this justice." He walked around the almost six feet of tree lying in her living room. Half inside and half out.

"I started picking up the glass."

"Well, let's finish that then." Dan pulled gloves out of his light rain jacket pockets. "Do you have another box?"

"Yes." She ran into her garage and came back, and they set about picking up the glass.

After steady work of half an hour, they felt sure they'd gotten the worst of the mess. "I probably won't walk around barefoot until I've had professional cleaners do their work."

"Good idea. Next thing is to relocate this tree. It doesn't exactly fit your décor."

"No, you're right. George said to call if we needed help, but I'm not sure if the exertion would be good for him. He's had a few heart issues. Hopefully, we can wrestle the tree together."

"The plan is to drag the tree from the living room to the patio. Then we can use the tarp to close this opening."

"Dan, I have a dolly in the garage. Could that help?"

"Worth a try. Bring it in."

Holly scurried to the garage and returned with the dolly.

"Good girl. This will help. If we can get the heaviest part of the tree on the dolly, I'll pull it, and you get the lighter end."

It took many maneuvers accompanied by lots of grunts and laughter, but they finally got the tree up on the dolly. "Oh, my gosh, even the light end weighs a ton."

"The dolly is helping a lot," Dan said. "Without it, we'd need to call George or someone else. Hate to admit, but I wouldn't be able to lug this tree by myself." After much moaning, groaning and more laughter, they finally got the entire tree outside on the patio as darkness settled over the complex.

"Your whole neighborhood must be out."

"Yeah. The only sliver of light is from George's house. His generator will make his house a popular place for our neighbors."

"Not sure where my head is. I left a big flashlight in the car. Be right back." Dan tapped on his cell-phone flashlight and went out the front door, returning with a giant lantern, hammer, and a brown paper sack. "I brought nails." He held up the sack. "I want to get the tarp hung up. Not much protection but better than an opening in the wall."

Holly turned on her flashlight. "Between the two flashlights, this isn't bad."

"Do you have a step stool or ladder?"

"Sure. Also, in the garage. Hang on a minute." She hurried to the garage and quickly returned carrying the ladder with both hands.

"Let me take that from you." Dan carried the ladder outside in front of the patio opening. Holly followed him dragging the tarp. Dan put a couple of nails in his mouth and others in a pocket. Then he grasped a corner of the tarp and climbed about three-fourths of the way up the ladder. Tap, tap, tap.

Several good whacks with the hammer, and he secured the corner. He climbed down, moved the ladder, and climbed back up. Holly passed him more of the tarp, and he repeated the process. Twenty minutes later Dan had secured the tarp including both sides as well as the top. A person trying to enter that way could manage to get in, but the tarp would slow him down.

"Okay, let's go around and come through your front door."

"Good thing I have a code because I didn't remember to bring the key. Actually, I didn't think past what we'd do after you got the tarp up."

"Be careful of the steps."

"You, too. I'm more familiar with this than you are." As she stopped talking, her foot hit the corner of one of the steppingstones, and she lost her balance. Dan's quick response, his hands around her waist, saved her from what could've been a bad fall.

"Oh, my gosh. Thanks. Guess I shouldn't have been bragging." Dan didn't remove his arm from her waist, surprising Holly. She not only tolerated his touch, but she enjoyed the feeling. At his care, warmth spread through her system. Hmm. She hadn't enjoyed a man's touch in years. Not even dancing, which she used to love, having taken lessons at a local studio for years. But that all ended with Joe—

Stop. Don't go there. She had enough on her plate without dredging through those nightmare memories.

As they rounded her house, they noticed flashlights piercing the dark—her neighbors checking out the damage and on each other. She put in the code—thank goodness for batteries—and let them into her house. Her house she loved and felt safe in. Well, you couldn't do enough to protect against an angry Mother Nature.

"I'm bushed. And I didn't do the hard part. Can I get you a glass of wine? I want one."

"Good idea."

She made her way to the kitchen and set her large flashlight on the counter with the light pointing toward the ceiling. She pulled a bottle of wine off the rack and uncorked one of her favorite Texas wines. After she found the glasses and filled them, she handed one to Dan. They settled on the loveseat.

"Thank you."

"No. Thank you. You've been amazing." She squeezed his hand. "Seriously, I don't know what I'd have done without you."

"You'd have managed on your own. You might've taken longer, but you'd have completed the job. Perhaps you'd have called on George's help, but I'm glad I was here, and you didn't need to ask him." He tipped his glass against hers. "Here's to getting through the worst of the storm. Cleanup's such a pain."

"Still, what a relief for the storm to have passed through quickly this time. We've had storms where the rain and wind lasted for over several hours. Those were dreadfully dangerous because flooding became an issue. I've never liked this time of year because of the storms. Everyone waxes poetic about spring and goes on about its beauty, and the wildflowers are gorgeous, but it's not my favorite season." She gulped from her glass.

Dan patted her on the thigh. "Take a few deep breaths, Holly. You'll get through this. Did you report the outage?"

"You know, I haven't even thought about doing that. The sun came out right after the storm, and judging from the darkness now and the flashlights, many in the complex lost power."

"Go ahead and text in the outage. Then you'll get messages telling you when to expect your power to come back on."

Holly nodded, pulled out her cell, and texted the company. A message popped up. "They say they know and hope to have the power back up by morning. That's not bad. I've known of places that have been without power for a week or more after one of these storms."

"Are you planning to go to one of your sisters', or do you want to come to my place?" Dan's gaze met hers over the rim of his glass.

"Oh, wow, I hadn't even thought about tonight. I don't feel comfortable leaving my home with the open doorway, even with the tarp over it, especially since the main gate is open."

"I understand your feeling. I'll stay here then...in your guest room. How will that be?"

"Uh, uh, yeah, thanks. That will be fine." Dan spending the night with her. Well, not with her, but.... Hmm.

"First, I vote for supper. Afterwards, we can stop by the grocery store and pick up a couple of sacks of ice. Whatever foods you regularly use can go in an ice chest, then you won't have to keep opening the refrigerator door."

"Right, we can try not to lose too much food. Let me put on my lipstick, and I'll be ready to go."

"You look beautiful without it."

"Oh, my goodness. That's nice of you to say, but I've always valued your honesty, Dan. Don't make me doubt you now after all these years."

"Just calling it like I see it, ma'am."

Holly laughed. "Be right back."

Dan took Holly's arm as they stepped outside the front door. Holly pressed Lock on the automatic door lock. They made their way to Dan's car. As they drove out, they passed George standing on a corner talking with a couple of the residents. Holly rolled down the window.

"We're going for supper. Can we bring you anything, George?"

"Just information. Let me know how far the power outage goes. News on my cell doesn't help me figure out where the power is out. I've heard from a few residents who plan to spend the night in a hotel."

"Not a bad idea. I'll text you what we find."

Dan drove out of Holly's complex, grateful he'd found her all right, even if shaken up. She'd come through more than most people did in one lifetime. Losing her home on top of everything else would've been unfair. Oh, she had plenty of money, and she could afford to rebuild, but that trauma on top of all the others would be a lot. How much could one person deal with and not fold in on herself and decide to become a hermit?

He didn't believe Holly would react that way, but still she'd been through a lot. Resiliency could only get you so far.

"I checked. Traffic lights aren't working on Camp Bowie," he said. "Let's go south on Bryant Irvin."

In a few blocks, things looked normal. "Ah, here we go." Holly breathed a sigh of relief to see the stoplights working and shops open. She pulled out her cell and tapped a number. "Hey, George. Yes, it's me. Looks like the lights are only off in our area along Camp Bowie and a little south. As soon as we went over the railroad tracks on Bryant Irvin, we found the lights working." She paused for a second. "You're welcome." She disconnected.

"How about Pinstripes in Clearfork? That's not far. Afterwards, we can hit Whole Foods. That's only a block or so down the road."

"Sounds like a good plan to me."

Moments later, Dan parked in the shopping center's garage and helped Holly maneuver down the long driveway to the street. "We could've taken the elevator."

"But this way I get my steps. Gosh, from all the people on the streets here, you'd never know we had a storm."

"Yeah, this area doesn't even have standing water." He glanced around. "They've done a great job on this development. You know the saying, if you build it, they will come? The people have certainly come here. I thought about getting a condo in one of the places here because I could walk everywhere I needed, but decided all the people and constant noise would get on my nerves."

"I like your place in Mistletoe Heights. Such a great example of Craftsman design with a super porch."

"That's why I bought the house, and I've put that porch to good use over the years." The times he hid away from the disaster of his marriage. Rocking and reading and pretending his wife wasn't out with another man. After she'd shown up on the arm of the other man at a social event he attended, he'd immediately filed for divorce. Probably a good thing she didn't realize he planned to attend, too. He might've let the relationship drag out longer. Not healthy for either of them. He'd seen many divorces, and he hadn't wanted to join the statistics, but he deserved to be loved for himself and not his position. Interestingly, the guy his ex-wife had teamed up with went bankrupt. Karma.

"I'm surprised there's such a little line." Holly interrupted his dark thoughts. And why would he be thinking about his ex when he could hang out with Holly? Such a beautiful woman. Her head reached right to his shoulder. Her body while slender had curves in the right place. And her blue eyes were like her sisters', but hers held more than a hint of sadness. But she was strong. To recover from her abusive marriage and then the incident. Yeah, she was strong. He'd admired her for a long time.

He admitted to himself that he'd come to care for her. But he knew with her background, he'd have to move slowly, and that's what he continued to do—keep hoping for a sign she'd be amenable to his advances.

The server took their drink orders and quickly returned to take their meal orders.

"I never do this, but I'm ordering the chicken fried steak."

Dan ordered the salmon. His regular go-to when eating out.

Holly raised her glass. "I need to replenish the well and to celebrate being alive and the house being okay. Celebrate my sisters are okay and that you, my friend, are okay." She clinked her glass with his.

"I'll celebrate you're okay, too, because you were lucky. If all you must do is have your rug and floor professionally cleaned and put in a new patio door, you'll come out fine."

"I agree. From the sound of that wind, I wasn't sure at all. Yeah, I'm one of the lucky ones. Do you think it was a tornado or just straight-line winds?"

"As I drove over, the weather reporters were guessing straight-line winds, but of course, they'll know more accurately tomorrow."

Their food arrived, and they focused on their meal.

Holly pushed her plate away with its half-eaten meal. "Oh, I'm so glad I ordered that. It's one of my favorite meals, and I don't allow myself to indulge often. I don't know why they serve such big portions. Do you want to finish my steak? Otherwise, I'm asking for a to-go box."

"Hand it over" Dan's eyes twinkled.

Holly slid over her plate then sat forward. "Oh, my gosh I never thought. Did you hear whether the zoning commission cancelled their meeting?"

"Yes, they did and have rescheduled for the nineteenth."

"Good. I'd have hated to miss a chance to plead our case."

After Dan finished her meal, they headed for Whole Foods, where they picked up a couple of sacks of ice, fruit, and sweet rolls for breakfast. Before long, Dan turned into Holly's complex.

"Thanks for the wonderful meal. Going out and seeing others with power gave me hope."

"You're welcome, and I'm glad you enjoyed the meal. Let's get this ice into a chest and rescue whatever food you might need to use before the power comes back on. Keeping the refrigerator door closed will save everything in there if the power comes on tomorrow sometime."

"It seems strange to walk in and have to use our flashlights and lanterns after being where we had light. Those lights gave me a false hope. I somehow thought we'd come back and find the power had returned." Holly's chuckle made him smile. Her ability to laugh at herself counted at the top of a long list of the many things that had drawn her to him.

"Hopefully in the morning or by midday. Since it's not the whole city, but only your part, they can get the work done quicker."

After salvaging the various food items they thought they'd frequently need, Holly poured them each another glass of wine, mixing hers with a La Croix lime drink. A spritzer type drink seemed in order with no AC.

She settled on the love seat next to him, but after one sip of her drink, she popped up. "I'll check to make sure the guest room is okay."

Dan took her hand. "I'm sure the room will be fine."

"Okay."

He gently pulled her down, and she settled next to him. "I hate the delay in getting approval for Grant Gardens."

"Yeah, you'll be pushed back a few weeks or possibly a month, but that shouldn't be too bad unless they don't grant the waiver because the neighbors make a big stink."

Holly stifled a big yawn. "Okay, all the stress, hard labor with the tree, the great food and drink, and I'm done in. I better check on the guest room before I fall asleep on you."

"Probably not all bad—except for the crick we'd both have when we woke up in the morning." Did he manage to make a joke about that? The words had popped out before he could stop them. He'd been spending more time than he should thinking about Holly as more than a friend.

Holly ran a hand around the back of her neck. "Oh, those are dreadful. Come on." She stood and took his hand to bring him along but dropping her hold too soon.

Of course, her guest room was immaculate. The ensuite even had fresh towels.

Dan woke up the next morning to the smell of hot coffee. He wandered into the kitchen shoving his shirt tail into his pants. "You brilliant woman. How did you manage fresh coffee?"

Holly waved a long grill starter around like a sword. "While the flame wouldn't come on by itself, my magic wand provided the spark. Here you go, kind sir. I knew I'd eventually find a good reason to hang on to this old percolator. I've forgotten how many times I've almost chunked this old pot into the Goodwill bin. Glad I didn't." She held out a cup to him.

"Blessings on you. I figured we'd have to forage into the community for the nearest coffee shop." He blew on the coffee and then took a tentative sip. "This will do nicely."

"How'd you sleep?"

"Out like a light." He wouldn't share the sensuous dreams about lying in a king bed on a beach with his hostess. They were both naked, and people stood around applauding. Wonder what the audience meant? Did he want others to know how he felt about Holly? Maybe.

"We've got sweet rolls, but they're not warm."

"That's okay. I'm starving. Anything would do and this looks excellent, hot or cold." Dan picked up a large bear claw. Of the many pastries, this ranked as one of his favorites. "What's on your calendar for today? What can I help with?"

"First thing is getting back with the insurance company and Home Depot. I've got to get this door repaired ASAP, and I'm not waiting for insurance money for that. Then contact a roofer to come check. I haven't seen any leaks in the house, but I want to be sure it's okay."

"You sound like you've got a full day before you. I'll head home, shower, change, and go to the office."

They finished the coffee and rolls in comfortable silence. Holly took her plate and cup to the kitchen. Dan followed with his. She turned and put her arms around his neck. "Thanks for coming right away last night. And for staying. That meant everything to me. I'd have been scared here by myself."

"Of course. Any time. You know that." His mind cantered back to the incident and getting her terrified call in the middle of the night. Yeah, he'd been there for that, too. That experience made everything else seem easy.

She hugged him again. He let his hands rest on her slim waist, not tugging her closer as he'd like but enjoying the feel of her so close. She stepped back, and he immediately let go and swallowed a sigh. He needed to get control of his emotions. Holly might never be up for more than a friendly hug.

If that was all she could offer, he needed to decide if he could live with it.

Chapter Seven

Holly spent a busy morning on the phone assuring her sisters she'd managed fine. Brad, Lee's son in Dallas, had no storms at all, and Sarah, Kay's daughter at TCU, only got a smidgen of rain. She didn't tell her sisters about Dan. At least not now. They didn't need to know he'd stayed the night, which had surprised her even as his presence brought comfort. She'd had a bit of trouble falling asleep realizing he slept in the other room. Her sisters stayed there once when they had to leave early the next morning on a trip, which made sense, but she'd been in the house by herself except for her sweet dog. But last night felt good. Having Dan there allowed her to sleep soundly after the initial tossing and turning.

Thankfully, she'd gotten hold of her handyman. She'd met him at Home Depot to pick out the new door, and he would do the installation that afternoon. That meant no need for Dan to spend the night again. Hmm. Did that disappoint her a little? Surely not, but yeah. If she were honest, she felt a hint of disappointment because having him around brought comfort.

And he'd always been there for her. She'd started working with him when she'd first gotten into the development field. He worked quickly and efficiently with contracts and made sure as much as possible that while they were fair, they favored her. Her business deals had made him quite a bit of money over the years. She'd bought land out in the boonies, and now the city had annexed much of the property and increased the land's value. She'd sold and sold. And continued to buy as she had the property with her sisters. Dan had kept her from making a few property mistakes, too.

Knocking at the door pulled her from her woolgathering. She peeked through the glass and then opened the front door.

"Hey, Les. Come in." She welcomed her handyman.

"Do you know the front gate is open?"

"Yeah. Someone was pulling in when the power went off, and the gate froze in the open position. As soon as the power comes back on, I'm sure the issue will be resolved. At least that's the hope."

"When do you expect power to be restored?"

"Well, the last text said this afternoon. Anytime now, I hope."

"I've got the door in my truck. Let's see what your situation is."

Holly pointed toward the tarp. "My friend Dan put this up last night."

"Well, yes, I can see he did. I'll go around to the patio and start by taking down the tarp. This made for a good stopgap until I could get here." He moved toward the front door.

"Thanks, Les. Holler if you need anything."

"Sure."

Holly took down the ruined drapes while Les worked outside. After he removed the tarp, she smiled at the light pouring into the main room. One of the many things she'd loved about this house. All the light. Lovely.

Holly wandered into the guest room. Might as well pull off the sheets and put on fresh ones. She couldn't wash them yet, but better to get done what you could when you could. Like last night, the room was ready to go when Dan needed to stay there. The pillow still had a dent where his head had lain. His scent still clung to the case. A hint of spice.

She yanked off the case. Get busy. She was being ridiculously foolish. She and Dan had been friends. Had been forever. Don't do anything to screw up that invaluable friendship.

She'd finished taking off the old lavender sheets and remaking the bed with the peach floral set when Les called out to her, "Hey, Holly."

She dropped off the dirty sheets in the laundry room and returned to the main room. "Do you need anything?"

"No, I've got my portable generator, and it's fixing to get loud. I thought you might want to take off. I should have this done in an hour."

"Thanks for the heads up. I'll take your advice. Maybe by the time I return, we'll have power, too. I've got ice in this chest if you need any for your drink."

"Thanks. See you after a while." Les went back to work.

Holly picked up her purse and keys and opened the doors to the garage and her car as the noise level increased. Les had been right. Drat! She just remembered she couldn't click a button and open the garage. With all her strength, she tried to push up the door. Finally, she gave up and went in search of Les. "I hate to interrupt you, but I can't get the garage door up. Can you help?"

"Sure." Putting down his drill, he followed Holly to the garage. In no time, his extra strength and reach had the door rising.

"Thanks, Les." Holly waved and drove off, not sure where she'd go but wanting to get away from the noise of Lee fixing her patio door.

At first, she went to the La Madeline near where she lived. Duh. They still didn't have power either, but she'd come through a storm and needed to reward herself. She hoped the one off Hulen would be all right. The storm, while strong, had been spotty. After driving down Southwest Boulevard, she merged onto 820 and then turned onto Hulen and into the shopping center lot that had another La Madeline. She parked, noticing lights in all the stores. Nice. She went into the bistro and ordered a cup of coffee and a Napoleon and settled on the patio. The traffic sounds didn't even bother her, and the spring air only caused a smidge of trouble with her allergies. Easily handled with a quick pop of a pill.

With time on her hands and nothing else to do, she thought about the rescheduled board of adjustment meeting. She'd been ready to do her presentation, and now she had to regroup with the week's delay. Hopefully, they'd see the importance of what she and her sisters wanted to do—provide houses for those who were unhoused. Maybe if something like this had existed, her aunt, her mother's sister, wouldn't have killed herself. Aunt Lee's situation turned her parents on to this important area of service. She and her sisters had joined the fight. Better not to warehouse people in giant dorm buildings but to recognize their dignity and provide them with a home.

She savored every bite of the decadent Napoleon, licking her fork to get the last bit of lusciousness.

Her cell beeped. "Hey, Les. Everything okay?"

"Just giving you a heads-up. I'm almost finished, and the power came back on about ten minutes ago if you want to come home."

"Great news. I'll be there in less than twenty minutes."

Sure enough, as Holly drove into the west side of town, streetlights flickered red and green. The gate to her complex stood closed. It opened with not a moment's hesitation like nothing had ever been wrong. The garage door closed after she drove in, she let herself into the kitchen, and walked toward the patio door.

"Oh, Les, you've done it. Thank you. You're a lifesaver. I feel like I can breathe again."

Les's smile met hers. "We were lucky. Your door had standard measurements. Otherwise, we'd have been special ordering, and you'd have been waiting for weeks."

"Sometimes going fancy-fancy is not the best thing. When I bought the house, I considered making the opening larger and putting in a new, larger patio door. Fortuitous that I didn't." She walked outside to get a good look from that perspective. "Yes, this is perfect." She entered. "What do I owe you?"

Les handed her an itemized bill for the door itself and his labor. "Not bad to assure myself I can sleep here safely tonight. Let me get you a check." She hurried to her office and filled out the info on a check and then returned to the main room.

"Thank you again, Les. You always do great work, and I appreciate you being able to get here today." She hugged her handyman.

"Anytime for you, Holly." He stepped back. "Call me if you need anything else." He grabbed his tools and walked out the front door.

Holly moved out to her patio. Two large pots lay on their side, their greenery and dirt spilling out. Guess she'd need to replace plants here, too. But lots of progress had been made. She'd need to buy new drapes, too, but that could wait. She looked up the number for the restoration company that fixed things after a storm. The floors had to be professionally cleaned to make sure they'd gotten all the glass, and no water remained. After scheduling the company, she took a broom and dustpan to sweep up the dirt from the patio.

"You slept at Holly's house?" Jon Baxter's eyebrows soared up his forehead. Dan's partner and best friend sat up from where he'd slouched in front of Dan's desk. "Man, was that smart?"

"Maybe not smart, but necessary." Dan explained what the storm did to Holly's house and how the gate on the complex had stuck in the open position. "I couldn't leave her there with only a tarp for protection."

"You're a glutton for punishment if I've ever seen one. Do you plan to ever tell her how you feel?"

"Maybe. For a moment last night, I thought I picked up a tiny spark of interest. I felt a flare of hope."

"It's gotta be hard though working with her the way you do and wanting more."

"I knew that going in. I met her after she and her husband had divorced. I knew she'd had hard times, but then when he got out of prison, he stalked her. The surprising thing would be if she got to the place where she wanted any kind of a physical relationship with any man. If she ever comes around, I want to be that man."

"A real Boy Scout."

"Eagle Scout."

Jon laughed. "Proud to be your friend."

"**G**lad you could meet for lunch, Kay." Lee hugged her younger sister. "La Madeline is one of my faves. Great food and ambiance." They went through the line, and each ordered iced tea and salads then settled in at one of the tables for two.

Kay raised her glass. "I'm celebrating because I've finished that commissioned painting."

"Congratulations, Kay. I'm happy for you." Lee clinked her sister's glass. "I'm celebrating, too."

"Why?" Kay sipped her tea and set the glass on the table, resting her chin on her hands.

"Because Dan spent the night at Holly's house the night of the storm."

"What?" She stopped while a server brought their salads. "Thank you." The server nodded. "Holly didn't say anything to me, but I'm excited for them." Kay raised her glass and clinked Lee's a second time. "Definitely something to celebrate." She sipped her iced tea and then sampled her chicken salad. "Yum. This is the best. Definitely a celebratory meal." She ate two bites. "You know he's the most patient man. I was afraid Holly would never come around."

"Well, she didn't exactly." Lee bit into a giant strawberry.

"What do you mean?"

"He stayed in the guest room."

The stuffing went out of her sister, and Lee struggled not to laugh out loud. Kay slumped in her chair, and the corners of her mouth turned down.

"That's a terrible way to joke, Lee. You got my hopes all up."

"Well, I took their decision as a good sign." Lee picked up her glass. "She could've come and stayed with either of us, but she chose to stay there with Dan."

"I get she didn't want to leave her house at risk with the gate open, but wow. Yeah, I guess this is some kind of a big deal."

"None of us has a good track record with men. But our situation is totally different than Holly's. Her husband nearly killed her."

"Well, I might've said I'd like to kill Bill, but I spoke the words only in jest. We weren't right for each other, plain and simple. He never understood my need to paint and that made him wander. He kept after me to quit and do something that would make money."

"Who's laughing now?" Lee tipped her glass toward Kay. "How much is this latest commission?"

"Forty-five hundred, but who's counting?" Kay touched her glass to Lee's, and they both laughed. "What's that saying, the person who laughs last, laughs longest?" Kay set down the glass. "Seriously, is there anything we can do to push Holly off dead center?"

"I don't know. I guess pray for them both." Lee pushed aside her salad plate. "Do you want to split a dessert?"

"Split? No way. I'm having my own. Remember we're celebrating." Kay rose and Lee followed her sister to the dessert case.

Barrett Armstrong wandered over to Roger's house and knocked.

The man opened the door. "How're you doing, Barrett? You want to come in?"

"Doing fine, and no, I don't need to. I wanted to remind you the board of adjustment meeting is tomorrow night. Do you have your speech written out?"

"Sure do. We've worked hard for what we've got. I don't want no lazy bums moving in and messing with our neighborhood."

"Why don't we drive together? Parking is a nightmare down there."

"I was going to pick up Maxine, but if you want to drive, that works."

"I'm on the way to check with Maxine now. Be at my house at six thirty. I want to make sure we can get a good seat. Sometimes there's no one at these meetings, and sometimes they're packed."

"You got it. See you at six thirty tomorrow."

Barrett walked to the end of the corner and turned toward Maxine Krause's house. The woman's yard impressed everyone. Not surprising. She worked there every day. Barrett found her cleaning out flower beds, her red hair tied back with a bandana. For the life of him, he couldn't see any weeds. Guess that's why her yard won most of the neighborhood awards.

"Hey, Maxine. You ready for tomorrow night?"

"Sure am. Got my remarks all printed out. Even timed it. They won't interrupt me."

"Good to hear. Roger's meeting at my house at six thirty. We can all ride down together."

"Works for me. I'll see you then." She turned back to her weeding.

Barrett walked off. He wasn't taking any chances that those two wouldn't show up. They needed to present a united front to the board of adjustment. No reason for them to give Holly Grant a waiver to put up a bunch of homeless losers across from their neighborhood.

Chapter Eight

Holly stepped out onto the front porch as Dan drove up. She didn't even wait for him to get out to hold the door for her. She'd worn her power outfit with the short red jacket and flared black skirt that fit smoothly over her hips with black pumps. Sensible heels, but heels nevertheless.

"Hey." She climbed in, put on her seat belt, and slammed the door.

"Hey, to you, too. You doing okay? You seemed a bit impatient. I'd have come to your door."

"I'm eager to get this over and done. Get our waiver and move on." She grasped the strap of her purse. "What's your opinion? Will we get the waiver? Will Jon be able to help?"

"Jon won't be able to vote. I figure he'll have to abstain because he and I are partners, and he knows you. Declaring our connection will help. We'll see what the other members say."

"Gosh, I want this to go through. Mom and Dad would be so proud for us to be able to make even a small dent in the homeless population. I know others are out working, too. But Grant Gardens— Oh, my goodness, I've got to show you the plans we're working on with an architect."

"I'm surprised you went ahead with the architect before you knew you could move forward." Dan stopped at a traffic light and shot Holly a glance.

"My sisters and I decided we wanted to put the idea out there in the universe. You know. Declaring something to be true before it is. Manifesting our dreams."

"Oh, I get it. Hope this doesn't end up being a waste of your money. Do you know something about the board members I don't?"

Holly laughed. "No, I don't. Do you?"

"Well, at least one of them, Marilyn Chambers, is known for voting no on any requested waiver. Marilyn is strait-laced, by-the-book, wearing suits no matter how hot, and she sprays her bubble hair to within an inch of its life. No wind will alter her hair style. Her thing is everyone should know what the rules are and abide by them. If the rules say only six-foot fences, don't show up begging the board to let you put in an eight foot one for whatever reason."

"I get that. But we're only asking to make smaller and more houses on the property, but not so much as to mess up traffic or make it difficult for fire and ambulances to get through."

"In Marilyn's mind, that's an adjustment that's not necessary."

"No matter how much good the waiver would accomplish?"

"The rules are the rules are the rules to Marilyn. Well, look at that, a parking spot." Dan pulled in. "I'm taking that as a sign of our good fortune. Are your sisters on their way?"

"They left about the same time we did and drove together. They're glad I'm doing the talking, but they want to be seen as supportive partners."

Dan grasped her hand. "You're beautiful. You'll do great. Let's go do this." He squeezed once and let go. He came around and held her door while she got out, and then they walked the short distance to the entrance. They went through security and then rode the elevator to the top floor where they found Lee and Kay waiting.

"You look great, sis. Love the power jacket. Impressive. Looks competent." Kay, the color person, would notice that.

"The heels show off your legs well, too," Lee observed.

Holly chuckled. "I don't wear them often. But if they impress, they're worth the strain." She glanced at Dan, whose gaze locked on her legs. Interesting.

"Okay, ladies, let's go get our seats." He opened the double doors and led them into the chamber, a large room, with raked theatre style seating so everyone could see well. The board of adjustment sat on a raised, curved platform behind a built-in desk. A speaker's stand and mic stood in the center facing the board.

Holly let her sisters go into the row before she did. She followed, leaving the end seat for Dan. Once they settled, she took both sisters' hands and sent them an encouraging smile. Holly appreciated Kay coming. She was such an introvert, happiest in her own home slapping colors on a pallet. Their issue wouldn't appear until around midway through the agenda.

A hand on her shoulder made Holly jump. She turned her head to find Bentley Stevenson standing in the row behind her. Dan and she rose.

"So glad you could come, Ben." Dan shook the hand of the older man in a dark business suit.

"Of course. I'm excited about your project, Holly." Ben extended his hand to her, and she clasped his with both of hers. "This is right on track for what we're trying to do. Find real homes for these people and get them off the street and out of the shelters."

"Thanks, Ben. We're excited to be a part of the effort."

Ben spoke to her sisters before the chairman of the board of adjustment called the meeting to order.

After the opening ceremony, the meeting got started, and the board moved through several items on the agenda. Holly felt like ants crawling all over her as she waited with anticipation and a small part of fear for the chairman to call their item number. She needed and wanted them to get approval so they could move forward with the work on the complex. The need was great out there. If they didn't get approval, they'd have to make changes to their plans and try again or look for another piece of property. Either action would slow down their ability to help put their plans in place to help people out of homelessness.

Trying to distract herself from her worry, she glanced around the room. Huh. She nudged Dan's arm. When he looked at her, she angled her head toward the far-left side of the room. His gaze tracked her direction. He looked back at her, his lips a straight seam, not any happier to see Barratt Armstrong than she was. Guess they'd find out where he stood when he spoke. Forty minutes into the proceedings, the secretary stated the number of their agenda item and called Dan's name as the first speaker.

He rose and went to the podium. "Mr. Chairman and members of the board, thank you for your time tonight. My name is Dan Morgan, and I live in District 9. I'm here representing Hollister Grant and her sisters, Leeland Grant Kennedy and Kaitlan Grant Clayton, in their request for a waiver of the minimum size of house on properties with the A10 designation. In the interest of your time, we will have Ms. Grant and Bentley Stephenson, President of the Homeless Coalition, speak."

"Yes, we have both Ms. Grant's and Mr. Stephenson's names," the chair acknowledged. "Which of you is speaking first?"

Dan turned toward Holly, and she rose. "I'm speaking first." Dan stepped to the side. He smiled and nodded at her. She walked toward the podium and leaned toward the mic. "My name is Hollister Grant, and I live in District 7 in west Fort Worth. Our request is personal to us. My mother's sister became homeless and lived in a shelter. She struggled with mental health issues, and despite all our grandparents' and parents' efforts, they weren't able to help her. But my mother remembered her sister saying her fondest wish was to live in her own space. Not to have to share with another person as she did in the shelter. My mother and father set up a trust for my sisters and me, which we inherited at their deaths." Holly swallowed against the pain of losing those two wonderful people. "My sisters and I—" She gestured for Lee and Kay to stand. They did and then sat down. "—decided the best thing we could do with the money is to make a development for people who'd been homeless, giving them a space of their own, as our aunt had wanted.

"The parcel of land is near health care facilities and on the bus lines to get to shopping and jobs. Our plan is to build thirty tiny houses that would each house one or two people. We're not talking about building a three-story apartment complex that would significantly increase the density. We call the development Grant Gardens, with the intent of having lots of green spaces and actual vegetable gardens that the residents would tend. We've been communicating with agencies that serve the homeless, including Bentley Stephenson, president of the board of the Homeless Coalition. We'll have social workers on site and bring in people with expertise to help the residents with their needs. We appreciate being heard and hope you'll grant our request for a waiver." She turned to the chairs behind her. "Ben."

Bentley rose and crossed to join Dan and her. Holly shifted to the other side of the podium and Ben began by identifying himself and stating where he lived. "Agencies who work with people who are homeless are focusing more and more on figuring out ways to get people out of the shelters and into spaces of their own. The kind of community that Ms. Grant and her sisters are proposing is exactly the kind of thing we're looking for. The need for these communities is great, and we'd love to see Grant Gardens become a reality."

Dan moved behind the mic. "Do you have any questions for any of us?"

The chairman looked to his left and right to see if members had questions. Jon Baxter's light glowed green.

"Okay, Mr. Baxter. You have the floor," the chairman said.

"Thank you, Mr. Eisley. I want to make clear my relationship with Mr. Morgan. He and I are law partners. And I know Ms. Grant, too. I will abstain from any vote we take on their issue." Low mumbling from the audience and the board filled the air.

"Thank you, Mr. Baxter. I appreciate you being upfront about this." The chairman glanced around. "Anyone else?" No one punched his speaker button. "Well, my first question is, have you spoken to your neighbors? Based on the maps I've seen, there's a neighborhood across the road from where you propose to build your community. Have you contacted them?"

Holly smiled at the chair's use of the term community. She nodded at Dan for him to respond.

"Mr. Eisley, Ms. Grant and I met with the High Trails Neighborhood Association on April 6. We understood that they voted not to oppose this work.

"Thank you, Mr. Morgan, Ms. Grant, and Mr. Stephenson. You may be seated."

Holly, Ben, and Dan returned to their seats.

"I have several other people who've requested to speak on this issue. Barrett Anderson, Maxine Krause, and Roger Tyler. Which of you would like to go first?"

Maxine rose and strode toward the front of the room. She fiddled with the mic before beginning. "My name is Maxine Krause, and I live in the High Trails neighborhood. We don't want those kinds of people living near us, and I'm against you granting the waiver of the rules. The rules are the rules are the rules, Mr. Chairman. People must abide by them. Thank you."

Holly felt the stab of the woman's glare as she returned to her seat on the other side of the room.

"I'm Roger Tyler, Mr. Chairman and board members. I also live in the High Trails neighborhood. "Folks..."

Holly realized Tyler must be making eye contact with each member of the board as his head pivoted from one end of the table to the other.

"Folks, we worked hard for our money and scrimped and saved so we could move to this safe, beautiful neighborhood. We don't want any undesirables moving in across the road from us. This proposed development will hurt our property values. And that's the bottom line."

As he returned to his seat, Barrett took his place at the podium.

"Good evening, Mr. Chairman and members of the board. My name is Barrett Armstrong, I live in the High Trials Development, and I'm the president of the High Trails Neighborhood Association. Reducing the size of the houses on the property across from our neighborhood isn't a good idea, and as Mr. Tyler stated, will devalue our property. And as Ms. Krause stated, the rules are the rules for a reason. We ask that you not grant the waiver."

Armstrong turned to go but the chairman stopped him. "For clarification, Mr. Armstrong, did the neighborhood association take a vote, and are you speaking for the association or yourself?"

Holly made eye contact with Dan. He shrugged his shoulders as if to say, "I don't know what he'll say."

"Well, uh, well, Mr. Chairman, when the neighborhood discussed the issue, they were evenly divided on whether to support this project or not. I'm speaking for a significant number of dissenters."

"But not the neighborhood association as a whole?" The chairman pushed to pin down Armstrong's position.

"No, not the whole association, but a very concerned group."

"Thank you, Mr. Armstrong."

Holly squeezed Dan's arm. Surely his answer helped them.

"Any discussion from the board members?" The chair looked to his left and right.

The light in front of Marilyn Chambers glowed red.

"Ms. Chambers, you have the floor."

She adjusted her mic. "Mr. Chairman and fellow board members, you know my position, but I want to go on record to make it clear. As Ms. Krause stated, the rules are the rules are the rules. I will vote no to granting the waiver. We must protect our neighborhoods."

"Thank you, Ms. Chambers. Anyone else?"

The light in front of Charlotte Jessop turned green.

"Yes, Ms. Jessop."

"Thank you, Mr. Chairman. I want to go on record as being one hundred percent behind this project." Her gaze met Holly's. "I too had a family member who found himself homeless for a time. He'd grown quite ill and couldn't keep up his house payments. Anyone can find themselves in this situation. I thank you for what you're doing."

Holly smiled and nodded.

"Anyone else? I see no lights. Can I have a motion then?"

Charlott's Jessop's speaker light glowed.

"Yes, Ms. Jessop." The chair acknowledged her.

"I move that the board of adjustment approve the request for a waiver of agenda item BA 23-19."

Without pushing his speaker button, Arturo Hernandez said, "I second that motion."

"Any more discussion?" The chair looked to his left and right. "If not, all in favor, vote yes."

Holly held her breath as she counted one, two, three, four, five, six green lights.

"All opposed, vote no."

Marilyn Chamber's lone red light glowed.

"We have six votes of yes and one vote of no and one abstention. The agenda item passes. The next item on the agenda is..."

Holly never heard what he said after that as she, Dan, her sisters, and Ben made for the exit. She could hardly keep her excitement in check. She wanted to scream and holler and jump up and down. She contained herself until the doors closed behind them.

"Yea! We did it." She hugged her sisters and Bentley. "Thank you, Ben." Then she hugged Dan. And oh, my that felt amazingly good. "I can't thank you enough, my friend." Yes, he was her friend, nothing else. She needed to keep that in mind, but oh, she liked the feel of his arm around her shoulder.

"How about we go out to celebrate? We can grab drinks and appetizers at Bob's Steak and Chop. It's only a couple of streets over."

"Sounds good to me." Holly smiled at Dan. "What do you say, sisters? And, Ben, you must join us."

"I'd love to, Holly, but I've got a board meeting in the morning and have a bit more to do to get ready. Not the least of which is to report on your good news. Dan, will you be there?"

"Sure will."

"Congratulations then and keep us in the loop on your progress. If you need anything or have questions, I'm here for you."

Holly hugged Ben. "That means a lot, Ben. Thank you for tonight. And I'm sure we'll be asking as we go along."

"We'll come but only for a short time." Lee answered, and Kay nodded as they headed to where they had left their car.

"Let's go then." Dan took Holly's hand and walked outside, and they walked back to his car to drive the short distance to the steak house.

Holly's tummy turned over at how good her hand felt in Dan's. They were just friends, weren't they?

Chapter Nine

Dan emptied the last of the second bottle of champagne into the sisters' glasses. Laughter had flowed along with the bubbly. Listening to the sisters chatting about their plans filled him with excitement about their project. Holly's responses filled him with more than excitement, something more like anticipation. He enjoyed being a part of her business life, but what he wanted was to be involved with her personal life. They had a lot in common, both working to make people's lives better through the development of new and better properties. He wanted to go home to her every evening and get up with her in the morning. Jon was right. Dan had it bad. Would he ever get to the point where he would go after what he wanted? What he wanted was a life with Holly Grant.

Lee set her glass away. "Okay, this has been a great celebration, but we need to get on home, and I can't have another drink if I'm safely driving Kay and me home." She laughed. "I'm kidding, I'm perfectly fine to drive us, but even the best of times needs to come to an end. Come on, Kay, let's hit the road." Lee slipped her purse strap over her shoulder.

Kay grumbled but complied. "Thank you for the wonderful meal, Dan. We could've gone Dutch treat."

"Well, yes, you could have, but I insisted. We needed to celebrate getting your waiver. Now you're almost ready to go full steam ahead with the plans for Grant Gardens. We just need approval from the council, but they usually go along with whatever the board of adjustment recommends."

They all rose, and they exchanged hugs and kisses. "Thank you for coming out, Kay. I know it's difficult for you." Holly returned her sister's hug.

"You're welcome and being in attendance wasn't that bad. Didn't hurt that we came here afterwards for the meal. It's my favorite. Thank you again, Dan. We appreciate how you keep an eye out for our sister."

"Oh, she does all right on her own." Dan slid an arm around Holly's shoulders.

"Thank you, kind sir. I believe I do quite all right. I'll talk with y'all tomorrow about next steps." They wandered outside onto the street and gave the valet their tickets. Two young men went off at a run to bring around their vehicles.

In no time, they were back and after another round of hugs, Holly's sisters climbed into Lee's large SUV and carefully merged into the downtown traffic. Dan reached over and grasped Holly's hand. "I'm happy for you."

"I'm happy for us, too." Holly returned the squeeze of his hand. "I guess I'll contact the architect tomorrow and let him know we're almost a go. I know we still need the city council to agree, but this is a win for sure."

After the short drive home, Holly activated the gate opener. Dan pulled in and around to the back of the complex where Holly's house stood. Should he make a move tonight? He found her celebratory mood encouraging. He'd like to help her celebrate even more.

"Why don't you come in for one more drink, Dan?" Holly held out her hand to him as they went up the steps to her house.

"You sure it's not too late?" He'd give her an out. He'd never force her, but oh, he wanted to make love to this woman.

"No, no. Come on in." And so, he followed her into her house. She flipped on a few lamps, which spilled their soft glow across the terrazzo tile floors. "Can you open this bottle, Dan? I want to get more comfortable. I can wear a suit with the best of them, but..."

"You go ahead. I'll have your glass ready by the time you return." After uncorking the bottle and pouring two glasses, he carried them into the family room. Holly joined him before he set the glasses on the coffee table. She had slipped off her high heels and left her jacket in the bedroom. The black skirt fit across her hips and flared at her knees. The silk blouse draped sensually across her breasts. Desire stirred within him.

He clicked his glass with hers. "To a beautiful woman."

"How kind. Thank you." She sipped. "Ah yes. The champagne we had with dinner was excellent, but this is my favorite wine. Nice hints of plum and blackberry."

She settled on the sofa, and Dan dropped down beside her. With his thumb, he rubbed gentle circles on the back of her hand.

"Holly."

"Dan."

They chuckled as they both spoke at the same time. Dan decided to make his point. He set both glasses on the coffee table. He grasped her chin in his hand and ran a thumb over her lips. She gasped but didn't pull away. "I care about you, Holly. More than as a friend. I have for a long time, but I haven't wanted to do anything to cause us to lose our friendship if you didn't feel anything for me. But I decided I needed to gut up and tell you how I feel."

Her eyes grew large, and her breathing quickened.

"Well, I—"

"You don't have to say something because I have. I don't want to pressure you," Dan interrupted her. He didn't want her to stop him, or for her to ask him to leave, but he had to tell her.

"Dan, I want to say something."

He held his breath. What was on her mind?

Her gaze searched his face. "I care for you, too."

"That's good, but do I hear a *but*?"

"Not exactly a *but*; however, I feel I need to tell you more of my story."

"Holly, I know what happened when your ex attacked you. It was fifteen years ago, but it's not something I'm ever likely to forget."

"Yes, you do know about what happened when he attacked me, I shot and killed him." She shook her head to remove the images of Joe clutching his stomach and the blood from his shoulder mixing with the wound in his middle spreading across his shirt and through his fingers before he tumbled to the ground. "I'll forever be grateful to you for how you stood by me and helped me through the legalities. But I'm talking about what happened before that." She'd never told Dan about the specifics of the abuse. Oh, she'd had to share the emergency-room reports with the lawyer who represented her in the murder investigation. But Dan had never heard the sealed grand jury testimony. At the time, she hadn't wanted her friend to know what she'd been through. But if they had any chance to be more than friends, he deserved to hear all the gory details.

"I know you know Joe abused me. It's the reason the grand jury decided not to indict me for murder. But before that, way before the divorce, his abuse did a number on me...psychologically and physically. I don't have children not because I didn't want children, but because I *couldn't* have children."

Dan gripped her hand. His lips stiffened into a straight line.

She gulped a sip of wine. She could get through this. She had to. She owed this man the truth. "And despite therapy, I still have difficulty believing a man would desire me, or if he did, that I could respond appropriately."

"Oh, Holly. I'm sorry. I had no idea. I should've talked with you about this."

"Had you asked, I wouldn't have told you. I wasn't able to or ready to. I think I am now." She took a couple of breaths before beginning her story.

"You know, Joe and I met in high school, dated, fell in love. We went to the same college and after two years decided to get married. My family wasn't too thrilled. They wanted me to finish school first. But I was hell bent to have that fancy full-blown wedding with six bridesmaids and the country club reception. Many of my sorority sisters were getting married. People didn't live together back then as easily as they do now, and that's not how my parents brought me up." She paused, drawing in a deep breath.

Dan took her hand and rubbed his thumb across the back. "Take your time."

She paused. She could do this. "It didn't take long for the marriage to start falling apart. We argued over money, his friends, my friends. Joe thought any guy who spoke to me wanted in my pants. He was insanely jealous, and for no reason. I could never convince him of that." She shook her head. "The absolute worst night in many ways happened when he held a shotgun under his chin and threatened to kill himself if I didn't promise not to talk to a guy, we both knew from school. It's crazy, you know. My mind kept flashing towards what would happen if he pulled the trigger. The blood, the police, the utter desolation of having someone you love taking his life and right in front of you."

"What'd you do?"

"I promised, of course. After much crying and begging, he finally lowered the gun. But then he hit me, blaming me because he'd almost killed himself. You know how in the old cartoon shows, the character gets something dropped on his head and stars dance around? That really does happen when you're hit in the head." She looked at him.

Dan pulled her into the shelter of his arm. "I'm listening."

"We rocked along for several years. If things were going well with him, he acted the perfect gentleman. Talk about Dr. Jekyll-Mr. Hyde. But if he had any trouble at work, and I was doing well... Life got scary. My first year in real estate, I had phenomenal sales. The company nominated me to represent them in the competition for first-year realtors. I went on to win out over all the nominees from other companies."

"Wasn't he proud of you for that? Sounds like quite an accomplishment to me."

"No. Unfortunately, the recognition happened at the same time he was having difficulties at work. I never knew whether people picked on him or if he had screwed up. I only heard his side of the story. I found out later he had a gambling problem, making our financial situation worse. He made such a stink about the dinner, I went alone to the banquet to receive my recognition, something most people took their significant others to. When I came home, I found Joe drunk and furious with me for going without him even though he'd refused to go. He beat me up so bad. I couldn't go into work for several days."

Dan's hand clenched on hers and then softened in comfort.

"I'd fallen into that all too common mindset of abuse victims. If I hadn't made a higher grade than him on the accounting test, if I hadn't gained those ten pounds, if I'd kept the house cleaner, if I hadn't won the prize. On and on went the abuse. Usually not bad enough to land me in the hospital, until that year, when I missed a lot of days. I felt bad about letting down my clients, but my bosses were incredible.

"They kept encouraging me to call the police to report him, as did my parents. But you know that's hard to do to someone you've loved. I'm not sure I still loved Joe by then, but I loved the idea of us and hated to admit I'd been one of those brain-washed victims. I mean I let him do that to me."

She paused for a sip of the deep purple liquid. A glance at Dan showed his face drawn with wrinkles between his eyes, a muscle clenching and releasing in his jaw.

"The last year we were together, Joe escalated. The third time I wound up in the hospital, my bosses called the police and reported the abuse themselves. He broke my left arm in two places and a rib and caused a concussion from the blows to my head and face. Kicks to my middle killed my ability to have children. So, I filed charges. My testimony sent him to prison. We were officially divorced after five years of marriage.

"As you know, the moment they released him, he came after me. That's when I shot him."

"Your story blows my mind, Holly. I don't know how you've coped."

"It hasn't been easy, but I had support. Parents, employers, my sisters. I worried Lee and Kay would try to kill him. They were livid about everything that had gone on. When they heard he'd been released from prison and had harassed me again. Well..." Holly shook her head. Her sisters were something else.

"So that's who I am. I've not felt safe or strong enough for anything more than a rare kiss, much less anything like a fulfilling sexual experience since Joe's abuse. I want to try with you, but I can't promise anything."

Dan's arm came around her, and she nestled against his chest. She felt safe. Cared for. And oh, my goodness, she desired this man. But what if she couldn't go through with it? What if in trying, they ruined their friendship, which Holly valued above everything except her sisters?

"We can go slowly, Holly. I'll do anything to make you feel safe. I'm sorry you experienced this. I'm honored you felt safe enough to trust me with the details. Reliving the events couldn't have been easy."

"Thanks, Dan. No, telling you wasn't, but you deserved to know what you were getting yourself into. If you've changed your mind, I totally understand."

Dan took both her hands and drew them to his lips and tenderly kissed them. "You couldn't say a thing that would make me care less. If anything, I'm more determined to make this work. You deserve to know and believe how beautiful and how desirable you are. If I can help you accept that, I'm all in for however long we need."

Tears slid down Holly's cheeks. Dan reached up and brushed them away with his thumb. "Don't cry. We'll get through this. Can I stay with you tonight? We won't do anything, except sleep in the same bed. I want to hold you."

The huge grin spreading across Holly's face almost embarrassed her. She nodded and kissed his cheek. "Yes, I would like that very much."

B arrett walked out his front door and headed to the front of the complex. He stared across the road to the land he considered his own. Damn the board of adjustment. His friend Marilyn Chambers had disappointed him. Yes, she voted against the motion, but she hadn't been able to convince any of the other members to join her. He had a chance because the waiver still had to go to the city council, and he'd have to convince them to oppose the waiver. However, the city council had been facing a lot of pressure to deal with the vagrants and panhandlers on the street. If they saw Holly Grant's project as a tool to help with that, they'd be inclined to go along, especially since the board of adjustment had given its seal of approval.

He scuffed at the dirt with his boot as he stepped out of the road when a car roared by. Crazy kid drove way above the speed limit. Barrett walked on considering his options.

In the past, he'd hired a guy to cause disruptions to the site when they began work, and that had been successful. The past owners decided the cost of the accidents made their projects cost-prohibitive to continue. He wasn't certain that would work this time. Holly Grant seemed determined to make this happen. Hmm. Was the key Holly Grant herself? If he took her out of the equation, perhaps the sisters would let go of his land. He could at least gain time while they dealt with their grief. One corner of his mouth hooked up in a smile. Yes, that's what he'd do. He needed to figure out how, but he could do that. He whistled on his way back home to research the woman to find out where she hung out. Glad he'd resolved a way to keep his property.

Barrett went directly to the liquor cabinet, opened the door, snagged the bottle of Bourbon. He filled a glass, took a sip, enjoying the burn as the liquid slid down his throat. That hit the spot. He settled in front of the computer and googled Holly Grant. Lots of links came up about the woman, including a shocking story about her shooting and killing her ex-husband. Damn. He tapped his fingers in a pattern on the desktop. Guess he'd have to be trickier than the woman. That was his land, and he'd do whatever needed to keep control. She didn't appear to work at an office. That limited the places he could gain access to her.

His next search pulled up her address. Man, he loved the internet. You could find anything. Time for a little excursion. He downed the rest of the bourbon, set the glass in the sink, lifted his keys from the hook by the door, and headed for the garage. He loved how quietly the door went up. He'd paid extra for that perk. Before leaving the garage, he tapped in Holly Grant's street address he'd found when he'd researched her. Not close but shouldn't take more than fifteen to twenty minutes depending on the traffic.

The warm spring weather urged him to put down his window and let the breeze blow through. In Texas, you couldn't often do this, and he sang along to a tune on the radio.

Traffic hadn't been bad, and he soon turned onto the woman's street. The internet map he'd looked at seemed to indicate a gated community. Wonder how her neighbors would like those worthless homeless people across from their property? Of course, houses lined the street across from the walled complex with no chance to build new. Only two gates allowed entrance. He kept driving and circled the golf course behind the complex. He wanted to see if the wall went all the way around. He drove down the street and circled around the golf course before returning to the complex. He had trouble seeing the complex from the other side of the golf course. He didn't often play golf, but he had a couple of friends in that country club. Might be time to set up a game. He traveled north on the street but didn't see any numbers to give him a better idea of where the house was, though the internet map seemed to indicate her house sat on the northwest back side. He pulled onto a side street, made a U-turn and parked so he could keep an eye on the gates. He needed to figure out a pattern for people coming and going so he could squeak through after one of them.

After an hour of sitting and watching, he decided he needed to be better prepared for this surveillance next time. Snacks and drinks were a necessity. Results of his time were slim. He'd seen only a couple of cars leave and only one enter. He needed to see more entering to give him a chance to follow one inside. Looks like he'd have his hands full with this stakeout. His mouth hooked up a corner in a grin. He'd always wanted to play detective.

Chapter Ten

The city council handily approved their request, not only unanimously, but with words of praise for what the Grant sisters wanted to accomplish. Armstrong had shown up with his buddies and spoken against the motion. Holly brought her sisters, Ben Stephenson and Dan as she had at the board of adjustment meeting. And they had prevailed again. Holly had waited no time to let her architect and contractor know they had permission to proceed with the project.

She could hardly contain her excitement, which bubbled up inside and then would subside. Then she'd think, we get to build the tiny homes, and her excitement bubbled up again. Like riding on a roller coaster. The architect called and told her he'd finished the preliminary plans he'd shown her earlier and wanted her to sign off on the final product. She'd worked with Juan Lopez on a couple of other projects, but not many because mostly she bought and sold property, for others who built warehouses, malls, office buildings, whatever. She'd been fortunate to buy property when the market was depressed, and then she sat on it until the market grew hot. Yes, the real estate gods had done well by her. They were fickle, and she could've lost her shirt on any of the projects.

Now she and her sisters had property they would build on themselves. Somehow this was way more satisfying. Especially considering who they were building houses for. She steered into the architecture firm's garage and lucked into a spot on the ground floor. Juan's office filled the entire third floor. Entering the building, she took the elevator. The doors opened to lots of glass with offices off to the left and right. Several employees bustled by. One stopped.

"Are you Holly Grant?"

"Yes, I am." Holly tipped her head at the young woman who looked to be a college student.

"I'm Anna Rodrigues, and Juan asked me to keep an eye out for you. Come this way, please." The beautiful woman with dark hair worn in a long braid down her back led Holly into a room surrounded on three sides by glass. One wall had windows to the outside, and the windows in another wall overlooked the hallway. The third wall of windows overlooked the entryway with a tall atrium that went all the way down to the ground floor. Clients in the meeting room could look outside from those windows providing an open and airy ambiance. A long wooden table filled the center of the room. Comfortable swivel chairs were drawn up all around. The one solid wall had pictures of different projects the company had worked on.

"Can I get you anything? Coffee or water?"

"Coffee would be lovely, thanks. I take mine black." Eight-thirty in the morning wasn't too unusual for Holly to be at work, but she welcomed more coffee whenever someone offered her a cup.

In only a few moments, Anna returned with the requested coffee in a white mug with the blue logo of the company on the side.

"Thank you." Holly sipped the coffee. "This does the trick."

"Juan should be in here soon."

"And here I am." A dark-haired man of medium height entered the office carrying a large portfolio in one hand and his own cup of coffee in the other. "Thank you for covering for me, Anna. I had an unexpected phone call come in as I headed this way."

"Good to see you, Juan. And absolutely not a problem. Anna has taken good care of me." Holly smiled at the woman as she stepped from the office closing the door behind her.

Juan set his cup on the table and reached to clasp Holly's hand and then settled into a chair next to her. "Anna is amazingly efficient. She's my cousin's daughter and is considering whether she wants to be an architect. Before her family pays for further schooling, they thought giving her a taste of what the life is like in the profession would be a good idea."

"Makes sense to me." Holly took another sip of her coffee. Once the papers were spread out, she would set aside the cup. "Juan, I can hardly wait to see what you've come up with."

"I'm excited to show them to you. This has been a fun project. Malls are great, but I'm proud to be involved with you in this. Let's put our cups on this sideboard, and then I'll show you the plans."

With the cups safely stored, Juan opened the portfolio and pulled forward the first large paper. "This is the overview of the whole property." He pointed to how the tiny houses were set out around the center main building. "This is the clubhouse and is where the office, a large meeting room, and a small kitchen will be. We've also added two office-type areas for other agencies that might need space."

"Oh, that's good. I'm sure we'll need that."

"The houses are on streets that go out in spokes from this center area. Much like you'd find in a regular neighborhood."

"Oh, Juan. I like this." Holly rose and leaned over for a closer look. A grin split her face ear to ear. "I can't wait to see the various house plans."

"We came up with five different designs and each street will have a mixture of each."

"That's perfect. As you said, we have the feel of a real neighborhood. Okay, show me the first one."

He slid out a page showing the front elevation of one house and the floor plan. "Oh, I love this cottage design with the porch on the front." She slid the floor plan closer to her. "What's the square feet for this one?"

"Three hundred and fifty. The bedroom is in the loft on this one. Only two designs have loft bedrooms. I felt like we might be dealing with older people or young people with disabilities."

"Yeah, that is the case. What else do you have?"

Holly spent the next two hours poring over Juan's designs. She loved the houses with the lofts, but her favorites had the bedroom on the main floor. They might have a loft, but the space could be used more for an office or extra storage. One of the designs even had a setup for bunk beds for siblings.

"Juan, I can't wait to show these to my sisters. They both will want to give their input into the selection process for decorating."

"Of course. This set I've prepared for you to take with you. Let me know when you're ready for another talk about these, and we can set up a meeting."

"That's terrific. After we've studied these, I'll call you, and we'll do that." Holly rose. "Thank you, Juan. I love these. Such great ideas. I can't imagine either my sisters or I will make many suggestions, but I'm glad we get the opportunity."

"Of course. Glad you're pleased, Holly. As I said, I'm proud to work with you on this project."

Holly shook hands with Juan, picked up the portfolio, and proceeded to the elevator. Normally she walked down but decided with her hands full she'd be safer not to take a chance with the stairs. She loaded the drawings into the back of her SUV where they could lie flat. Before turning on the ignition, she texted both sisters.

I've got the designs for Grant Gardens. You want to come to my place for supper tonight? We can look at them together.

She waited a bit but didn't get an immediate response. Hmmm. They knew she had a meeting scheduled with Juan this morning, but hey, they were busy people. And with Kay painting, they might have to go to her house. When she dropped into the zone, she never heard the phone.

Holly chuckled and punched the button to turn on the ignition. Where to next? She glanced at her to-do list on her cell. Oh, yes, cleaners and Walmart, then home to return calls about other pieces of property. One of those calls had to be to Dan to check where he stood with their documents. Her heart did a little skip at the idea of talking to him. She sighed. What about him? What about her? What about them?

Holly put the finishing touches on the pasta salad she'd made for supper with her sisters when they came over to look at the plans for Grant Gardens. The black and green olives popped. The red flecks of pimento were a nice touch. Yellow squash, green zucchini, purple onion and bright green bell pepper filled the bowl of bowtie pasta. After a quick mix of all the ingredients together with a splash of Champagne vinaigrette dressing, she snapped the cover on and placed the bowl in the fridge. Fresh butter lettuce, croissants, and wine would finish out the meal.

As she thought about her call with Dan, warmth spread up her cheeks. My goodness. What was the matter with her? They were friends. Had been for years. He'd seemed serious about wanting something more than their friendship, but had her story scared him off? He had stayed the night, and the experience had been wonderful. They slept in each other's arms. No expectations. Did he mean what he said about waiting for her to be ready for more? But what if she couldn't act on those feelings? If she couldn't make love with him, would that destroy their friendship?

"I can't wait to see those plans." Lee had let herself into Holly's house. "Kay is right behind me."

Thank goodness. Her sisters would take her mind off the handsome lawyer. "Hey, Lee and Kay. The papers are on the dining table."

"Do you have wine?" Kay dropped her purse on the entryway bench and made her way to the dining table. She clapped her hands together. "It's exciting to have gotten to this place in the process."

"It certainly is, and of course I have wine. It's that south Texas brand we all like so much. Here you go." Holly handed a glass of Merlot to each of her siblings and took one for herself. She raised her glass. "To Grant Gardens. It's for sure happening." Her sisters clinked and took a sip.

"WhoHoo!" Kay yelled. "Show us. Show us."

The women gathered around the long side of the table, and Holly walked them through the drawings. They oohed and aahed. Kay liked the house that looked like a train. The cottage-like one with the bedroom on the ground floor caught Lee's attention.

"I like the layout of the grounds, too." Lee took a sip of her wine. "It looks like a neighborhood you'd find anywhere. That's important. And we get to pick out all the stuff on the inside?"

"Yep." Holly smiled at her sister, who set her glass down so she could literally rub her hands together.

"Oh, this will be sooooo fun."

"Sarah and I put together several options for what the sign at the entrance should look like," Kay said. She went back to the entryway and picked up a much smaller portfolio than the one with the tiny house designs in it. She brought the case to the table, pulled out several large pieces of paper and spread them out for her sisters. "What's your opinion of these?" She laid out three different designs all using leaves and flowers surrounding the words *Grant Gardens*.

"Oh, Kay. You and Sarah worked together? They're really special. I've always known you are both talented, but these...I love these. Which do you like best, Lee?" Holly looked to her sister for guidance.

"I like this one with the dark letters on the white background. Easier to read. Can you do the leaves and flowers in colors, or will that cost too much?"

"We can swing that, Lee, if we decide that's the better look. And of course, you'd raise the practical issues involved. If people can't easily read the sign, there's not much point to the sign. Should we do the design in metal, or will wood suffice?" Kay looked at each of her sisters.

"From a cost standpoint, the wood will be cheaper, even if we must repaint every now and then. And I like Lee's idea of the added color. Not sure we can get color in the metals." Holly leaned over to get a better look at the design.

Kay studied the plans. "Sarah and I scotched the idea of neon. That's not at all the right feel."

"Have we reached agreement on the sign?"

Holly's sisters nodded.

"Good work, Kay. Make sure to tell Sarah how much we like y'all's work." Holly patted her sister's shoulder.

"I'm afraid all our design decisions may not be quite as easy. And you know we'll have a kazillion of those. We're not talking about one house. With five different house designs, we can decorate them all differently." Lee paused and looked at her sisters. "However, repetition will save us on costs and make planning easier. How does that sound to you, Holly?"

Holly walked around the table and picked up one of the house plans. "I'm afraid you're right about the cost if we make each and every house different. Let's find a middle ground. If we have thirty houses and five designs, maybe we will have five different decorating plans. Then if my math is correct, every fourth house will be the same. Or—I don't know, this is your bailiwick, Lee. You figure out the math."

The sisters all laughed. Finally, Holly said. "Oh, my gosh, we forgot to eat supper. We can leave the papers here on the dining table and eat outside." She opened the sliding doors to the patio. "Let's enjoy this unexpectedly pleasant evening. The breeze is delightful. If y'all would help set the patio table, I'll plate the meal."

"I'm glad you were able to replace the doors after the storm, Holly," Lee said. "They let you enjoy the outdoors more and expand your living area." Lee and Kay finished putting napkins, placemats, and silverware on the table. Before long, they all settled on the patio.

Holly raised her glass. "To progress on Grant Gardens. Thanks, Mom and Dad."

Kay raised her glass. "To Grant Gardens."

"To Mom and Dad," Lee said.

"One of my favorite meals, Holly. Thanks for making it." Kay speared a ripe black olive. "Yum."

"Glad you're enjoying the food. You know it's super easy. You chop up everything and then cook the pasta and throw everything all together. Hard to mess up this recipe."

"Except one time when you mistook the bottle of barbecue sauce from the fridge for the salad dressing and didn't notice until you'd coated the pasta and veggies."

Holly laughed. "Yeah, not my finest hour. If my memory serves, we went out for burgers after bravely trying to eat the salad."

"Best burgers ever," Kay added.

Barrett left his friends in the bar of the country club. He'd had no trouble convincing one of them to ask him to come. The golfing had been fun, and getting away from his buddies hadn't been hard either. He made up the excuse of being out of shape. He put his clubs in his car and then wandered out across the grounds searching for Holly Grant's house, which backed up to the golf course. He knew its approximate location.

A stone wall separated the complex from the golf course. He came over a hill and sucked in a breath. He'd found her house. He heaved himself up into a tree for a better view. Holly Grant pushed open sliding doors to her patio. She and her sisters talked and laughed like they had nothing to worry about. Could he take out all three women? He studied the situation. Tossing a stick of dynamite or a hand grenade in there right now would end all his problems. But he didn't have either of those with him.

Yes, he could crawl up over the stone wall. Shouldn't be any harder than getting up in the tree. But this tree gave him an excellent vantage point. Maybe he didn't need to get onto her property. Then he wouldn't have to climb the wall. He could shoot the woman. And if the sisters were there at the time, he'd get them, too. That would put an end to their plans for his land. Slowly he made his way down from the tree and ambled back to his car enjoying the beautiful greens, the tweeting of the birds, and the breeze. He reached his car in the parking lot, got in, and drove out to his neighborhood. In twenty minutes, he parked in his garage, got out, and locked his car. He crossed the road to his grandfather's land and wandered over to a log that had fallen in the perfect place to sit and enjoy an evening. In the daytime when he came, the large oak shaded him. He loved this spot where he'd buried his grandparents. No one would ruin this for him. He clenched his hand into a fist. No one.

"Hey, Jon. Come on in. I'm about to put on the steaks. Your timing couldn't be better." Dan welcomed his friend and partner into his home. Work kept them super busy, and he wanted to run ideas by Jon about issues with Grant Gardens.

"Thanks, man. I'm never turning down the possibility of one of your steaks."

"Grab two beers, and we can sit outside while they cook. The ceiling fans will keep us comfortable." Dan pushed open the sliding doors to his patio carrying a platter with two large T-bones on it. He'd seasoned the steaks with garlic, salt and pepper and had added a dollop of butter on each one. He plopped the steaks on the grill. The sizzle and aroma made his mouth water, and he closed the lid.

"The timing of your invite fits fine for me. Janey has rehearsals tonight. My menu consisted of a frozen dinner. I cook only when she'll be home for supper." Jon handed a beer to Dan. "This is much better." He raised his bottle to Dan and then took a glug. "Ah, yes."

Dan settled into a navy Adirondak chair. "I've got something I want to run by you while the steaks cook."

Jon sat in a white Adirondak chair. "Sure. What's on your mind?"

Dan rolled the bottle back and forth between his hands. "I'm concerned about the neighborhood association—not the association itself, but Barrett Armstrong in particular. He seems single mindedly against the development of Grant Gardens. Well, he seems against anything going on that property."

"It's not even his property. According to what you've said, it belonged to his family years ago but doesn't anymore. Why should it matter what his opinion is?" Jon took two swallows of beer. "Mmm, that's good."

"He's acted weird you know. Oh, some of his supporters are NIMBYs, you know, those Not-In-My-Backyard folks who don't want low-income people living near them, but his opposition seemed to be on a different level."

"Why don't I do a little digging about Mr. Armstrong and see what I can find out?"

"That'd be great. I may be overreacting about him, but I'm concerned about the Grant women."

"And maybe one Grant woman in particular?"

Dan rose and crossed to the grill, keeping his back to his friend. "Well, yeah, but..." He lifted the grill lid and turned over one of the steaks.

Jon came and stood beside Dan at the grill. "Boy, these smell good."

"We've got another three minutes, and they'll be ready."

"What are your concerns about the Grant sisters?"

Dan settled on top of the low stone wall around his patio. "Nothing specific, but I got a dull ache in my gut. Like something bad is about to happen."

"Are you talking about you and Holly?"

"No. I feel pretty good about that. She shared stories with me of awful stuff from her time with her ex. Made me understand why she'd be reluctant to have a physical relationship with anyone." He rose and pulled the steaks from the grill, and he couldn't stop the grin from spreading across his face. "But I feel good about the possibilities with her."

"Glad to hear that, man." Jon took the plate Dan handed him and set it on the outside table. "I'm ready to dig in. This smells great."

"I'll bring out the potatoes and the salad if you can you grab us another beer."

"Sure."

Before long, they had settled in with their meal. "You could open a restaurant. Have you ever thought about that?" Jon pointed his fork with a piece of steak on the end at Dan. "Not that I want you to leave the firm, but man, this is good. Once you and Holly are together, you can grill for the four of us every week."

Dan leaned back and laughed from deep in his belly. "How about once a month?"

"You're on." Jon went back to gobbling down the steak.

"Thanks for researching Armstrong. I'll feel better about Holly and her sisters if you come back with findings that he's a kind, law-and-order dude who never even speeds."

"Guess we'll see."

Chapter Eleven

Holly rode the elevator up to the third-floor office of her architect, Juan Lopez. He wanted her to meet the person who would be lead on carrying out their designs. Again, Anna met her as she got off the elevator. "Hey, Ms. Grant, come this way. Juan is ready for you."

"Thanks, Anna." Holly followed the young woman into the glass conference room.

Juan rose and came around to shake her hand. "Thanks for coming in, Holly. This is Samuel Ramirez. He'll manage the construction on your project."

"Hey, Mr. Ramirez. Nice to meet you." Holly extended her hand.

The middle-aged man with not an iota of hair on his head clasped her hand. "Please, call me Sam."

"Sure. And I'm Holly. Glad you're on this project with us."

"I am, too. I had a cousin who became homeless after a bad car wreck, and he lost his job. Eventually, he got out of the hole, but this project would've helped him get there a lot sooner."

"I'm surprised by how many people I know who know someone who's been homeless or nearly so," Holly said.

"Have a seat, and we'll go over a few things." Juan gestured to a chair on one side of the table.

Holly sat, followed by the men.

"Go ahead, Sam. Tell Holly about the permits."

"Bottom line, Holly, they take a long time. I've started the process, but...you know how the city works."

Holly chuckled. "Yes, I've run into issues there before. What's your best guess for when you'll be able to turn dirt?"

"I'm hoping for September. We can have everything ready to go then. We can order the materials and hopefully even get them delivered. If you can go ahead and make all the selections for interiors that will speed things along."

"So how long until we could have the occupancy permit?" Holly drummed her fingers on the table. She'd hoped this would get off the ground soon.

"Probably early next year." Sam's gaze hooked with Juan's who nodded.

"Well, that's disappointing. But some things we can't change. My sisters and I want it done right. Whatever is required, we'll jump through all the hoops."

"Thanks for being understanding, Holly, and I want to assure you we're making this project our priority." Juan smiled at her.

"Sure. In the meantime, we will put together our ideas for the insides of the tiny houses, and we'll work with your interior design people. That way you won't be waiting for us."

"That should work. You'll be working with Jenny Aldrich. Let me know when you've got your ideas together, and we'll set up an appointment with her."

"We know we can keep costs down by doing repeats of design, but we want to have variety for the community."

"Jenny will be able to help you with that."

"My sister Lee is an interior designer herself and between the two of them, I'm sure we can design pleasant, warm homes. I don't suppose there's anything we can do to speed along the permit process?"

"Nah, the city doesn't have enough staff to handle all the building going on. It's crazy down there."

"Okay. We will set our expectations appropriately. Anything else, Juan?"

"No, we've got our plans in order. If you have concerns or questions call Sam or me."

"Will do." She rose. "Thanks, guys. We'll be in touch." They shook hands, and Holly left the conference room. She walked down the stairs, using the exercise to help her deal with the disappointment threatening to swallow her. Guess she hadn't been realistic. She bought and sold property all the time but didn't usually get into the building of buildings on that property. She needed to tell her sisters. She'd invite them for supper and tell them tonight.

L ee sailed into Holly's home in The Oaks followed by Kay. "You don't have to keep hosting us, Holly. I'm sure we're way overdue to play that role."

"But, Lee, Holly has this amazing patio. With the ceiling fan and all the trees, we can still enjoy sitting outside. My patio faces west, and it's already a nightmare in the late afternoon and evening. I'll never again buy a house with the patio facing west."

"But, sweetie, you focused on making sure you had great morning light for painting. And you've got that." Holly hugged her sister.

"There's that." Kay laughed. "Can I do anything to help?"

"Sure, set the table on the patio. The meal will be ready in two minutes. And, Lee, please open a bottle of wine and fix us some spritzers."

"She loves giving orders." Lee laughed as both sisters went about doing Holly's bidding.

"Well, I said *please,* didn't I?"

They laughed and rolled their eyes.

In minutes, they had settled at the patio table. Holly had made a spinach and artichoke quiche and a salad.

"As usual, this looks yummy." Lee raised her spritzer. "To us."

"To us."

"Have you missed hanging out with us, Holly or is there a purpose for our get together?" Kay took a bite of the quiche. "Yum. Sooo good."

"Thank you, Kay. Glad you like the meal. I've got news to share with you about our project, and it's not particularly good."

"Yeah? What's going on?" Kay raised her glass for a sip.

Holly explained about the delay due to the length of time getting the city permits.

"Well, that's disappointing, but that gives us time to get all our ducks in a row with the various agencies we'll want to work with." Kay took a bite of the quiche. "This is one of my favorite meals. Thanks."

"You're welcome."

"And, Holly, this will give us plenty of time to get all the decisions made about the interior of the homes." Lee spoke in her role as the encourager.

"Well, I like y'all's positive attitudes." Holly sampled the salad. "Lee, can you arrange to meet with Jenny Aldrich? She's the interior designer with Lopez Architecture."

"Absolutely. Actually, I'm pretty certain I've met her at an association meeting. Do you want us to come up with ideas and present them to her or the other way around?"

"Let's take her our ideas first, and then she can help us finalize them." Holly sipped her spritzer.

"Works for me. I'll put together ideas and get input from Leeann. She's excited about this project. Then I'll show y'all based on the discussions we've already had. How does that work?"

The sisters nodded, and they all proceeded to discuss color options and styles for the cottages.

Barrett ambled across the green rolling hills of the golf course dragging his golf bag behind him. Besides his golf clubs, the bag held binoculars and his rifle. He'd get rid of Holly, and all his trouble would be over. Without her, the sisters would never follow through with the project. Their grief would overwhelm them. Yes, he'd get to keep his land. His grandparents' land.

He eased up behind a tree close enough he could see they were talking but couldn't hear voices or make out what they were saying. Climbing the tree the last time had gone pretty well. He felt confident he could do it again even with the addition of a weapon. He glanced around, and seeing no one near, he pulled the rifle from the golf bag and slid it up into the branches. This tree had several low limbs that made climbing easy for him even if he grunted on the last push to settle himself. Looking at the scene with the binoculars, he saw Holly dressed in a bright orange blouse. What an easy target. He carefully leaned down and lifted the gun from the lower branch and settled it against his shoulder. Ah, yes. This would be easy. He sighted down the barrel and drew in a breath.

"I'm getting the wine bottle. We need a refill." Lee rose.

Bam! They all jumped.

Lee screamed as she reached for her shoulder. Her scream curdled Holly's blood.

Lee slumped to the floor.

Two heartbeats later, Holly sprang toward Kay, who'd risen. "Get down! Get down!" She cradled Lee in her arms. Holly prided herself on being good in a crisis, her emotions shutting down, and her critical mind kicking into control. She needed that ability right now.

"What's going on, Holly? Was Lee shot? Is she okay?" Kay's voice trembled.

"I don't know. It's a lot of blood. Stay down but call 911 and then call Dan." Holly tugged a cloth napkin from the table and thrust it against the wound on her sister's shoulder. Lee moaned. That's good, isn't it? Holly mumbled a prayer. "Please let her be all right. Please let her be all right."

"My sister's been shot," Kay said to the 911 operator and gave the address. Then she used Holly's phone to call Dan.

After what seemed forever, Holly heard sirens in the distance.

"Holly, they're sending the EMTs, and Dan should be here soon after them."

"Hang in there, Lee. Help is on the way." Holly added another napkin when the first one became soaked with her sister's blood.

Pounding from the front of the house sent Kay crawling toward the front door. She returned, followed by officers with guns drawn. The EMTs rushed in. They pushed Holly out of the way and began to treat Lee.

"Is she on any blood thinners?"

"No." Holly managed to respond though her voice trembled. "She's the healthiest one of us. I can't believe this happened. Will she be all right?"

"Ma'am. I'm Officer Kent. Can we get you all inside? Can you move your patient?"

The EMT nodded and lifted Lee onto a gurney and rolled her inside.

"Please identify yourselves," the officer said to Holly and Kay. He had his notebook out.

Holly did, proud her voice didn't quiver much. "Can we go with our sister?"

"You can follow her, but I need details from you first. Do either of you have a weapon?"

Kay shook her head but glanced at Holly.

"I do, and when it was required, I had a concealed handgun permit."

"Can you get the weapon for me?"

Holly nodded and hurried into her bedroom. Did he suspect she had shot Lee? Holly returned carrying the gun. "Here you go." She handed it to him butt first.

The officer smelled the barrel of the gun and emptied the bullets from the magazine before handing it back to her. "Is there any reason someone would want to hurt your sister?"

"No." Holly and Kay both shook their heads. Holly set her gun on the coffee table.

"Other officers are checking out the area now to try to find the person who shot her and to make sure the area is safe."

Holly and Kay stood with their arms around each other when a disturbance at the front of the house got their attention.

"Let me in. I'm Holly Grant's lawyer, Daniel Morgan."

Holly left Kay and rushed to Dan as he entered the living area. "Thank heavens you're here."

"Tell me what happened." Dan took her in his arms, drawing her close. One hand made comforting circles on her back.

Holly pulled in several deep breaths, drew back, and explained. "We were eating supper on the patio. Lee got up to get the bottle of wine, and we all heard a loud sound, and she yelled. Blood flowed from her shoulder, and she fell. Kay and I got on the ground, and she called 911 and you while I put pressure on Lee's wound. The EMTs have taken Lee to the hospital." Holly gasped for air. She had spewed out the story in one breath. Her legs wouldn't have held her if Dan hadn't kept an arm around her. She held out a hand to Kay who came and joined them.

"We need to go to see how Lee is." Kay's voice wavered.

Dan raised his voice. "Officer, can I take Holly and Kay to see their sister? I can assure you they are not going anywhere."

"Yes, I'll have an officer escort you outside since we're not sure if the shooter is gone or still around. Ms. Grant, we'll be in touch."

"Thank you. Dan, let me wash my hands and change my clothes."

"Sure."

When she reached her bathroom, the image in the mirror drew her up short. Blood covered her shirt. She pulled off her bloody clothes and dropped them in the tub. She stepped into her walk-in closet and pulled out a purple short-sleeved T-shirt and a clean pair of black slacks. Found a pair of slide-on sandals and sped back to the living room where she found more officers had arrived. George Sanderson, who acted as the mayor of their little community, had pushed his way in. "My gosh, Holly. What's going on? Is everyone all right?"

Holly briefly explained what had happened. "We're on our way to the hospital. Can you lock up for me when the police finish up here?"

"Sure. You go on. Don't worry."

The police officer stopped her before they left. "Can I have your phone numbers?"

They all complied, leaving the chaos behind, not knowing what chaos lay ahead.

B arrett Armstrong made his way off the golf course, cursing his luck that he'd hit the wrong woman. He had Holly in his bead, but as he shot, the other woman moved. Well, maybe this would still work. He could only hope. If not, he'd still have to take out Holly Grant. The land belonged to him and his family. He walked to his car and stowed the golf bag in the trunk and drove slowly away from the area, taking a circuitous path to his home.

Chapter Twelve

Holly's knuckles turned white in her clenched hands. Kay's soft sobs came from the rear of Dan's SUV. Kay had the softest heart of any of the three of them. She could hardly kill a wasp or bee, and if she accidentally hit a squirrel in the road, she turned into a basket case for days.

"She'll be all right, won't she, Holly?"

The worry in Kay's voice tugged at Holly's heart, but she had to be strong for her sister. But gosh, there'd been so much blood. Still, for Kay's sake she dug deep. "I'm sure they can fix her up. I certainly hope and pray they do."

"Was this some sort of random act? How could someone shoot a gun in a neighborhood? People are nuts."

Holly glanced at Dan. He nodded. "Well, you're right about that, Kay. People are sometimes nuts."

"Oh, my gosh. I've gotta call Lee's kids." Holly groaned at how she dreaded making that call.

"I bet Brad can get here quickly from Dallas. Leeann may take longer. You know how the drive from Austin can be. Glad you thought of that," Kay said. "I'm calling Sarah. I don't want her hearing about this from some third party."

Holly called Lee's children and filled them in on what little they knew. Brad said he'd be able to leave within the hour. Leeann said she'd leave in an hour or two, and then it would take her a good three hours to get to Fort Worth.

"Be safe, Leeann. Your mom needs you to get here in one piece." Holly disconnected. "Well, those were two of the worst calls I've ever made."

"I told Sarah she didn't have to come. She's preparing for a test. If things look bad, I'll get her to come to the hospital," Kay said.

Dan found a parking spot near the emergency room, and they all hopped out and dashed inside. Holly went to the check-in desk and identified herself.

"Can we see our sister, Lee Grant Kennedy? They brought her in a little while ago. A gunshot wound."

The nurse looked at her and then at Kay and Dan, then at her computer screen.

"Yes, I have a Lee Kennedy here, but no, you can't see her. I'll let the doctor know her family is here. Why don't you take a seat in the waiting room?"

Dan shepherded them both to chairs gathered in the corner away from the entrance. Kay dropped into a chair and crossed her legs, one of which kept up a nervous swing, swishing her long skirt back and forth. Dan settled on the middle chair. Holly sat and then hopped back up and paced from one end of the room to the other. And back and forth and back and forth.

"Holly, you should sit down." Dan rose and stopped her mid-pace. "You're wearing yourself out."

"I can't sit still, Dan. I have to do something."

"And there's nothing you can do right now. It's hard." He rubbed the back of her neck, and she rolled her head in response.

"Better?"

Holly nodded. "Thanks. I can sit now." She settled next to Kay and took her hand.

"The family of Lee Grant Kennedy?" A tall, slender black man in scrubs with a mask hanging below his face looked around the waiting room. All three of them jumped up and hurriedly crossed to him.

"I'm Holly Grant, and this is Kay Grant Clayton. We're Lee's sisters. Our lawyer, Daniel Morgan, can hear anything you have to say."

"I'm Dr. Garvel. We've stabilized your sister, and we're taking her up to surgery. You can wait up there on the third floor. I'll be out as soon as we finish to let you know how things went."

He turned to leave, but Holly stopped him with a hand on his arm. "Dr. Garvel, is Lee going to make it?"

"We're hopeful. She's lost a lot of blood and will need transfusions. If any of you are available to give blood, that would help."

"We can certainly do that. All three of us have the same blood type."

"Good. I'll set that up. The lab is down that hall. Now I've got to go. See you after the surgery."

Kay hugged Holly. "Well, at least we have something to do now."

"Yes. Let's go to the lab."

When they got to the lab, Holly went up to the desk and explained, but at that point, the lab hadn't received the doctor's orders.

"I'll call you as soon as we've got it. Y'all just take a seat for now."

"Hurry up and wait," Kay muttered. "My favorite thing to do." She dropped into a chair and her leg took off swinging again. Dan settled next to her. Holly paced the entire length of the room, making a giant figure eight.

"Ms. Grant."

Holly turned sharply toward the desk. "Yes. Are you ready for us?"

"We need to get your names and birthdates. Dr. Garvel didn't have specifics."

"Of course." Holly and Kay gave the nurse the info she needed.

"Ms. Grant, if you'll come back here? Ms. Clayton, we'll call you back in a bit."

Holly hugged Kay and Dan then went through the door the nurse held for her.

"When I give blood for testing, I have the nurse poke a vein in my hand. It's easier to get to. Can you do that now?" Holly asked.

"For a pint, we'll need to draw it from your arm."

"Okay." Holly settled in the chair and put her left arm on the rest. The nurse proceeded through the steps to draw her blood. Holly looked away when the needle went in. She didn't mind giving blood, and even if she did, she'd still donate to something this important, but looking at the needle made her queasy. Her mind drifted to happier times like when she and her sisters planted the Sold sign on their property. And their visit to the tiny home community. Any and everything except why she sat in this room having a pint of her blood drawn. Despite her best efforts, she came back to worrying about Lee and whether she'd really be all right and why had this awful event happened. For crying out loud, they'd been sitting on her patio. They should've been safe.

The nurse's voice yanked her from her dark thoughts.

"You feel okay? Woozy at all?" The nurse removed the needle and placed a cotton ball over the spot where she'd inserted the needle. "Hold this tight and hold your arm up." She marked the bag and set it aside. Then she used a pink elastic bandage to hold the cotton ball in place.

"I'm not woozy at all. You did that well because I barely felt the prick."

"Thanks. Nice to hear. You can head on out that way."

Holly walked through a different door than the one she'd entered as she heard Kay's name called. "See you in a bit, sis," Holly said to her back. Kay waved her hand and disappeared.

Holly stood in the middle of the room. Now what?

Dan's strong hands on her shoulders turned her to him, and she went thankfully, dropping her head on his chest. Her soft sobs filled the room. He rubbed her back and placed kisses on her head for the longest time.

Finally, she sniffed in a big breath and raised her head. "Thanks, I needed that."

"Yeah. You've been through a lot. Good to let it out."

They settled in the chairs to wait for her sister, not talking, just waiting.

"Boy, that nurse was good." Kay entered the waiting area about fifteen minutes after she went in, pulling her sleeve down over a similar pink elastic bandage.

"Yes, she was." Holly brushed the tears from her face. She didn't want to worry Kay.

"How about we head up the surgery floor now?"

"Good idea, Dan." Holly smiled at him, grateful for his support.

He led them out, and they rode an elevator up two floors and got out to a room done in soft pastels with greenery and lovely scenic paintings on the wall. They settled in surprisingly comfortable chairs. How long would they have to wait?

"How're you holding up, sis?" Holly asked Kay.

"I'm scared. We can't lose Lee."

"Yeah, and not knowing is the pits. Hopefully, the doctor will come out soon and tell us something." Holly leaned over and squeezed her sister's hand. "At this point all we can do is pray." And she bowed her head and prayed more than she had about anything since facing down Joe with a gun. And here another gun incident faced her. Guns. She shuddered. Glad she had one but hated the reasons she needed to have one.

As Kay said earlier, people were nuts, and if one of those nuts came after you, it paid to be prepared. That's why she took her gun to the range monthly and practiced. A weapon had saved her life once before, and she'd never risk not being prepared again. Even though that meant someone else died.

Please, God, let Lee be okay. Guide the doctor's hands.

They'd been there about thirty minutes when a Hispanic man got off the elevator. He stood there and looked around before striding toward them. "Ms. Grant?"

"Yes." Holly stood as did Kay and Dan. "Are you another doctor?"

A half smile creased his face. "No. I'm Detective David Vela. I'm following up on the shooting at your house." He flipped open a wallet, showing his ID.

"Have you caught anyone?" Dan stretched out a hand to the detective. "I'm Daniel Morgan, a friend and Ms. Grant's lawyer."

Vela shook Dan's hand. "Does she need a lawyer, Mr. Morgan?"

"I don't see any reason she should, but as I said, I'm a friend. To repeat my question, have you caught whoever shot Ms. Grant's sister?"

"No. The officers didn't find anyone suspicious in the vicinity, even after checking with all the homeowners in your complex. They're checking the golf course now. You have any idea of anyone who would want to hurt Ms. Kennedy?"

Holly looked at Kay, and they both shook their heads. "This is our younger sister, Kay Grant Clayton," Holly said.

Kay held out her hand. "Detective. If there's anything we can do to help you solve this, tell us, and we'll do whatever."

After holding her hand for too long, Vela let go and nodded. "Thank you, Ms. Clayton. Why don't you tell me about your sister? Maybe as you talk, something will come up." He pulled out a small notebook and pen.

Dan pulled up another chair, and the four sat in a small, tight circle.

Holly spoke first. "Lee is an interior designer with her own company. She's divorced with two kids, both out of college. Brad works in Dallas, and her daughter Leeann works in Austin. We called them early on. They are both on their way."

"Can you give me their contact info?" They did, and he wrote the names and numbers in his book.

"You said she was divorced. Any problems with her ex?"

"Charles?" Holly looked at Kay and they both chuckled. "No, they had an amicable divorce. After fifteen years of marriage, Charles came out and wanted to be his authentic self. Lee wished him well. They've remained friends even with his new spouse. They join us for family gatherings."

"Okay. Has she made any enemies in business? Anyone she stole a client from?"

Kay smiled at Holly, and then she answered Vela's question. "Officer, my big sister is the kindest person. Everyone loves her. She'd never steal anything, much less someone else's client. She helps out beginning designers and has shared clients with people in the early days of their careers."

Vela dragged his gaze from Kay and made notes of what she told him.

Holly looked at Dan and raised her eyebrows in question. He shrugged. They'd have to discuss this later.

"What about her children? Could any of them be involved in something that would cause a person to come after their mother?"

"I can't even imagine something like that, Detective Vela. When they get here, I can have them call you. Would that be okay?"

"Yes. Perfect. Here's my card." He handed one to each of them. "Thank you for your time. I hope Ms. Kennedy comes through surgery well and makes a full recovery. If I have more questions, I'll be back in touch. And please have her children call me."

"Of course, Detective Vela. Thank you."

After shaking hands with each of them, he walked to the elevator. The door closed behind the detective. Another door opened, and Dr. Garvel entered. The three rose and rushed to him.

"How is she, Doctor?" Holly rushed to ask.

"Ms. Kennedy came through the surgery well. Fortunately, no bones were broken, but we did use the two pints of blood you two donated. She's doing well. She'll need to follow proper steps to take care of the wound, and she may need therapy to get back the full use of that shoulder, but we'll set that up before she leaves here."

Kay spontaneously hugged the doctor. "Thank you so much. I don't know what we'd have done if we'd lost our sister." Then she turned and buried her head on Holly's shoulder and sobbed.

Holly patted her back with one hand and held out the other to Dr. Garvel. "Thank you. When can we see her?"

"We'll move her to a room in another hour or so, and we'll let you know where that is. In the meantime, you can stay here, or you can go down to the cafeteria for a change of scene. By the time you return, we should know which room she's going to. If we get her moved before you return, we have your contact info and will call you."

"Thank you, Doctor." Dan shook the man's hand, and Dr. Garvel went back through the door.

"How about we go to the cafeteria and grab a bite to eat?" Dan rested his hand on Holly's back.

"Sounds good. And I need coffee. You going to be all right, Kay?"

Her sister stepped away from Holly, wiped her eyes, and smiled. "I sure am. That super news overwhelmed me."

"Indeed." Holly took Kay's hand and Dan's, and they set out for the elevator.

Chapter Thirteen

Barrett Armstrong parked in his garage. After lowering the door, he dragged out the golf bag, stowed the bag and with the rifle in it in a corner behind boxes. As good a place as any. He didn't expect anyone to come checking, but best to have stowed the bag out of the way.

He entered his house through the kitchen. He walked to the cabinet he kept his liquor in, lifted a bottle of whiskey from the shelf and poured himself a straight shot. The burn trickled down his throat. He slammed the glass on the counter and drew in a long breath. He refilled his glass and walked over to his recliner where he settled. Such a comforting place. The recliner next to him had been where his wife always sat. They spent many lovely evenings sitting here. She sipped wine and read. He sipped his whiskey and watched sports. He missed her, but he had his interests.

His land across from their neighborhood topped his list. His land where his grandparents were both buried. He'd do anything to keep that a sacred place.

Just as he'd done today. Too bad he hadn't hit Holly Grant, but hopefully her sister's accident would slow down their work.

The land needed to stay open, free, and uninhabited except for the ducks, squirrels, and the deer. He'd done the right thing. And he'd repeat the attack on Holly's family if they didn't stop the work on his property. No one would build on that property—ever. And certainly not a bunch of tiny homes for the homeless. Who wanted those people, a bunch of losers, as neighbors? Not in his neighborhood and absolutely not on his property. He finished up his second glass of whisky savoring the burn.

Holly pushed away her half-eaten egg salad sandwich. For hospital food, it was actually good, but her stomach tied itself in knots as they marked time waiting to go upstairs to see Lee. Holly's phone pinged, and she glanced down where it lay on the table. Was the hospital calling with updates on Lee? "It's Brad."

She connected with her nephew. "Hey, sweetie. Your mom came through surgery well. Where are you?" She listened and then explained the situation and told him they would wait for him in the cafeteria. "Okay, see you in a bit. Love you."

Holly disconnected and turned to Kay and Dan. "He's driving in circles trying to find a parking space. You know how frustrating that is. Hopefully, by the time he gets here, we'll have a room number for Lee."

And just then, her phone buzzed. A number she didn't recognize. She answered and listened for a moment. "Oh, that's good news. We'll be up there soon. We're in the cafeteria waiting for her son to arrive. Thanks for getting this information to us." She disconnected, and her cheeks almost cracked with the giant smile spreading across her face.

"They moved Lee to room 312. She's waked up and is asking for us."

Kay rose. "Let's go then."

"What about Brad? He's expecting us to be here." Holly literally wrung her hands.

"You two go ahead," Dan said. "I'll wait for Brad here, and we'll come up as soon as he arrives."

"Okay." Holly rose. "Thanks, Dan. Let's go, Kay." She took her sister's hand and headed for the elevator.

Dan carried the leftovers from their meal and drinks to the trash. He turned to find a dark-haired young man as tall as he at six feet, obviously looking for someone.

"Hey, Brad." Dan made his way across the cafeteria and extended his hand to the young man dressed in slacks and a sport shirt.

"Dan. Good to see you. Do you know how my mother is? Where are my aunts? I thought Aunt Holly said y'all were in here."

"You missed them by only a few minutes. They've already gone upstairs. Right after Holly talked with you, she got the information that your mother had been moved to her room and had awakened. She and Kay headed out fast. Come on. I'll take you."

Dan led Brad to the elevator and pushed the button for the third floor. "How was the trip over?"

"Like usual." Brad grimaced. "Crazy traffic. I'd have gotten here sooner, but a wreck slowed me down."

They got off the elevator, but Brad stopped Dan from heading for the room. "Dan, can you tell me what's going on? You said the sisters were on Holly's patio when someone shot Mom? How could that happen?"

Dan patted Brad on the shoulder. "We don't exactly know. Maybe a random shot. Can't figure out why someone would've targeted your mom or if someone did. There's a detective who wants to talk with you and Leeann when she gets here, but let's go see your mother right now."

A nurse directed them toward the room but cautioned them about too many people at once. "You go in, Brad. Tell Holly I'm here in the hall."

"Thanks." Brad straightened his shoulders and entered his mother's hospital room.

Voices came from inside as the son greeted his mother and aunts. In a few moments, Holly came out and walked directly to Dan, surprising him with a hug. He held her loosely but savored the contact.

Holly pulled away. "Thank you for being here. I'm relieved Brad's arrived. Kay wanted to stay a while longer, and they've limited us to two people."

"How's Lee doing?" Dan reluctantly let go of Holly as she stepped away.

"She's doing way better than could be expected. She did lose a lot of blood, but she's doing well and will be released in a few days. The doctor said putting pressure on the wound the way I did made all the difference."

"That's great news. You have any more thoughts about why this happened?"

"It must've been a random crazy person." Holly brushed her hair behind one ear. "Gosh, I'm tired. Now that I know Lee will be okay, all I want to do is climb in my bed and sleep for hours."

"Not sure you can go home, Holly. My guess is your house is still a crime scene."

"Oh, my gosh. I bet you're right. Just like before." Her brain flashed visions of the yellow tape the last time her ex attacked her over fifteen years ago. "Boy, I hoped to never see that yellow tape again."

"You can sleep at my house tonight. When the police finish with your place, you'll need to get a cleaning service in before you can return. If they dusted for fingerprints, I bet you've got a mess."

"Why would they do that? The shot came from outside."

"Are you sure, Holly? From the golf course?"

Holly stopped pacing and faced him. "It must have. But why would someone be on the golf course with a gun?"

"Do they know what kind of gun?"

"The doctor said he thought the wound looked like the bullet might have come from a rifle."

"Hmm."

"I'm changing the subject to something maybe better." Holly cut her gaze at Dan. "Did you pick up on any vibe between the detective and Kay?"

"He did hold her hand longer than was technically necessary, and Kay's face did turn a shade of pink."

"Well, she's been alone for a while now and only recently got back to painting, which is her life. I don't want anyone coming along and spoiling things for her."

Dan hoped that wasn't how Holly thought about their relationship or whatever it was they had. "Well, maybe something good can come of their meeting, Holly."

"Yeah, guess we'll see."

The door opened then, and Brad and Kay left Lee's room.

Brad hugged Holly. "Thank you for saving her life. If you hadn't acted quickly, well...." He hugged Holly again. "Thank you."

"You know your aunt Holly, the one you want around in an emergency. She even got me to get down on the floor when I stood up. Crazy me." Kay gave a rueful laugh. "What do we do next?"

"We all go home and get a good night's sleep. Lee will be all right. It may take longer than we'd like, but she'll be fine. You've all been through a lot. She's in good hands tonight and will need your support more later."

"Dan's right. I grabbed your mom's purse when we left my place. Her key is in it, and you can sleep at her house, Brad. Or you can sleep at Aunt Kay's. I'll be at Dan's. Can't get back in my house yet."

"Aunt Kay, do you mind if I come home with you? Don't feel like being alone tonight."

"Of course." Kay linked her arm through Brad's. "We need to call your sister and give her the good news, and I need to update Sarah."

"Oh, Brad, here's the detective's card. He'd like you to call him."

Brad took the card from Holly. "Sure, any reason why?"

"They're trying to eliminate all possibilities for why this happened. They want to eliminate that you might be involved in something that would cause someone to go after your mother."

"Okay. I'll give him a call when we get to Aunt Kay's, and I'll call Leeann. She'll be relieved, and I bet she'll want to crash at your house, too." He smiled at Kay.

Dan led the way toward the garage. "Why don't we meet at the Pancake Palace for breakfast in the morning before we go see Lee?"

"That's one of my favorites, and I haven't eaten there in ages. Thanks again. See you in the morning." Brad led Kay toward his car.

Dan took Holly's hand as they walked to his. Who would've shot at Lee? Did they have a random occurrence? Those did happen. Or could Holly or one of her sisters be the target?

"Were you able to get any sleep, Brad?" Holly scooped up the last of her syrup with the last bite of her blueberry pancakes.

"Actually, yeah, I did. Aunt Kay's guest room has a great bed. And knowing the good news about Mom making a full recovery was a relief."

"Thanks for letting us both crash with you, Aunt Kay." Holly's niece, Leeann, a slender young woman dressed in straight jeans, a purple blouse, and low-heeled boots, held a cup of coffee in both hands as if needing to get warm. A cold that had everything to do with what was going on and not the real temperature.

Kay patted Brad's hand. "Y'all are both welcome whenever, and hopefully next time will be a better reason." Kay sipped the last of her coffee. "I was relieved when you arrived last night, Leeann. I worried about the traffic."

"I wanted to leave immediately, but I had to arrange for a friend to keep my pup and had to pass off a couple of work projects. Now I'll be able to give Mom my undivided attention."

"I know she'll appreciate having you both here." Holly turned her cup around and around.

"Have you talked with the detective yet, Brad?"

Holly smiled at the lawyer in Dan kicking in.

Her nephew nodded. "He plans to meet us at the hospital, which I appreciate. I want to spend as much time with Mom as I can before I have to go back to Dallas." He glanced at his sister. "Leeann, he can talk with you right after he talks with me."

"And why does the detective want to talk to either of us? I'm not sure I get that?" Leeann's eyebrows crinkled in confusion.

"They're investigating all the possibilities of who shot your mom and why." Dan reached for the check. "I've got this, shall we head on over there?"

Holly smiled at Dan and rose. "Thanks for the excellent breakfast. I definitely overindulged. Stress eating, I'm sure."

The group went out into the already hot morning with the temperature pushing ninety degrees. Forecasts predicted another hundred-degree day. Holly hated hot weather and did everything she could to stay out of the heat. Heat was the main downside to her job in development. Sometimes you couldn't avoid being outside in the beastly summer heat.

Holly rode in Dan's car. Brad drove Kay and his sister. "Better to have a car and not need it than to need one and not have it," he'd reminded them all.

After parking in the garage of the hospital, they rode the elevator upstairs to see Lee. The other elevator doors opened, and Sarah stepped out. She hugged her mom and then turned to her cousins.

"Great to see you, but not this way."

"Thanks for coming up. We'll talk later. We're about to go in and see Mom." Brad and Leeann went in first.

Kay hugged her daughter. "You didn't have to come. I know how busy you are right now."

"Not only did I have to come, I wanted to come. We're family. It's what family does. Stick together."

Holly paced waiting for her turn.

"Be patient, Holly. One of them will come out, and you can go in."

"I know Brad and Leeann needed to go in first, but waiting is hard, Dan."

Kay gripped her hand and pulled Holly into a chair next to her and Sarah. "Sit. They'll be out soon."

Holly smiled and dropped into one of the chairs near her sister. "Sorry. Good to see you, sweetie," she said to her niece.

"You, too, Aunt Holly. No worries."

Before long, Brad came out. "Y'all can join us. Mom is doing remarkably well, and the nurse said we could bend the rules."

Holly, Kay and Sarah hopped up and headed toward Brad. Then Holly stopped and turned back to Dan.

"It's okay. Y'all go on. I'll wait here."

"Thank you."

"Hey. Brad said y'all were in the waiting room. And Sarah's here, too." Lee's upbeat tone surprised and cheered Holly.

"Well, look at you, all bright-eyed and bushy tailed." Holly leaned over and gave her sister a gentle hug, careful not to bump into her injuries.

Brad stepped away, allowing Kay to take a space on that side of the bed. He slid an arm around his cousin. "Mom, you gave us quite a scare, but you're already looking better than last night."

"Thanks. Though I must've looked like death warmed over—to use an old cliché—so anything would be an improvement." She turned her gaze to her daughter. "You didn't have to come, Leeann. The doctor said I should be able to go home tomorrow."

"Well, of course I had to come. Are you kidding? And I've arranged to be with you for several days after they release you."

"What'd I say, Mom? No stopping Leeann." Brad squeezed his sister's hand. "Wonder where she gets that." He winked at his mother.

After a knock on the door, Dan stuck his head in. "Lee, the detective would like to talk with you. He planned to meet Brad and Leeann here at the hospital. Are you up to talking with him first?"

Holly worried her sister would try to do too much too soon. Despite tubes hooking Lee up an IV, Holly wouldn't be surprised to find her sister walking the halls and pulling the IV stand behind her. She was a determined person.

"Thanks, Dan. Yes, you guys get out and send in the detective."

"Holler if you need anyone. We'll come running." Holly led the group out of Lee's room. "Good morning, Detective Vela. Lee can see you now."

Brad held out his hand. "Detective, I'm Brad Kennedy, Lee's son and this is my sister, Leeann. And this is my cousin, Sarah. We'll be here when you conclude your business with my mom. Please don't stay too long with her. We don't want to tire her out."

Detective Vela shook hands with Brad and Leeann and nodded to the others. "Thank you, I appreciate that, and I won't tire her out. I promise."

"Detective." Holly placed her hand on his arm before he stepped through the door to go in to see Lee. "When can I get back in my house?"

"You can go back now. I just got a text they finished. I'd like to visit with you again, Ms. Grant."

"Sure, text me, and we'll arrange a time and place."

After Detective Vela went into Lee's room, Holly turned to her nephew and nieces. "Would you mind if I went home? I'd like to see what I have to deal with and make a few calls."

"Of course not. It looks like Mom is doing remarkably well, and Leeann, Kay, Sarah and I can handle anything. You go take care of your home."

"Thanks." Holly stretched up and kissed Brad on the cheek and then hugged Leeann. "Don't let your mother do too much too soon. Kay, keep me posted. Sarah, glad you could come up, but don't feel you have to stay."

"I have a break in my classes, so I scooted on up here."

"Dan, can you drive me back to my place?"

"Of course. Let us know if you need anything, Brad." Dan took Holly's hand, and they rode the elevator down to the ground floor and then got on the garage elevator to ride up to their floor. They climbed in the car and drove toward Holly's complex.

When did they fall into this habit of holding hands? Holly hated to admit how much she liked the closeness. Standing on her own had become an imperative after the chaos of her first marriage. After all these years, she felt like all that had happened to another person in another time. She shoved the memories into a dark hole, where they belonged. They were no part of her life today.

"Holly. Holly."

"What?"

"You seemed to have drifted off."

"Maybe I did for a minute."

"We're at your house."

"Oh, my goodness. I did drift away. Missed the whole trip."

"The police turned the house of one of my client's upside down when they went over it looking for clues in a robbery. I want you to be prepared for what will probably be a real mess."

"Okay, then, forewarned." Holly unhooked her seat belt. "Let's go check out the situation." She led the way up to her house, her stomach turned flip-flops at what she might find.

She went in with Dan right behind her. Her gaze skittered across the floor of the front entrance. So far so good. Nothing out of the ordinary here. Stepping into the main living area, chaos struck her in the face. Fingerprint powder was everywhere. Still, the room looked all right. She stepped through the glass to the patio where they'd been when the bullet struck Lee. Chairs lay on their sides, and blood stained the floor. The two napkins she used to staunch the flood of Lee's blood lay where the EMTs had dropped them. She gulped in a shaky breath. Dear God, they'd almost lost her. Her legs gave out, and she staggered. Strong hands came around her waist and lowered her to the patio sofa.

"You okay?" Dan settled on the sofa next to her and slid an arm across her shoulder.

"It's not the house. It's realizing how close we came to losing Lee." Holly faced Dan. "I don't get it. Why would someone be shooting from the golf course? Who were they aiming for? Were kids pulling a stupid prank?"

"I don't know. Hopefully, the police will find out. But if we're dealing with a random incident, which makes more sense, we may never know."

Holly rose and stood in the middle of the patio and pivoted three hundred sixty degrees. Her gaze went to the crack in the patio wall. She reached out her hand before she jerked it back. "That must be where the bullet hit. The bullet that went through my sister." She ran a hand across her forehead, down the back of her head and began to massage her neck.

"Let me do that."

Before she knew what happened, Dan moved to stand behind her, and his strong hands kneaded the muscles which had bunched into knots. In moments, her head dropped forward, and a long sigh slid from between her lips. "Oh, my gosh. You could get a job doing that."

Dan laughed. "I'll keep that in mind if I ever get tired of the law and taking care of my clients."

Holly straightened. "Seriously, you're talented. I can go on now."

He gave her shoulders a last squeeze. "What's next?"

She rolled her shoulders, relaxing them down her back. They'd been hiked up almost to her ears. So much better. "I'll call Gretner again to schedule them to clean it all up. They did a good job after the hailstorm. I hope they can work me into their schedule." They walked back into the house.

"You're welcome to stay with me until all this is put back together."

"Seems like I did that after the storm. I hate to impose."

"You're never an imposition, Holly. You must know that."

Holly swore her heart skipped a beat at the look in Dan's eyes. My goodness. She did enjoy whatever was growing between them. "Well, thank you."

"Will you be okay here by yourself for a while? I need to head to the office for a meeting."

"Of course. Don't let me keep you."

"Call me and let me know when you're ready to come over, and I can come get you."

"That's okay, I'll drive over, but I'll text you when I'm on the way. I'll bring supper."

"Nice. See you later then. Good luck with Gretner."

"Thanks."

Dan waved before turning and heading out the front door. Holly spun around and flopped on the sofa. Someone had shot her sister, the police had wrecked her house, and she couldn't stay in it, and yet happiness bubbled just below the surface. Yes, definitely happy. What part did Dan Morgan play in that happiness?

Chapter Fourteen

A week later, Barrett trudged across the street to visit his grandparents. He found the site under the giant oak tree and knelt to arrange the flowers. He brought new flowers every couple of weeks and tended the ones that grew there.

"Well, Grandpa. I'm trying to keep our property. You know Dad stupidly lost it gambling, but no one has been able to build anything on our property. I've made sure that didn't happen. I've successfully fought off all invaders and kept it for you and Grandma.

"Now there is this woman who is crazy determined. Would you believe she wants to build tiny homes on the property? Crazy she is. And the worst part is she wants to set up homeless people in those tiny homes. Those people would let whatever she built run down. They'd trash the place. The development would devalue our property across the road. And I'd have trouble coming here to visit you. I can't let that happen. I won't let that happen.

"Rest easy, Grandpa. I'll protect you."

Barrett pushed himself to his feet. If Holly Grant thought she was determined, she didn't know him. Protecting his grandparents. Nothing would keep him from accomplishing that mission. He crossed the road to his house and went into the garage where he found his golf bag sitting in the corner.

Holly happily settled back in her home. She appreciated Dan's hospitality, but she wasn't sure how good it was for her heart to stay in that intimate situation for an extended time with him. It felt like they were playing house. Well, of course, they weren't. They didn't. Nothing untoward happened. Still sipping coffee in their pajamas in the morning had an intimate feel to it. It just did.

Holly filled her bag with papers she needed for a meeting with the owner of a property that she had interest in. Buying and selling. That's what she did. Keeping the property and setting up Grant Gardens was different from anything she or her sisters had done. They all three owned properties, but for their own use. Not for someone else to use. The excitement she originally felt about this project had only grown and had steeled her determination to make homes for people who needed a hand up. They had pulled together several agencies to collaborate with them to make sure the people had the support they needed to get their lives on track.

A misconception many people had is that the homeless didn't want to work, or they were bad people. The reality was that many people were only a car wreck or medical bill away from losing their house. If rent increased two hundred dollars a month, many people would be in real trouble. The City of Fort Worth and the agencies they worked with focused on finding housing for people who'd been on the streets. Once they had a safe place to live, then they could find a job or get training. For both of those, they needed an address. A tent city in the trees by the railroad tracks didn't provide that.

A smile spread across Holly's face as she considered the improvement in Lee's health. Such a relief. Lee's son, Brad, stayed only until she got out of the hospital. Her daughter, Leeann, stayed for several days before she headed back to Austin. Sure signs everyone felt Lee had reached a good place. Sarah had been a big help keeping her mother from getting too strung out.

The Gretner Company had come out quickly and done a super job putting her home back together. She chuckled. Nita, her housekeeper who came every other week, would feel like she'd gotten a new house to work in. The place was spotless.

She entered the garage, got in her SUV, and backed out, heading for a meeting in an office building in the Clearfork area. Not at all far from her house. She liked the work she did, putting together buyers and sellers.

I n the car on her way back to her home, Holly's cell chirped with Lee's song. She hit the accept button and answered, "Hey, sis. What's going on? How are you feeling?"

"I'm fine, thank you for asking. I wanted to run ideas for the tiny homes by you. If you and Kay and I agree, I'll get them to the architect's interior design person, and we'll try to finalize the plans. Then they can get materials on order."

"Sounds like a good idea. I didn't know if you'd had time or felt like working on these since the accident." Holly refused to believe someone had intentionally shot her sister.

"I've worked on them while I recuperated. Planning helped take my mind off my injury. Kay came over and provided her good color eye as well as providing my arms. Anyway, we're ready to show you. When are you free?"

"I'm free this evening. I have papers to file digitally and in real folders, but I'll be free after six. Should we come to your house?"

"No. I don't feel like straightening the house." Lee's chuckle came through the cell. "Kay can drive, and we'll bring pizza. You provide the wine, and we'll all make decisions. I love making decorating decisions. It's creative hard work and makes the brain cells stretch."

Holly chuckled at Lee's enthusiasm. Important to love your work. "Okay by me. See y'all later." Holly disconnected and continued on her way home. After parking in her garage, she went inside and settled at her computer where she finished putting away the files for the southeast Fort Worth project, a grocery store and pharmacy in a lower income part of town. Pride filled her at the thought of the dent the project would make in the food desert of that area.

Standing, she stretched her arms way up and then leaned over from side to side. Sitting in one spot too long made her stiff.

"Hey, Holly. We're here. You ready for us?" Lee opened the door, carrying a giant pizza box. Kay followed her inside, carrying an overlarge portfolio.

Time had flown while she worked. "Oh, and would you smell that Mama's pizza. Haven't had theirs in a long time. It's the best. Come on in. As much as I want to see your designs, I'm starving. Let's eat first, and then you can show me what you've got."

Holly poured wine into her sisters' glasses and then set out the parmesan cheese and red pepper flakes.

Kay made Lee sit down and served up the pizza. "Here you go, Lee, two for you and Holly and two for me. You're on your own for more. No judgment from me." She wiggled her eyebrows at her sisters. "Do you have ranch dressing, Holly?" Kay opened the refrigerator. "Oh, good, you do."

Holly loved having such a close relationship with her sisters. She realized everyone wasn't as lucky as they were. They finished their meal with lots of teasing and laughter. Kay and Holly cleaned away the food off the table. "You just sit, Lee. We'll make you work extra hard after you're back on your feet."

Lee laughed. "I'm sure you will. In the meantime, I'll enjoy being waited on."

"Okay, sisters, show me what you've got." Holly could hardly wait.

Lee lifted her portfolio and laid it on the table before slipping out several three by four feet sample cards. "Kay and I had the best time working on these. I hope you'll be pleased. Here's the country cozy one with lots of white and beiges."

Holly studied the samples. "Nice."

"This one is our beach house, and we've used three shades of turquoise and white."

"Oh, I do love that one." Holly leaned over, studying the swatches. "What else do you have?"

"This one is modern with black, white and gray."

"Probably not for me," Holly said, "but I'm sure somebody will love it."

"You'll love this Cape Cod. It's got a bedroom with two cute windows with flower boxes and storage upstairs." Lee pulled out the next card and showed Holly.

"We chose navy and white, and we even put in wainscoting," Kay pointed to the wood sample.

"Oh, yes! You gals are rocking it! That's four. What's the fifth one?"

"A mountain cottage." Lee held up the card. "Rustic and yet soft. Look at the plaids."

"And look," Kay pointed to each card. "We've put a small dishwasher and a combined washer-dryer in each unit. You know, like in Europe."

"This is wonderful. Y'all did a great job. People will be so happy to live in this community. Run these ideas by Jenny Aldrich at Juan's firm, and if they both agree, tell them to go ahead with ordering the materials.

"Here's to Grant Gardens." Kay lifted her glass, and Holly and Lee joined in the toast.

"Spread out all the cards, Lee. I want to take a couple of pics so I can show Dan."

"Show Dan?" Lee glanced at Kay, but she moved to do what Holly asked.

"Sure. He'll be interested in this. You know he serves on the board of the Homeless Coalition." Holly pointed her phone at the boards, then took shots of specifics of parts of each one.

"Of course. For his board work." Kay grinned.

Holly paused. "What are you smiling about?"

"I've noticed you seem to spend quite a bit of time with Dan these days. Even spending the night at his place. Lee and I can't help but wonder if it's more than business with you two."

Holly finished shooting her pictures. "There, that will do. Thanks. Go ahead and pack them up."

Kay held the portfolio as Lee slid in one large card after the other. When Lee had them packed away, she pinned her gaze on Holly. "Don't you plan to respond to what Kay said?"

"Well, no. I'm choosing not to respond to Kay's fishing exhibition. You gals did a super job. I'm pleased." She hugged Kay and then Lee. "I can't wait to see the real houses standing on the property. And now it's gotten late, and I still have work to do."

"What's this? Here's your hat, what's your hurry?" Kay picked up her purse from the entry bench, and Lee picked up the portfolio.

"Apparently we're being kicked out, Kay." Lee chuckled. "I'll get these to Jenny and Juan, and I'll let you know what they say."

"Thank you. Thank you. I know Mom and Dad would be proud of us and this project."

After a group hug, her sisters went out the front door, which Holly locked after them. Her sisters were gone, but Kay's words surrounded her. Holly could almost see them encased in a dialogue bubble floating around below the ceiling and sometimes dipping down to slide in front of her face.

Too bad they'd already cleaned up the kitchen. She needed something physical to do to take her mind off those words. A walk. She'd go for a walk. One of the reasons she loved her complex was because of all the different trails through which she could meander. She felt safe walking around the grounds even at night, despite someone shooting Lee while they were on the patio. That had to be a bizarre random event. Didn't it?

It didn't cool off much in the dead of summer, but tonight a good breeze rustled the leaves and caressed her cheek. The smell of fresh-cut grass greeted her. After walking for ten minutes, Holly let herself focus on Kay's comment. She had to face it. Ignoring her feelings wasn't working. Why had she felt it important to share the tiny house plans with Dan? Oh, sure, he served on the board of the Homeless Coalition and as her lawyer made sure everything she wanted to do she could legally do. And he'd ramrodded the process of getting approval from the board of adjustment and the city council. His support and work were invaluable.

She settled on a bench under one of the giant oak trees. Did she want more from her relationship with Dan? Could she give more to the relationship? She didn't know. Ever since the last time her ex-husband attacked her, she'd avoided men. Oh, she had men acquaintances and friends. Dan had been an invaluable friend during the mess with her ex. Her fingers clenched, and her heartbeat increased, making her gasp for breath. She'd made a mistake to come out here into the heat. The wind stopped. She fanned her hand in front of her face and finally leaned over, dropping her head between her knees. Her head spun and her stomach churned.

A moan escaped her clenched lips. It had been a long time—a couple of years—since she'd had one of these episodes, she hoped she'd gotten over this reaction to that night. That night fifteen years ago. The movie reel began playing in her head, a reel she was powerless to stop.

Holly dutifully locked the door after Rick, her private security guard, had already checked that the house was secure. She headed back to her bedroom to get into something comfortable before she ate her salad supper. She pulled out a pair of jeans and a t-shirt from her closet and went into the bathroom taking off her bra. She draped it across a towel rack, then slipped into the comfortable outfit. Oh yeah, so much better. She could feel her spirits begin to rise at the thought of a nice evening at home alone with her salad, a glass of wine, and a light-hearted sitcom on TV. That's what her weary mind needed. She stepped back into her bedroom, froze in her tracks, a scream lodged in her throat.

Joe Bryant sat on her bed leaning against the headboard, a wicked smile spreading across his face.

She opened her mouth to say something, but nothing came out. My god, was she hallucinating? How did he get in here? She'd scream. Would Rick hear her? Why hadn't they tested that? Her mind scurried around like a rat in a maze.

"What's the matter, Holly? Proverbial cat got your tongue? I wouldn't mind getting your tongue." He wagged his at her.

Bile rose in the back of her throat. Her stomach cramped. Her head spun. She couldn't pass out. She'd be at his mercy. Not something she remembered him having much of. She dug her fingernails into her palms. The pain brought her up short. He'd not get the better of her. Not again. She swallowed a couple of times and moistened her lips.

"What are you doing here, Joe? How'd you get in?"

"Well, aren't you being the cool one? Thought I'd at least get a holler out of you. You used to be a good screamer. Remember, Holly?"

"What do you want, Joe?" She struggled to keep her jaw from trembling. Counseling was fine. Self-defense training was fine. But Joe stood in her bedroom again, and she might die of fright. Her heart so fast she figured he must be able to see the organ thumping in her chest. This could not be happening again.

"You're not being very friendly, wifey."

"I'm not your wife anymore, Joe." She took a deep breath. She had to remember to breathe. To get oxygen to her brain. Maybe he didn't mean to do anything bad. Yeah, but he'd broken into her house. "We haven't been married since before you went off to prison."

"Yeah, but you never got hitched again, so I kind of figured you must be waiting for me to get out. It'd have been nice if you'd visited me during any of those long, lonely years, wifey mine." Joe moved to get up off the bed.

She couldn't help herself; she stepped back.

"What's the matter? You don't have any reason to be afraid of me. Of course, you did lie about me on the stand. You made sure I spent fifteen years of my life in that damned prison." He edged closer and closer to her.

Holly backed up until her back hit the wall. He reached out, grabbed hold of her breast and squeezed. She couldn't keep the gasp from escaping.

"Get your hands off me. A private security guard sits in his car out front. I holler, and you're back in jail forever this time. You want that, Joe?"

"No bra." He rubbed his hand over her other breast. "You waiting for me? Or you waiting for someone else?"

"Just get out of here, Joe. Please." Her voice trembled, and she hated her weakness.

He grabbed her arms and forced them behind her, pulling her close to him, rubbing his body against hers.

She gasped again and tried to get away, but he kept her hands pinned behind her with one of his hands. He slid his other between their bodies and began trying to unhook her jeans.

"No, you're not getting away with this. I swear, Joe, I'll kill you if you don't get your hands off me. Now."

"Sure, Babe." Joe laughed, an insane kind of sound. He left her jeans alone to fondle her breasts more, running his hand up under her t-shirt, stepping back to put more space between them.

Holly recognized the opening she needed and had prayed for. With all the force she could muster, she slammed her knee into his groin. Unlike in her self-defense classes where the men wore protective covering, Joe's muscle and tissue gave from the impact of her knee.

He yelled and doubled over. Holly leaped around him and grabbed the pistol from the top drawer of her bedside table, then ran for the front of the house. Glad she'd learned to keep a bullet in the chamber, she screamed while she flipped off the safety.

Thank God, the front hall. Almost safe.

Suddenly her shirt collar choked her. A sob escaped when she realized Joe had caught up with her. He slung her to the floor. She landed on her back, nearly losing hold of the gun. But she wouldn't give up without a fight. The namby-pamby woman who'd been married to him all those god-awful years had ceased to exist.

"You'll wish you hadn't done that. I planned to kill you quick, but now I'll make you suffer. Like you've made me suffer all these years."

Holly screamed again, pointing the gun in his direction.

"You won't use that. You never tried to stop me before. You know it's only what you deserve." Daring Holly, he stood tall with both hands on his waist and laughed at her, a scary ugly laugh.

She steadied the gun with both hands and fired, the explosion ringing in her ears, deafening her.

Joe reached for his shoulder. Blood seeped between his fingers. "I'll make you pay for that." He pulled a knife from his pocket, flicked it open and roared as he lunged for her. She fired again, and he landed on top of her.

The front door crashed in as Rick burst through the front door, gun drawn. "Get off her or you're dead."

Joe didn't move.

Rick rushed over. He leaned down and rolled Joe off her. He kicked the knife away.

"Is he dead?" Tears ran down her face. Sobs caught in her throat.

"Yeah." Rick knelt beside her and removed the gun from her hand. "The police are on the way. You okay? Did he do anything to you? Hurt you?"

She scooted against the wall, pulled her knees up in front of her, dropped her head, and sobbed. After a while, the sounds of people entering her house reached her. She raised her head to see the house swarming with police.

Holly shook herself from the nightmare, forced her legs to move, and made her way back to her home, locking herself safely inside. She went to the kitchen and poured a glass of wine. After a large gulp, she walked into her bedroom, stripped, and stepped under a steaming hot shower. Desperately trying to wash away the guilt of taking a person's life. Maybe you didn't ever get over that. Maybe that was a good thing. Despite so many years having passed, Holly had never been able to move past the experience. Oh, she'd become a successful developer. Had with her sisters cared for their parents and looked after their business interests. But she'd never had a successful romantic experience. Why was she even considering putting Dan through that? She wasn't being fair to him.

She shut off the shower, stepped out, and toweled off before slipping into stretchy pants and a soft t-shirt. With her glass on the table beside her bed, she climbed in and settled against the headboard. Could she continue to work with him when she felt this emotional pull toward him? A pull she didn't believe she could respond to. Leading him on would be wrong. How she wished she could make a different choice.

Chapter Fifteen

Dan finished the project he'd been working on for over two hours. Rubbing his eyes with one hand, he leaned back in his desk chair. Making sure all the changes his client wanted in the document said exactly what he'd intended was tedious work, but that's why they paid him the big bucks. Dan took pride in the clarity of his contracts. He emailed the contract to his client and signed out of his secure work site. He should've gone home hours ago. His stomach had almost stopped growling, but he needed to eat. If Jon had worked late, too, they could get a beer and a burger together and catch up.

Work had buried them both lately. A good thing for the law firm and his bank account. Not great for relationships. Any relationship. Dan realized it had been over a week since he'd seen Holly. Summer had almost ended, and she'd told him they still didn't have the permits from the city to allow them to start work on Grant Gardens. Disappointing. Fortunately, nothing else had happened to her sisters or to Holly. He'd been grateful to hear that information. The shooting must've been random, as scary as that was, he'd choose that over having a crazy person who had targeted Lee, Kay, or Holly.

Holly. What was he going to do about her? Oh, he knew what he'd like to do with her, but what if she wasn't ever able to be with him in a physical way? Should he give up on them ever being together?

Dan walked down the hall to Jon's office, but no light shone from within. After eight in the evening. Anyone with a family would've been gone a long time ago.

A family. Dan never had a family. Not really. His wife had left him for another man because he'd buried himself in the law. At the time, the choice seemed to be the right decision, working long hours for them to have all the things they both wanted. Building his practice and helping the firm. But all the shiny things hadn't been enough to keep her satisfied.

Well, he'd not make that mistake again. Of course, now he had a well-established legal practice and made more than enough money for him and anyone else. Holly was the one person he'd like to share his life with. He'd held out hope for something developing between them. They'd spent many hours working together on real estate projects over the years.

Oh, she appreciated him for all his support when she'd shot her ex-husband. Dan couldn't imagine how awful that must've been for her. Or how bad the situation must've been for her when she'd been married. Bad enough to get her husband arrested, tried, and convicted. But prison time didn't change him. The horrible result was his attack on her and her shooting him.

Dan left the office and went down the elevator to his car and drove out of the parking garage. Maybe he'd pick up fast food tonight. He didn't do that often. As you got older, you had to pay more attention to what fuel you put in your body if you had any chance of keeping yourself in shape. Oh, he wasn't an extremist, eating his share of ice cream, his dessert of choice, but he did limit fried foods. Tonight, he'd make an exception. Nothing beat a burger, fries, and beer as comfort food. All his thoughts about Holly made him sad. Yes, tonight cried out for comfort food.

D an finished filling out the last of his billing for August. After the staff did their thing with the info, he'd double check the figures before the secretary sent the bills to his clients. August had been a good month. His cell beeped. He smiled at Holly's face appearing on his phone screen. Too many weeks had passed since he'd heard from her.

"Hey, Holly. What's up?"

"Hey, yourself. Do you have a few minutes? You can bill me." Her laughter floated across through the connection.

"So, this is business, huh?"

"I'm excited. I got a call from Samuel Ramirez, our construction manager. We've got all the permits from the city. Finally! You were the first person I thought to share the good news with."

Dan's heart swelled at her words. She called him before her sisters. That had to be a good sign, right? "I'm happy for you, Holly. It's taken longer than any of us expected. Thanks for sharing the good news. Do you plan to celebrate?"

"Of course. We never miss an opportunity to celebrate. We could go out to the property. None of us have been out in a while. We celebrated the purchase there. It makes sense to celebrate getting the permits."

"Did Sam say when they'd actually begin work?" Dan doodled with a pencil on a pad he kept for such purposes. Sometimes the squiggles made a pattern, sometimes they were random like now.

"September 10. After all the delays, I can hardly believe we're finally doing this. Listen, I've got to let you go. I need to call my sisters. Bye." She disconnected before Dan could ask her about celebrating the good news with him. Maybe another time.

After Holly parked on the edge of her property, she climbed out of her car. She clapped her hands and spun around.

Sam laughed at her. "Pretty excited, huh?"

"Absolutely. Okay, walk me through the layout." She looked around the property.

Sam used pieces of stone to mark off the entrance. "The community building with the office is here close to the front of the project. We're planning on streets going back in spokes behind the center. You can name them what you want, but we're calling them A, B, C, D, and E. We'll have six houses on each street with three on each side in a staggered pattern to give everyone plenty of space." Stakes in the ground showed the intended streets.

"What about the trees, Sam? Will you be able to work around them?" Holly shaded her eyes with her hand even though she wore sunglasses. Despite the calendar saying they were in the month of September, in Texas that meant summer sun and weather continued.

"Yeah, mostly. We will have to take out one of the trees. That large one on the south side of the property. It's diseased and in a storm could fall on one of the houses."

He led her around the property, and they studied the area.

"I'm sorry to lose any trees. Glad it's not this one. Such great shade this tree provides, making a welcome place for sitting by the pond." She patted the tree trunk as if she might be patting a dog that could feel her touch. "Can we use the wood from the tree you'll take down to build a pergola? Residents will want lots of shady places to sit outside. Between the tree and the pergola, we'll provide a perfect place for meditation or visiting with friends, and I hope the residents will make good friends here."

"I'm sure we can make a pergola from the tree. I've got a buddy who does woodwork. He'd love to get his hands on that tree, give it a second life."

"Thanks. Makes me happy to hear that. I'm a bit of a tree hugger and can't bear to see them taken down."

They walked back toward the main part of the property.

"I'm expecting my workers to show up any minute, Holly. You want to stay to take pictures or anything?"

"I'm staying, and taking pics is a great idea. Lee and Kay wanted to be here, but Lee had a client appointment, and Kay is deep in creation mode. Nothing interferes with that." A loud noise drew her attention. "Oh, my goodness. What's that?"

"The grading begins today."

Holly clapped her hands again and barely kept herself from jumping up and down. Work started. Ultimately, they'd have a community here for people who needed a home. Her heart pounded with excitement. Her parents would be proud.

Holly stayed for over an hour watching the grader smoothing out the ground. Finally, the heat forced her to leave. Sweat trickled down between her breasts. Her hair clung to her head. When she climbed into her SUV, she immediately flipped the AC switch and sighed when the cool air made chill bumps prickle on her damp skin. Not a fan of Texas summers. She usually tried to get away from the heat for several weeks into the cool mountains of Colorado, but she'd been too busy. Pulling out on the road, she glanced through her back window at the work on Grant Gardens. Missing a summer vacation had been worth the loss, for her to see the progress being made on the Grant Garden's project.

B arrett raised the binoculars to his eyes again. There she stood. That awful
woman walked on the sacred land where his grandparents lay buried.
She'd pay for this. He would not let her build her stupid little houses for those
losers.

His heart raced as she and the man tramped across his land. They got close
to his favorite tree. The one that towered over his grandparents' final resting
place. She dared to touch the tree. She'd pay for that.

He heard the noise before he saw the ugly machine pull onto his property.
His fingers tightened on the binoculars. His stomach cramped. "*Ahhhhgggg.*"
The growl escaped through clenched teeth. Yes, she'd pay.

Lowering the binoculars, he made his way into his home, poured himself a
shot of whiskey. Gulped it back. The burn helped center him. Time to make his
plans.

To begin with, he needed to follow her and get a better handle on her
comings and goings. He could attempt to get her again from the golf course,
but he hated to push his luck. If he had to, he could crawl over that wall
behind her house. He walked into his garage and found the rifle in the golf bag.
Opening the trunk, he slid the weapon in its cover inside and pulled a blanket
over. He needed to make sure to have the weapon handy when he found the
perfect opportunity. He would stop Holly Grant if he did nothing else in his
life.

B arrett wheeled his car behind Holly's as she headed southwest of town.
Was she planning to drive to his property? After following her for over a
week, he found she went out to the site once a day. She didn't stay long.
Sometimes she went by herself, and other times she had her sisters with her. She
was the brains of the deal, so he didn't have to get rid of her sisters, too. They'd
be basket cases after losing Holly, and they'd let the project drop. Too bad he'd
messed up the first time.

Barrett discovered Holly to be a woman of routine. Every morning but
Saturday and Sunday, she left her home by seven and headed to a gym. From
there she'd grab breakfast at the same bakery and then drive out to his property.
She'd park, sip a drink in a travel cup, and eat her breakfast. Then she headed

off to another piece of property or a meeting with an apparent client. He'd researched her and discovered that Holly Grant was a dynamo in the development business, buying and selling property with a remarkable success rate.

But this time, she'd picked the wrong project. That land belonged to him and his grandparents. He had to strike soon because the workers were there every day defiling the land. He needed to take intermediary steps since he hadn't found an opportunity yet to get rid of her. Could he blow up the equipment? How much dynamite would he need? Did he want to do that and risk a fire? No. No fire on his property. He'd read you could put water in the gas tank of one of the pieces of equipment and that would slow down the work. Yes. And he could easily do that at night.

He glanced up as Holly grant shook hands with her next client. Hmm. That's okay. You do your thing, woman, and he'd do his. If he had to put water in the tank of the machinery every night, he could do that, buying him time to develop his plans to permanently get rid of Holly Grant. Tonight would be the start.

B arrett's watch showed straight up midnight. All the coffee he'd drunk to stay awake had him wired. He filled four, gallon containers with water and put them in his wheeled garden cart. The cart had been a good purchase, and he'd used it for lots of activities, including cutting down on the number of trips he made hauling plants and soil. One trip across the road, and he'd take out the two large pieces of equipment on the land.

No moon, and while the neighborhood association had lobbied the city for a streetlight at the turn into their addition, tonight the delay in the light installation proved to be an advantage. He stood on the street, looking left and right into the quiet darkness. He flipped on a small flashlight and cautiously made his way across the road, pulling the cart behind him. The stillness made his steps echo in his ears. He turned his head to check that no one watched him. He got to the first piece of equipment and opened the fuel tank. He siphoned out about half the fuel, then he emptied two gallons of water into the tank. He screwed on the lid and went to the backhoe, repeating the process.

A smile spread across his face as he put the empty water jugs back in the buggy. He made his way to his grandparents' tree. "Don't worry." His whispered words slid into the air. "I won't let them get our land." He rested his hand on the trunk before turning and heading home.

Chapter Sixteen

Holly finished up with her workout at the gym, showered, and headed for breakfast at the Bread Bakery. They had the best pull-a-part rolls, oozing with cinnamon and brown sugar. Sometimes she got an egg and croissant sandwich, but she did have a sweet tooth she worked hard to keep under control. Munching the roll and sipping her coffee, she drove out to the Grant Gardens property, expecting to see the property completely cleared. They'd been making good progress.

After pulling off to the side of the road, she used a wipe to clean the sticky from her hands. Stepping out, she brushed the crumbs from her slacks and shirt. The odd quiet surprised her. Usually when she arrived, the roar from the equipment greeted her. Today, workers stood around doing nothing. Hmm. What had happened? A man separated himself from the group and made his way to her.

"Hey, Holly. I'm afraid I've got bad news."

"Good morning, Sam. What's going on? Or not going on?"

"We suspect we've got water in the equipment fuel tanks. We're waiting for someone to come haul off these two bulldozers. Replacements will arrive day after tomorrow."

"How did water get in the fuel tanks? We haven't had rain in over a month."

"Yeah. That's the mystery. The humidity has even been low. Makes us wonder if someone may have done this on purpose. We found spilled gasoline on the ground by both dozers." Sam shoved his hands in the pockets of his jeans.

"What? Why would someone do that? Who would do that?" Holly ran her hand through her hair and down the back of her head and rubbed her neck to relieve the tension tightening there.

"I'm afraid I don't have a clue. It's probably teenagers acting out. But I don't see how we'd ever find out. We don't have cameras. The neighborhood across the way doesn't have entry cameras that might've caught something. So, I'm sorry, our costs will increase, but that can come out of the contingency, and we'll have a short delay."

Holly shrugged. "Not your fault, Sam. I'm sorry about this, but what can you do?"

"At this point, let's assume this was a one-off. If anything else happens, then we may want to move up the date for when we install a fence, and we can consider putting a trailer with a guy who can sit out on the property at night. That will run up our costs."

"Well, no one is keeping us from doing this project. Whatever the costs, my sisters and I are in. Sure sorry for your inconvenience. Okay, I'll head out. I guess I don't need to stop by in the morning to see what happened today. I'll see you in a few."

"Take care, Holly. I'll send you a report on the extra cost."

Holly nodded and walked back to her car. What a bummer. Crazy teenagers. Kay seldom answered her phone when an art project held her in its grip, so Holly called Lee.

"Hey, Holly. You caught me on the way to a client's house. What's up?"

Holly explained.

"Well, that's disappointing. Hey, why don't we catch supper together? I'll text Kay and see if we can roust her out."

"Sounds great. Text me with the details." Holly disconnected and drove back to her community. The sound of the gate clicking closed behind her provided a special feeling of security. A tiny niggle of worry ate at her over the water in the fuel tanks. Yes, school had begun, and teens shouldn't have any spare time, but teens did occasionally act out when they didn't have enough to do or enough to do that they wanted to do. But where did those teens come from? The neighborhood across the way was for fifty-five and up. There might be a couple of kids living with their parents or maybe even visiting with grandparents, but not many. Puzzling for sure.

Holly got to work on phone calls and emails, keeping up with her development business. She loved the work and never found what she did dull because a new project came along every couple of weeks or so. The challenge of getting the best price for a parcel of land, then finding the right buyer for that land never failed to energize her. Having Dan handle all the legalities made things easier. He'd been a good friend for a long time. She smiled a moment then pushed the thoughts of Dan aside and went back to work.

It was five p.m. before she realized she hadn't heard from Lee about supper. The salad she ate for lunch to make up for the cinnamon roll she'd eaten for breakfast had long since gone away. She left her office and wandered into the kitchen for something to nibble on that wouldn't spoil her supper, whatever that would be. Had Lee been able to get hold of Kay? They'd learned not to worry about their younger sister. Knowing how happy her art made her tempered their annoyance at Kay's lack of response.

Holly nabbed two small pieces of white cheddar and crackers, poured herself a short glass of wine and settled on the sofa, propping her feet on the coffee table. A long sigh escaped. She'd much rather sit outside on her patio, but the dog days of summer continued through September, and temps would be brutal out there until almost nine in the evening even with the ceiling fan going on high.

Her phone in the pocket of her slacks vibrated. She slid it out to find Lee's smiling face.

"Hey, sweetie. I finally reached Kay. She was ready for a break. How do burgers at Hank's sound to you?"

"I haven't been there in a while, and their burgers are the best. What time?"

"Six is early, but Kay worked through lunch and is starving."

"Sounds good. See you soon." Holly disconnected. The earlier time worked for her as well. She finished her cheese and crackers and carried her glass with her to her bedroom. Jeans with a white short-sleeved blouse and sandals were perfect for tonight.

Holly walked into Hank's and found Lee and Kay already there at a table toward the back of the restaurant away from the busier and louder section. Much as Holly loved the burgers here, sometimes the noise annoyed her. Made listening to conversation difficult. She exchanged hugs with her sisters and sat down as a waiter arrived with three cold brews in icy mugs.

"Such a good idea on such a hot day. Thanks for ordering these, Lee."

"Of course." Lee tipped her mug in Holly's direction.

"I'm dead tired of every day being over a hundred. Can't wait for fall temperatures to arrive."

"Me, too."

"But you never go out, Kay, especially when you're painting." Holly teased her sister.

"Well, if you can choose, no one with any sense goes out after noon. This heat can kill you," Kay said defending herself.

"You're right about that. After making a couple of stops looking at property, I've had to go home and shower." Holly sipped her beer. "Mmm. This is good." The buzz cooled her from the inside.

The waiter arrived, and they each placed their order.

"Did Lee tell you about what happened to the equipment on our property?"

"Yeah, she mentioned it. Weird, huh?" Kay's forehead crinkled into a frown.

"Sam thought maybe teenagers, but who knows," Holly sipped her beer. "It's also made our costs go up some. Delays have a way of doing that."

The waiter arrived with their meal. They were all quiet while they passed around the mustard and ketchup, getting their burgers fixed to their satisfaction.

"So, I have an announcement," Kay put down her burger, and her eyes gleamed with excitement.

"So, share. What is it?" Lee asked.

"I've made a sale."

"You've made lots of sales, girl. What's the big deal?" Lee asked.

"You know the four by six painting of the lake with the sunrise?"

"Yes, it's one of my favorites." Holly dipped an onion ring into the ketchup. "As Lee stated, you sell your paintings all the time. What's special about this one?"

"It went to a wealthy man who's a patron of the arts. Lots of people will see my work and get to know my name. This opportunity could make a big difference in my future."

"Congratulations!" Lee raised her beer mug, and Holly and Kay did too.

"No one deserves this more, Kay." Holly patted her sister on the shoulder.

They chatted a while about the sale and how excited they were for Kay to be able to support herself with her art. Not many artists were this lucky. They could be super talented, but luck wasn't with them. Making a good living in any of the arts was a challenge.

Holly noticed Kay and Lee making eye contact. What's with those two? They looked like they were plotting.

"So, Holly, when did you see Dan last?" Kay popped a French fry in her mouth and followed with a swig of her beer.

Holly lifted her mug and took a swallow, buying time. What were her sisters up to? She set down the mug and said, "We met last week over a project in southeast Fort Worth."

"But that was business, Holly. Have you been out to dinner?"

"Yes, sometimes we conduct business over dinner." Holly tried to wiggle out of where she suspected her sisters planned to take this conversation.

"But you like him, don't you? I mean really, really like him." Lee took the last bite of her burger.

"Of course, I do. I wouldn't do business with him if I didn't. Besides, we've been friends for many years." The incident with Joe popped into her head, and she shoved the ugliness away. She wouldn't have survived without Dan.

"Well, Kay and I have been talking, Holly."

"Oh, you have, have you?" Holly braced herself for what she suspected the sisters might have discussed.

Kay reached over and took Holly's hand. "Sis, if you do like Dan in that way, and you say you do, don't you want more with him? Isn't it time?"

"We get how not only physically, but emotionally hurt you were by what that dreadful scum you were married to did, but you've got to move on from that. We want you to be happy." Lee lifted her mug and paused. "Hey, and we want Dan to be happy, too."

"Haven't you seen how he looks at you? Because we have." Kay squeezed Holly's hand.

"Thank you both for being concerned about me and Dan. I do care for him."

"Sis, if you can't act on your feelings about him, you might be kinder to cut him loose."

"Oh, wow!" Holly leaned back in her chair. Lee was known for straight talking, but her words took Holly's breath. Was she being selfish to keep Dan hanging on, hoping she'd get over all her hangups? She sipped her beer. Were her sisters right? But oh, my goodness, the idea of Dan not being a part of her life sliced through her heart like a cheese slicer through a block of white cheddar.

"Honey, we're sorry if we hurt you." Lee patted Holly's hand. "I'm frequently too blunt."

"We just want you to be happy, Holly. And I don't know if I could've spoken the message better than Lee. Will you at least consider what we said?"

"Yes, I can promise you that." Under the circumstances, Holly could only manage a tight smile. She certainly would think about Dan and their relationship or lack thereof. That topic might be all she considered for quite a long time.

Later that night, Holly poured a glass of Merlot and settled onto the end of the sofa, propping her feet on the coffee table. Think about Dan. That's all she'd been doing since leaving her sisters at Hank's. She didn't doubt that she cared about the man. How could she not? He'd literally saved her life by getting her a lawyer who kept her out of jail after Joe attacked her, and she shot the man.

Did you ever get over killing another human being? How did people in war times deal with that? Of course, often the killing wasn't done close up the way she'd shot Joe, but still taking a life should make you different. And taking a person's life should make you not want to ever do that again. Well, that's certainly where she was. Oh, she had her gun, but she prayed she'd never be in the situation where she ever had to use it again.

As for Dan. He'd stood by her, supporting her, encouraging her, and not letting her give up on herself. He helped her get counseling. And oh, those blue eyes. He had the darkest blue eyes, almost navy, and his beautiful thick white hair and beard. He looked good in a suit or in jeans and a tee. And he was kind and hardworking. And yeah, when she pictured him, tingles grew in her middle and worked their way down to her girly parts. Girly parts that were apparently not dead, despite not getting any kind of personal attention since the Joe incident.

Dare she try to see if she could have a relationship with Dan? What if she tried and froze up? What would that do to him? What would her failure do to their friendship?

What should she do? Stay in a frozen state until she died? That would be like letting Joe win. And she refused to let that happen. She stood, determined to take a shot at happiness with Dan. Scary as the idea was. She might be able to make this work. It darn sure couldn't work if she didn't at least try. A smile spread across her face in anticipation of trying.

If her sisters were correct and he felt something for her, was this the time to proceed with her pursuit of him? Her breath caught as she considered having a physical relationship with Dan. The idea of him seeing her naked...well, my goodness. No one had seen her naked in too many years to count. She did Pilates and walked and watched what she ate, mostly. But wow. Her face warmed at the idea. On the other hand, who better to have a physical relationship with than Dan? No one. Dan had meant everything to her for many years. Their friendship was the bedrock of her life. Was that why she hadn't been able to see him in a romantic role? Gosh, now she'd begun to look at him that way, she felt stupid to have taken this long to recognize the feeling. He'd told her he wanted more, but could she do it?

Holly opened the door for Dan to enter her home. "Hey, Dan. Glad you could come over. And thanks for quickly getting those documents completed. Your speed is what pushed this project over the top. The buyers couldn't be happier." Holly had asked Dan to stop by her house to celebrate the conclusion of a multimillion-dollar deal. She'd dressed carefully in a long, gauzy skirt and a silky black tee with a plunge neckline that showed a good bit of cleavage. Not her usual attire, but if you were going fishing, you needed to bait the hook. Holly smiled at that adage her father, an avid fisherman, used to say. The words applied to lots of situations.

"You're welcome, Holly." His gaze darted from her head to the tip of her feet clad in black sandals. His mouth quirked as he took in her red toenails. Then his gaze rose to that dip in her top before settling on her face. He smiled his appreciation, at least that's what Holly chose to believe that smile meant. "Your deal fell between other jobs allowing me to focus entirely on your project. That part of southeast Fort Worth has been booming."

"Come in and sit down." Holly sat on the sofa indicating he should join her.

"We've made good profits on those ventures, too. I figure it's about to slow down for a while. Only a little undeveloped land remains. I'm okay with that. I need to focus on Grant Gardens."

"I sure was sorry to hear about the delay out there." He squeezed her hand.

"Certainly odd. How in the world did water get in those fuel tanks? We may never know. Since nothing has happened again, we all figure teenagers must have been blowing off steam."

"That makes sense. I remember doing a lot of dumb stuff after consuming a couple of six packs with friends late on a Friday night."

Dan's rueful grin made Holly smile.

"I ordered a special blend of Merlot from that winery in New Mexico we like. It's just arrived. Can I tempt you to stay a while?" Gosh, she hoped her face didn't heat with her suggestion.

"I remember the last time you had that brand. Sure, I'd love to stay and share a bottle with you. Do you mind if I get comfortable? I've had on this suit and strangling tie all day because I had a bar association meeting at noon. And it's too damn hot to stay trussed up this way."

"Of course." Holly nodded as she opened the bottle. She let it breathe while she got down two crystal goblets and set out cheese, crackers, and grapes. Her gaze flicked to Dan as he dropped his coat on the back of the wingback chair and tore off his tie.

"Ah, this is much better. Hate wearing the tie in this heat."

"Dan, you know you never have to stand on ceremony with me. If you get the bottle, I'll bring the glasses and the snacks."

"Of course." He grabbed the bottle, and she set a tray on the coffee table in front of them. Holly filled each glass and handed one to him.

"Thank you. May I say you look exceptionally lovely tonight, Holly." He tipped his glass toward her, and she met his glass.

"You may indeed. Thank you. Kay helped me pick out this outfit. It's less tailored than I usually go for, but it's cool, and that's been a necessity. I get you wanting to ditch the tie and jacket as soon as you could."

Dan sipped his wine and then reached for a cracker and white cheddar cheese. He popped a bite in his mouth and followed with another swallow. He leaned against the sofa's back. "Ah, yes. This is nice."

"Yeah." She breathed out a long breath. "The only way to improve the situation is if we could sit outside."

"You and your thing about being outdoors. You usually escape this heat by heading to Colorado for part of the summer. And I have clients who routinely spend all summer in Maine or Michigan. Though I'm glad you didn't do that. I'd have missed you." He took her hand in his.

Holly smiled. "What a nice thing to say." She squeezed his hand and didn't let it go. "I'd miss you, too, if I did that. I've always enjoyed my time in Colorado in the past, but this year, I haven't wanted to get away. The work is the work, and you do it when it's there because there will come a point the work won't be there anymore."

"Yeah, I get that. This cheese is my favorite. It's the Vermont white cheddar, right?"

"Yes, I discovered the brand on a trip up there one fall. I buy it all the time now. I'm spoiled."

"Well, I guess I am, too, then." He popped another cracker and cheese in his mouth and finished his glass of wine.

She lifted the bottle. "More?"

He nodded. Holly refilled his glass and topped off hers.

"I don't have to be anyplace at any set time. I'm even taking off tomorrow. It's one of two Saturdays I've determined not to be workdays this month. My goal is to not work on any Saturday, but I'm not sure I can pull that off."

"Well, this is an excellent start. If you drink too much and don't feel like driving home, you're welcome to stay here." Gosh, she was such a goose at this. She should've watched a YouTube video on how to seduce a man. "And on Saturday mornings, fresh blueberry pancakes and bacon are on the menu."

"And now that's the way to tempt me. In fact, you tempt me in many ways." Dan outlined the deep vee of her silk tee with his index finger.

Holly's breath caught. She took his hand and raised it, planting several kisses on the knuckles, which caused him to catch his breath. He set his glass on the table and did the same with hers and then drew her toward him for a soft tentative kiss that deepened and left them both panting and wanting more.

"Oh, my goodness. You are a good kisser, Mr. Morgan." Holly drew in several deep breaths.

"If I am, it's only because of my partner, Ms. Grant." He tipped her chin with his finger. "And you know what? I'd like to do more of that. A whole lot more of that. But only when you're ready."

He must've seen her answer in her eyes because he lowered his mouth to hers. Holly felt him drawing her soul from her body. She wanted, no needed to be the life's breath for this man as he was to her. He gently laid her back on the sofa and curled in next to her. He trailed fingers from the vee of her shirt down her belly and up again. "We'll go slowly, Holly. If at any time I do something that makes you feel uncomfortable, you say the word, and I'll stop."

"Thank you, Dan. That's what gives me the courage to do this. I know I can trust you." Holly gulped in a ragged breath; her heart raced. And they'd only just begun. Could she continue to the end? God, she hoped she could for her sake and for Dan's.

The next morning, Holly blinked open her eyes to the sun barely squeezing through the slit in the curtains. She turned her head, and her gaze found Dan's naked back. Her breath hitched as she recalled their night together that made rainbows filling the sky seem tame. He'd made her feel things she never had before. Hard to believe what had happened. He put her in charge, which kept her from ever freezing up. He made her feel beautiful and cherished and very glad to be alive. The whole experience had been more than Holly could've hoped for. Fireworks sparkling in the night sky. A symphony orchestra. And such a sense of relief and celebration. Holly slid from the bed, draped her silk robe around her shoulders, and padded into the kitchen to start the coffee and the blueberry pancakes she'd promised Dan.

Once she had the coffee perking, she mixed up the batter, added fresh blueberries, and chopped walnuts, humming a little under her breath. After taking the bacon from the fridge, she laid pieces in the skillet on top of the stove. In moments, the sizzling sounds and the wonderful aroma of bacon hit her senses. Ah, yes. She'd stuck her head in the fridge to retrieve the butter when suddenly, arms came around her waist, making her jump.

"Good morning, Beautiful."

She barely missed hitting her head as she spun around into Dan's arms.

"I missed you when I woke up."

"I promised you blueberry pancakes, and I don't have a magic wand to make them appear with no labor on my part."

"It smells great." Dan released her, moved to the coffee, and fixed himself a cup. After two gulps of the hot stuff, he sighed. "Yes. I needed that. Can I do anything to help?"

"You can set the table while I keep my eyes on this bacon. I don't want to burn it. You know where the placemats and forks are." Holly returned to the stove, removed the bacon and set the pieces on a paper towel to drain. After adding a tad more olive oil, she poured batter for a giant cake into the large frying pan. She used to make two small pancakes, but one morning more batter spilled out of the bowl, and she made a larger cake. Much easier to cook and not so much flipping. From then on, she'd switched to making one large cake. She grinned at the thought that she could say she ate one pancake instead of two.

When Dan finished setting the table, he came up behind her and slid his arms around her waist and rested his chin on her shoulder. "Can I help you this way?"

Holly chuckled. "It's nice even if a bit awkward flipping the pancakes. Why don't you pour us each another cup of coffee? I'm about to pull out this cake and then start the second."

"Okay, if you insist, but I sure like having my arms around you."

At that, Holly turned and threw her arms around him. "I like it, too." She planted a quick kiss on his cheek and returned to her job with pancakes. "Dan, can you heat up the syrup in the microwave? I use that tiny pitcher." She pointed to a small burgundy colored piece of pottery. "It's the perfect size." She flipped the second pancake.

Dan took the syrup bottle from the cupboard and filled up the pitcher before placing it in the microwave. "Twenty seconds?"

"Twenty-five will be perfect. Twenty isn't long enough and thirty is too hot."

In moments Holly served the second pancake on a plate and drizzled butter on top. "You do want butter, right?"

"Well, yeah. Who eats pancakes without butter?"

"Actually, Kay does. It's something she started several years ago while on a special diet. Even though she eventually went back to regular eating, she still doesn't use butter on her pancakes."

Dan held the chair for Holly and then settled next to her. He poured a generous amount of syrup on his pancake and dug in.

"Oh, this is excellent. Light and fluffy with blueberries and pecans."

"Not pecans. Walnuts. They're healthier."

"Whatever, this is great."

They ate in silence for a while with only the clink of the fork and the sound of the coffee cup hitting the table.

Dan cleaned his plate.

"You want another pancake?" Holly smiled at him. The way he'd cleaned his plate convinced her he'd enjoyed the meal.

"No, I'm good, thanks. You can make this anytime you want."

"Even supper?"

"Sure. Why not?"

"Music to my ears. I love to eat breakfast for supper." Holly dragged a piece of pancake through the last of the syrup on her plate. This man was a real keeper. Happiness that she'd gutted up and taken this next step in their relationship bubbled up into laughter.

Dan leaned over and took her mouth in a long and lingering kiss. Yes, an excellent decision.

Chapter Seventeen

Barrett Armstrong closed the door on his departing guests, Maxine Krause and Roger Tyler. They'd stopped by after supper to complain about the work going on across the road from their neighborhood. Barrett had done what he could to reassure them that the homeless development would not come to fruition. That he had the situation under control. If he'd hit Holly instead of her sister, the project would be dead. Now it was rushing ahead like a dry river after a spring storm.

He walked into the kitchen and poured himself a shot of whiskey. He'd been sure he had things under control. Fixing the fuel tanks should've shut them down. Well, it did, but only for a few days. Barrett groaned as he considered the amount of land that had already been cleared. He must stop them. He would stop them. He'd hit the machines again. Tonight.

At two thirty in the morning, Barrett snuck out of his house carrying gallon jugs of water. No one would be up at this time of night. He hurried across the road and approached the first piece of equipment—something that looked like a medium-sized bulldozer. After siphoning off the fuel, he emptied the entire two gallons in the tank. He moved onto the second piece of equipment and did the same thing, emptying the water in the tank. That would slow them down. For a while at least while he figured out his next step.

Holly fixed scrambled eggs for Dan and her. He'd taken to staying every night, and she liked that very much. He had recently moved a few of his personal belongings into her house. She grinned at the good feeling she got when she walked into her bathroom to find his toothbrush in a glass by the second bowl. Maybe they'd never move in together permanently. Maybe this arrangement would only be a temporary sharing of space. But her smile spread across her face at the happiness Dan brought her.

Dan came up behind her and kissed her on the neck. "You smell like bacon. Makes me want to take you back to bed."

"Very sweet, sir, but I've got a busy schedule today. Lots of work-related meetings." She was setting the plates with the bacon and eggs on the table when her cell chirped.

"Huh? What does Samuel Ramirez want this early?" Dan shrugged as Holly clicked on the call. "Hey, Sam. You're pretty early. What's going on?" She listened and then said, "Wait a minute. I'm putting you on speaker. I want my lawyer to hear all of this." She clicked the speaker button. "Now can you repeat what you said, please?"

Dan moved over close to her and put his hand on her shoulder.

"When we got to the site this morning, we couldn't start either of the pieces of equipment. After we checked them out, we found what looked like fuel spilled on the ground and water placed in the fuel tanks. Same deal as last time. We'll be out of work for a couple of days. I'm sorry, Holly."

"Yeah, me too. This messes with everyone's schedule. Dan, what's your opinion? Should we see about putting a security guy on the property at night? I wouldn't have thought we have to do this until we were quite a bit further along."

"Normally that would be the case, after you've got the actual building taking place. You can do that, but at this point, you also should report the incident to the police. We can ask them to cruise by on a random basis." Dan shook his head. "I don't have a good feeling about this."

"I agree with your lawyer, Holly, about both reporting and hiring a security guard." Sam said.

"Okay, we'll do it. You call the police, and I'll hire a security guard. I'm sorry about this, Sam."

"Me, too. The police may want to talk with you after we report this."

"Yep. Okay. Well, I hope the rest of your day is better."

"We'll also go ahead and put up a security fence. We were waiting on that until we finished clearing the land. Sorry we didn't do that earlier even if it would've been inconvenient."

"That's okay, Sam. Talk with you soon. Bye."

Holly disconnected and hung her head. "Good grief. We can't seem to catch a break with this project."

Dan pulled her into his arms. "It will be okay, Holly. I know a guy who can be your security guard. He's a former cop. An injury took him out of full-time policing, but he's a great guard. Do you want me to contact him?"

"Yes, please. Well, this is a bummer of a way to begin the day, and now the eggs are cold."

"How about I take you out to breakfast, and then we can get on with our work?"

"Great idea. Let's clean this up before we go."

Barrett congratulated himself on how effective the water trick had been. He'd seen no work on the property for just about a week. But today, the equipment arrived again. His delaying tactics were only that. But the delay had worked. His actions cost them all money, and maybe the woman would decide she couldn't handle all the trouble and the cost increases. That's what others had decided. He didn't want to wait to attack again. He had his water jugs, and at two thirty in the morning, he set off across the road. He jerked to a stop.

What was that? He'd seen the new bulldozers arrive today, and the contractor had installed a new security fence. He could get around that, but now there was a small travel van parked toward the back of the property. Was someone in the van? He left his wagon with the water jugs and slipped across the road and along the side of the property. No lights on inside, but the presence of the van troubled him. He backed off the property and recrossed the road, dragging the wagon with the water jugs with him back to his garage.

The next morning, he got up early to check on the van. From his back balcony, he used binoculars to look across the road. Yep. A guy climbed out of the van, stretched and then walked over to the workers and shook their hands. Too bad he couldn't hear what they said. When the man turned to get back in his van, Barrett detected a gun on his hip. Damn. A guard. The van turned around and pulled off the property and onto the road, heading back north toward town. More workers arrived, and the engines roared to life, tearing up the beautiful resting place for his grandparents.

He stomped down the stairs. The flush of anger surged through his body making him struggle to get a breath. Despite the hour, Barrett poured himself a whiskey. If Holly Grant wanted to play this way, he could match that. He suspected he needed to go back to the original plan. What he was doing only caused a delay and did not put an end to the project. He'd make the woman sorry she ever decided to build on his property. Holly Grant's time had come.

D an looked up from his computer when Jon walked into his office. "How's everything going?"

"Pretty good. Our last big-deal client's check arrived today." A smile spread across Jon's face. "The project worked out to everyone's satisfaction, and we got a good payout."

"Good news indeed. That was a tough one, taking longer than either of us expected.

"You got a minute?"

"Sure, Jon. You've got your coffee. Let me heat up mine." Dan refilled his cup. "Take a load off." Dan gestured to the chairs around the small conference table and walked over to them. He slid out one and Jon sat in another. "What's going on?"

"I finished looking into Barrett Armstrong like you asked me to."

"Great what did you find?"

"No flashing red lights. I confirmed his grandfather owned that property, and his father lost it. Barrett and his late wife were among the first to move into that addition. He's a retired postal worker. Was pretty high up in Civil Service."

"Okay. Thanks for letting me know. Glad you didn't find anything. Guess I'm just overly worried." Dan sipped his coffee. "Don't I remember you talking about plans for a vacation? You and Janey wanted to head to Colorado for a long weekend before she got too deep back in school. Is that still in the works?"

"Yep. I'm looking forward to getting away with her and out of this heat. Summer has dragged into September with this streak of over seventy days of temperatures over a hundred degrees. With Labor Day falling the way it is, this weekend is perfect for us. Once her classes start in earnest, she'll be too busy, and we won't get another opportunity until Thanksgiving or Christmas."

"Is Janey excited about your trip?"

"Yeah, she is, and you know how she is once school rehearsals start with all the extra dance classes. It's like she's invisible." Jon's smile was rueful, and he shrugged his shoulders then wrapped his hands around his mug. "When they're little, they take all your time and energy. It's like you'll never catch a breath. Then before you know it, they're almost grown and gone. That's one of the reasons I stopped in. I wanted you to know we're taking off this weekend. I wish we'd been able to go earlier when she had more time, but I couldn't take off then. This is the best we can do."

"Don't you worry, Jon. You deserve to take off. You're a good father, missing only a couple of Janey's activities throughout all the years." Dan sipped his coffee, then set the cup on the table.

"Only because you've had my back. And I appreciate your doing that."

"I've been happy to step into work deals so you could see Janey perform. I've never understood how single parents manage. And then the bonus is I've gotten to go to many shows along with you." Dan sat forward. "We took her to New York that one summer. Now that was an experience. Besides, it's given me perspective on how the other half lives."

"The other half being people with kids?"

"Yeah." Dan leaned back in his chair.

"I know you missed having kids of your own. We don't talk about it, but I'm sorry because Janey's the best part of my life."

"Thanks for letting me piggyback along with you raising your daughter. I've enjoyed every minute of the experience."

"Holly never had kids either, did she?"

Well, that came out of left field. "No. Joe took away any possibility of that with one of his attacks. As things stood, she was grateful not to bring a child into that toxic environment. It took her a long time to get herself out of the situation. I don't know how she took the abuse for so long. Unless they've been there themselves, I'm not sure people can understand the difficulty of getting out of an abusive relationship. At least Holly didn't have children to be concerned about, and she had support from her family. The women who don't, well...many of them end up homeless. That's one of the reasons why what Holly and her sisters are doing is important. I wish they weren't having troubles out on the property."

"What's going on?"

Dan explained about the objections to the community from a few people in the neighborhood across from the project and the recent attacks on the equipment. "The sisters decided to put a security guy out on the property at night. So far, the delays haven't been too bad, but they are costly and that's not good. I connected them with Butch Hawkins."

"Glad to hear he's getting extra work. He's a good guy. So, on another subject, I drove by your house the other night and you didn't seem to be home."

Dan glanced down and then met his friend's gaze. "Nah, I wasn't home. I've been staying most nights at Holly's."

"Ahhh. Good for you. Good for both of you. Will y'all move in together or get married?

Dan chuckled. "Huh! Too soon to be talking about either of those. I don't want to rush Holly or scare her off. But honestly, I hope both of those eventually happen. I'm happy things are the way they are."

Jon rose and came around and clapped Dan on his shoulder. "I'm happy for you. Hope you can make it work the way you want. Keep me posted on the tiny home project. That's a genius idea. I've got a meeting in a few. Talk to you later." Jon left Dan's office.

He'd better get back to work, too, because he looked forward to seeing Holly at her place for supper at the end of the day.

Holly cleaned up the papers on her desk and shut down her computer. Good work today. She stood and stretched her hands over her head. Gosh, she wished she hadn't ignored the reminder buzz on her tracker. She should've gotten up and walked around the house. Contemplating going outside to get her steps when the temperature hit a hundred and five with the feels-like temperature even higher made her ill. The summer temps would not stop. Still, she should've moved. Stretching forward, she touched her toes, straightened and then twisted at her waist. Better. Time to begin making supper. She closed the office door and made her way to the kitchen. She expected Dan to arrive any time. A smile spread across her face as she considered their new relationship. Not something she ever expected to experience.

Because of the beastly hot temperatures, Holly decided on shrimp on ice, coleslaw, a fruit salad, and spritzers for supper followed by key lime pie for dessert. Her phone chirped, and a smile lit her up from the inside out. Dan. She clicked the gate for him to come through. She poured two glasses of wine with fizzy water and carried them to the front door to greet him.

"Hey. You look beautiful." Dan cupped her face with both hands and kissed her soundly.

Holly nearly dropped the glasses. "Hey yourself." She handed him a glass.

Dan took a sip. "Ah, yes. Nice and refreshing."

"That's what I figured we needed, and I planned a light supper. Shrimp and salads, and it's ready whenever you are."

"Sounds perfect. Just give me a minute to get out of my jacket and tie." When he returned from the bedroom, he slid one arm around her waist, and they wandered into the dining area. Dan held her chair for her. Such a nice touch in her own home.

"Did you make the red sauce?" Dan dredged a large shrimp through the sauce sitting in a small cup to the left of his plate.

"I did. Do you like the taste? Is it too hot? I like more spice than many people do."

"This is perfect."

They shared stories of their days with much laughter mixed in. At one point, Holly looked at Dan and asked herself when everything had changed. When did he go from being a friend to filling such an important part of her whole life? Holly raised her glass and toasted. "To you, Dan."

He met her glass with his. "I like to us better."

Holly sighed. Yes, having him in her life was the best.

Dan wolfed down more than a dozen shrimp and had seconds on the fruit salad and coleslaw. Finally, he shoved away his plate. "We should have this meal often. It's perfect for this time of year."

Holly laughed. "Glad you enjoyed the meal."

"Now, I understand we have key lime pie for dessert?" His eyebrows arched upwards, and a big smile spread across his face.

"You are correct. Give me a minute to cut us each a slice." Holly rose and went to the kitchen. Dan took their dinner plates and rinsed them in the sink before putting them in the dishwasher. She appreciated that he helped like he was a part of the family. Holly removed the pie from the refrigerator and cut generous pieces she put on peach-colored dessert plates. She set them on the table, and she and Dan settled in front of the creamy sweet.

Dan forked a bite first. "Oh, man. This is the best."

Holly followed suit and sighed. "My idea of how to end a meal." She licked her fork.

It didn't take long before Dan put his fork on the empty plate. "I have a better idea of how to end a meal." He reached for her hand, pulling her from the table. "How would you feel about working off those calories? I have a wonderful idea of how we could do that." He gathered Holly into his arms and kissed her. They ambled back toward her bedroom with their arms wrapped around each other.

Something woke Holly. She blinked in the darkened bedroom. A sliver of moonlight came through the curtains where she hadn't completely closed them. Must've been a dream. She opened and closed her bone-dry mouth. She needed water, but if she got water from the bathroom, she could wake Dan.

She rolled carefully from under his arm, eased off the bed, slid into her silk robe, and headed for the kitchen.

The low light on over the stove helped her see to take a glass from the cupboard. She crossed to the refrigerator, put the glass under the cold-water spigot, filled the glass half full, and then hastily swallowed. Mmm, good. Allergies and their medicines left her mouth dry like a crinkled fall leaf. She turned to set the glass on the counter when a movement caught her eye from the direction of the sliding doors. No one could be in her house. They'd locked the door and put on the security system. Hadn't they? At that moment Holly had no clear memory because after dinner they'd been completely absorbed in each other.

"Walk this way."

Did she recognize the voice? "Get out of my house," she ordered, proud of how strong she sounded.

"You're taking a little ride with me." The disembodied voice took the shape of Barrett Armstrong as the man moved closer.

"No. You will leave the same way you came in." Holly feared she'd pass out because of the racing of her heart. Oddly, she still held the water glass. Could she use it somehow to buy herself time? Did the man have a weapon? Could she reach for one of the knives on her counter? What about the meat mallet? Holly lowered the glass to the counter and glided toward the drawers where she eased one open on silent springs, the one with all the extra utensils. Her fingers grasped the handle of the mallet. Not much, but safer than no weapon at all.

"I have the deciding factor here in my hand. You will do what I say."

"Why are you here, Barrett?" She eyed the man holding the gun in his right hand. Maybe if she kept him talking, Dan would wake and call the police. She didn't want Dan to come in here. Then Barrett would have them both.

"My grandparents."

"What about your grandparents?" Holly grasped the mallet and eased it behind her back.

"You act like you don't know."

He waved the gun at her, and Holly nearly stepped back, but showing fear would be what he wanted. She'd been there, done that. And she wasn't repeating the behavior. Showing fear didn't help.

"Why don't you sit down and tell me about your grandparents?" The man didn't sit, but he didn't hold the gun pointing directly at her anymore.

"The land you're trying to build on is my grandparents' land. My grandfather bought the land for my grandmother as a wedding gift."

"What a nice thing for him to do, Barrett. But why do you say it's your grandparents' land? I bought it from Bud Henderson."

"It wouldn't have been his to sell if my fool of a father hadn't gambled the land away."

"I'm sorry, Barrett. That must've hurt you terribly."

"You don't even know. I've protected that land. Every time someone wanted to build on it, I've scared them away. I tried to stop you but got the wrong woman. I can't have people and buildings there when I want to visit Grandma and Grandpa."

What did he mean he wanted to stop her but got the wrong woman? Did he mean he shot Lee? "What do you mean, you visit your grandparents?" Goodness, the guy must be nuts. Holly had eased her way closer to Barrett. Her vague plan was to hit him with the mallet and take his gun. Not much of a plan, but better than no plan at all.

Barrett sank down on the sofa, tears spilling down his face. "I buried Grandma there and then Grandpa under the giant oak tree. I go see them almost every day."

A picture of the flowers under the oak tree skipped across Holly's mind's eye. A grave? Possibly.

"Well, Barrett." Holly dropped down on the coffee table in front of this sad, sad man. "You can still visit your grandparents after we build the tiny houses. The houses will be in front of the trees and shouldn't disturb your grandparents' resting place." Could she get through to him?

He raised his head, and his cold gaze met hers. "But you want to put homeless people there. You'll be defiling my grandparents' home." He raised the gun again.

Holly's gaze locked on the point of the barrel. Blood rushed in her ears.

"You don't want to do that, Barrett." Dan's deep voice behind Holly startled and comforted at the same time.

Barrett turned in Dan's direction and raised the hand holding the gun. Holly jumped to her feet and swung her mallet as hard as she could against Barrett's head. He yelled. Blood splattered. The gun went off. Explosion of sound. Chaos. She fell backward.

Dan kicked away Barrett's gun and then yanked her to her feet and away from the man who held his head and wailed.

"You okay?" The arm not holding Holly's gun came around her shoulder. Holly nodded. "You?"

"Yeah, he missed me. I'm afraid your mirror is toast."

Sirens split the night air, and soon flashing lights lit up their small, quiet community. In moments police swarmed Holly's house. Again. They collected Holly and Barrett's guns and the mallet and took statements from Holly and Dan. The EMTs treated Barrett, who wailed the whole time about Holly trying to kill him and her stealing his grandparents' graves.

Detective David Vela arrived in the midst of the craziness. He listened to Barrett and then asked one of the other officers to escort him out of the house, to read him his rights, and arrest him for breaking and entering, and attempted murder.

Vela joined Holly and Dan, who'd moved over to sit at the dining room table. Holly tightened the sash of the silk robe she wore over her pajamas. Dan wore a t-shirt and pajama bottoms.

"How'd you happen to come tonight, Detective Vela?" Holly squinted at the man.

"Because of what all's been going on with you, your sisters, and your property, I've put an alert out so when anything happens concerning any of you, I get a notice. A middle of the night alert didn't seem like a good thing to me. That's why I got over here as quickly as I could.

"You've told the first officers on site, but I'd like you to run through for me what went on here tonight."

Holly spoke first. "I woke up thirsty and went to the kitchen for a drink, not wanting to wake Dan. Fortunately, I didn't do a good job at that. Anyway, I'd filled my glass and turned around to head back when I caught a movement out of the corner of my eye. When I realized Barrett held a gun, I picked up the mallet from the drawer. And we talked." Holly glanced at Dan then turned back to the detective. "The land we bought used to belong to his grandparents. Apparently, his father lost the land in a gambling scheme, and Barrett believes the land should still belong to him. He claims his grandparents are buried on the property.

"I thought I'd calmed him down. He sat on the sofa and rested the gun next to him. I dropped onto the coffee table in front of him. He really had calmed down, and I naively assumed the worst was over. Then all of a sudden, he grabbed the gun and pointed it right at me. That's when Dan entered the picture." Holly turned toward him. "You want to continue?"

"Yeah. I rolled over and found you weren't in bed. I checked the bathroom, but you weren't there either. I started toward the main living area without turning on any lights. That's when I heard voices. I remembered you telling me about the gun you keep in the drawer of your bedside table. I eased back into the bedroom and found the weapon. After checking to make sure the gun was loaded, I hurried back to find Barrett pointing his gun at you. My heart dropped to my feet." Dan tightly gripped Holly's.

"Your voice made me feel better." Holly squeezed Dan's hand in return. "At the same time, it terrified me to realize you were nearby providing another target for Barrett. What if he shot you? When Barrett swung the gun in your direction, I used all the force I could muster to slam the mallet against Barrett's head. Good lord, the blood went everywhere. Will he make it? I didn't kill him, did I?"

"Holly, the man tried to kill us tonight and has probably been the one vandalizing your property." Dan's voice had a touch of incredulousness.

"Dan, he's a sad man. I almost feel sorry for him." She turned to Vela. "Detective, I'm not sure Barrett actually broke in. I can't swear we locked the sliding door, and obviously we didn't put on the security system."

"We'll determine all that as we continue the investigation. Your place is a crime scene again. You need to go somewhere else and let my forensic people do their work."

"We'll go to my place, Detective Vela." Dan crossed back to the bedroom and returned with one of his cards with his personal address on the back side. He handed it to the dective.

Detective Vela took the card. "You've got a few minutes to pack up and get out of here. I've got your contact info, Ms. Grant, and I'll be in touch."

Holly took Dan's hand and led him back to the bedroom where they both dressed, and she quickly threw together clothes for a couple of days, while Dan packed up all of his stuff. As they went down the front steps, George Sanderson, the mayor of their little community, met them dressed in pajamas, a robe, and house slippers.

"Holly, Holly. What's going on? Are you all right?"

She nodded.

"This is the second time we've had police come to your place. It's not what we expect from anyone in this community. I won't be surprised if we get complaints from your neighbors."

"George, I'm sorry to cause all the commotion. I believe it's all over now, and we won't have any more problems."

"Well, I certainly hope that's the case. Otherwise, we'll have difficult decisions to make." George turned on his toes and scurried off toward his own home.

"I'm not sure what's gotten into George. This behavior is not like him at all."

"That's a problem for another time. Let's see if we can get any shuteye for the remaining part of this night."

Holly nodded and climbed into his SUV. He set her bag in the back, and then they drove off toward his house.

Chapter Eighteen

Holly blinked her eyes open to the grittiness of too little sleep. She turned her head to the left. Dan wasn't lying on his side of the bed. The clock said 10:00 a.m. Good grief, she'd missed a nine-thirty call. She sat up and grabbed her cell phone off the bedside table and connected with her client. After explaining she'd had a break-in during the night, the man understood, and they rescheduled. Holly disconnected and hurried to Dan's beautiful ensuite bath. She took care of her business, brushed her hair, and went in search of the owner of the beautiful house. The tantalizing aroma of bacon and coffee drew her toward the kitchen.

"Oh, yum. This smells delicious."

Dan drew her into his arms. "Good morning. How are you feeling?"

"You let me sleep in, which was lovely. I missed a business call, but it's okay. I rescheduled. When I explained about the break-in, the client understood."

"I figured after what happened last night, whatever you had on your calendar could wait. You needed the rest." He set a plate of scrambled eggs, crisp bacon, and buttered toast on the kitchen island and handed her a cup of coffee. "Figure you may need this, too."

Holly sipped. "Oh yes. Way to get the blood flowing."

Dan pecked her on the neck. "Well, I can come up with a few other ways to do that, too, but first you need to eat." He settled her at the bar and joined her.

Holly didn't know what came over her. She devoured the meal, even eating a piece of toast.

"Seconds?" Dan's eyebrows went up in question.

"Gosh, no. You'll spoil me."

"I like spoiling you, Holly. What do you plan to do today?"

She shrugged. "Don't know when I'll be able to go home. Hopefully later today or at least tomorrow. Guess I'll bring my sisters up to date and let Sam Ramirez know they are good to move forward on the work at the site now. We'll have to figure out what to do with the graves of Barrett Armstrong's grandparents. Not sure it's legal to have them any old place, and we want to be respectful."

"You talk with your sisters and Ramirez. I've got a project I need to finish at the office. How about this afternoon we go to a movie and eat our fill of popcorn? It's too hot to head to the Botanic Gardens. I love that place in the fall."

"You know I like your ideas, Counselor. Can you drop me at my house to get my car?"

"Of course. But let's catch a shower first." Dan wiggled his eyebrows up and down and twirled an imaginary mustache.

Holly laughed. "I believe I've said this already, but it's worth repeating. I like your ideas."

When Holly pulled up to Lee's house, she found Kay's car already parked out front. Unusual for their sister who habitually ran late to everything. The front door opened as Holly stepped onto the porch. Kay threw both her arms around Holly and pulled her in for a giant hug.

"Oh my God! I can't believe you were almost killed."

Holly extricated herself from her sister's arms. "I'm fine, Kay. Let's go inside. The heat is brutal. When will this streak ever break?"

"Can you believe this woman?" Kay propelled Holly into the kitchen, where Lee filled tall, iced-tea glasses. "She's almost killed, and all she talks about is the weather!"

Lee smiled at Kay and gave Holly a hug, without the exuberance of their younger sister. "I'm sure glad you're okay. I've got tea. Let's sit down over here under the fan." She handed her sisters each a glass, and they settled in the living area. Holly chose a high-backed chair, and her sisters took the sofa.

"I freaked out when Lee called me to say to come over. I feared you'd had another incident." Kay rolled the glass between her two hands as if she could not be still. Her voice came out in a higher pitch than usual. Clearly the situation had upset her.

Lee patted Kay's hand. "I called to give her a heads-up, so she'd have time to process before we got together, but I'm sure we'll all feel better if you give us the whole show blow by blow so to speak."

And Holly did, starting with the nice dinner she and Dan had shared and sleeping together in her bedroom, excluding intimate details. Her sisters took in the story, not interrupting. Probably wouldn't be able to ignore that elephant in the room for long, but for now, Holly slid over her relationship with Dan.

"Tell me more about the man who broke in." Lee leaned forward on the sofa and set her tea on the glass coffee table.

"Barrett Armstrong lives in a development of people over fifty-five across the road from where Grant Gardens is going in. You remember he spoke at the board of adjustment meeting. While we knew he and a few others remained against our plans, others were supportive of the project. We felt like we'd done everything necessary to get the neighborhood association on our side. And we did. The association didn't oppose us at the board or with the council, but Barrett and a couple of others remained adamantly against the project. The others because of their misconceptions and prejudices about people who have lived in poverty. Barrett had those reservations, but his main concern had always been his grandparents buried on the property."

"What? Can you bury anyone just anywhere?" Kay sipped her tea. "I mean we can put our pets in our back yards, but humans?"

"Actually, you can. Dan investigated the subject, and many more states allow the practice than don't. In Texas in a rural area, you can. Not like if you lived in a downtown high rise for instance, but yeah, you legally can. Funny thing about the article he found that talked about being careful about the site you picked because you wouldn't later want to sell the land for development."

"And that's what's happened with the Grant Gardens property." Lee sipped her tea.

"Barrett told me his father lost the property in a gambling deal. It's now gone through several owners until it came to us. Because he'd buried his grandparents there, he believed and acted like the land belonged to him." Holly sipped her tea and set down the glass then used a paper napkin to wipe the condensation off her hands. "All in all, a very sad story."

"So, what happened when he got there, and how did he get in?" Kay's arms spread out to emphasize her question.

"He didn't break in. Dan and I forgot to lock up or set the alarm system. Can't believe we did that."

"Must have been otherwise pleasurably occupied." Lee's eyebrows wagged up and down, and her lips pursed.

Holly's skin heated, and she hoped the color wasn't too bright red. "Do you want to hear this story or not?"

"Yes, yes, we do. We'll be good, won't we, Lee?" Kay gently poked her older sister's shoulder.

Lee raised her arms in surrender. "Please continue, Holly."

"Finding someone in your house in the middle of the night is upsetting, of course. I'd gone to the kitchen for water when I realized someone was in the house, and I went from scared to terrified when I caught sight of the gun held in his hand. My gun lay in the top drawer of the bedside table, but I wanted something to keep from feeling like my world might be coming to an end. My fingers touched the heavy wooden meat mallet in the drawer, and I hid it behind my back."

"Not much protection against a gun, but a good weapon in any case." Lee nodded.

"At one point Barrett sat on the sofa, and I sat on the coffee table across from him."

"Are you nuts to get that close to a man with a gun?" Lee exploded.

Kay poked Lee in the ribs. "Shh. Let Holly tell the story in her own way." Kay nodded to Holly. "Go on."

"Barrett got upset and sad telling me about his grandparents dying and burying them there and how he visited every day. Tears ran down his face. I felt sorry for him."

"You felt sorry for the man holding the gun on you? That's too much even for me." Kay shook her head and stared at Holly. "Then what?"

"I told him he could still visit his grandparents' graves even after Grant Gardens opened and people lived there. After he explained to me where he'd buried them, I told him we'd make sure not to disturb them at all."

"Sounds like a great compromise," Lee said.

"Well, that's what I thought, but then his prejudice against the homeless kicked in, and he went nuts. Pointed the gun at me again, only now I'm sitting right in front of him. Then Dan entered the room and got Barrett's attention. When Barrett and his gun turned toward Dan, I brought the mallet from behind my back and swung hard at his head."

Holly rose and paced around the living area. "Oh my gosh, the blood. They say head wounds bleed a lot, and well, his sure did. The pictures in my head make me feel sick." Holly dropped her head into her hands, and her sisters rose and threw their arms around her, comforting her.

"You're okay."

"We've got you."

"I know." She patted each sister in turn. "Thank you. I'm okay. Let's sit down again. I need more tea. Talking makes my mouth dry."

"Go on, Holly," Lee urged.

"Well, then the police arrived, and later Detective Vela arrived, the one who came when you were shot, Lee. Because of what had been going on at the site and with you, he'd set an alert to get a notification if anything happened to any of us."

"Well, how nice of him to keep up with you." Kay nodded but didn't make eye contact with her sisters. Holly and Lee's gazes locked. Hmm.

"Barrett admitted shooting you, Lee. At least, I think that's what he meant. He said he tried to stop me and got the wrong person. He must be the person who shot you. I'm sorry."

"Honey, none of this is your fault."

"We're doing a good thing, Holly," said Kay, "trying to provide housing for those who are homeless. All the studies show this is the best way to help get people out of poverty. Give them a place to live. I mean gosh, you can't even get a job if you don't have an address. It's a shame this dude is messed up, but it's not your fault."

"There's our artistic Kay being logical. Thanks, sis. Anyway, that's the story. And I don't expect us to have any more trouble with the project. At least not like this."

Holly hugged her sisters, and they all laughed.

"Now let's talk about Dan." Lee pulled Holly onto the sofa, and she plopped between her two sisters.

"What about him?"

"Well, obviously y'all are sleeping together." Kay stated.

"And we are ecstatic, aren't we?" Lee nodded to Kay, whose smile stretched ear to ear.

"Well, yes, we are, and it's a good thing I might add. I'd have been in a heap of trouble if Dan hadn't been there last night." Holly's voice hitched as the reality of the statement hit her.

"Has he moved in?" Kay raised her tea glass for another sip.

"No. He doesn't stay every night. It depends on what each of us has going on."

"So has there been talk of moving in with each other or marriage?" Kay continued to probe.

"Oh, my goodness, Kay. No, we haven't been together for long."

"But you've known each other forever." Lee added. "Back to before you had all the trouble with Joe. It's not like your relationship is brand new."

"Besides, danger can increase the speed of a romance."

"What are you talking about, Kay?" Holly cocked her head at her sister.

"That's the way it is in all the books I read."

Holly and Lee both laughed, and then Kay joined in. "Well, it is, and I figured real life would work the same way."

"Okay, enough of this." Holly stood. "I need to go meet a client. I wanted to let y'all know what happened, and that we're both doing okay. Also, we can move forward with Grant Gardens with no more worries."

Lee and Kay rose, too. "Can you go back to your house?" Kay asked after giving her another of her giant hugs.

"Whenever the police finish their work. I'm guessing we'll find a mess similar to the one after you were shot, Lee, maybe worse because we were inside and not out on the patio."

Lee nodded. "You're welcome to stay with either of us, but figure you'd rather be with Dan, right?"

Holly hugged each sister. "Yes, if he'll have me. I'll be in touch. Love you both more than I can say." Holly scooped up her purse and set off to meet with her client.

Dan parked in front of Lee Kennedy's house. A car was parked in the driveway. He hoped Kay had arrived. He wanted to have this conversation with both of Holly's sisters at one time. Dan raised his hand and knocked on the door.

The door opened. "Hey, Dan. Come in." Lee stepped back to let him enter. You could tell what the woman did for a living. Every aspect of the room had a special touch resulting in a warm and welcoming feeling.

"Thanks for letting me stop by."

"Hey, Dan." Kay stepped forward.

"That must be your car in the driveway."

"Yep, the lime green makes me smile and makes the car easy to find in a parking lot."

"I'm sure that's true." Dan smiled at the two women. His finger traveled to the collar of his shirt. After the meeting with his client, he should've pulled off the tie. It about strangled him.

"Can I get you anything? Iced tea, coffee, something stronger? It's nearly five after all." Lee's smile twinkled in her eyes.

"Sounds like a good idea. Thank you. I'll take a Seven and Seven if you have it."

"Coming right up. Merlot, Kay?"

"Won't say no. Let's sit down, Dan. You've had some excitement."

Dan raised his eyebrows in silent question as he settled on the off-white sofa. He didn't want to go into any details if Holly hadn't already told them or tell them more than she'd shared. She might've been protecting them.

Lee walked into the living room with the drinks on a wooden tray. "Here you go, Dan." He lifted his glass. "Kay, your wine." Lee took her glass and set the tray on the bar. "Now we're all comfortable, and you are smart to wait to see what we already know before responding. Holly stopped by about midday and filled us in. Pretty scary stuff."

"And thank you for being there to save our sister." Kay laid a hand on Dan's arm.

He patted her hand. "I'm not sure who saved who in the situation. Probably fairly mutual." He raised his glass and took a healthy sip. This should be easy to do, but for reasons he didn't understand, he struggled to find the words. He took another swallow and set the glass on a coaster with a picture of an orchid on it. Lee had several live orchid plants sitting on that table and around the room.

"I wanted to talk with you about Holly." He rubbed his hands together. Okay, okay, tell them. His gaze hit each woman. "I've known this for a long time, but last night made me realize I need to act on the knowledge. I love your sister, and I want to marry her. I'm here to ask for your blessing. I know that's old-fashioned, but I know how much each of you means to her."

Neither woman said anything. Lee sipped her wine then locked gazes with him. "Let me ask you this, if we said nuhuh, nothing doing, what would you say?"

Smart woman. He nodded. "I'd ask her anyway and keep working to win her and you over."

Lee caught Kay's gaze. They smiled at each other. "Well then, Daniel Morgan, we say welcome to the family. We've always needed a good brother." Both women enveloped him in a hug.

"Now you know, if you ever hurt Holly, you'll have to deal with us." Kay punched his shoulder. "Got it?"

"Absolutely." Dan laughed and rubbed his shoulder.

"Seriously, Dan, we'll be over-the-moon happy for both of you." Lee's smile lit up her face.

"Thank you. I know how much Holly loves you both, and I'm grateful to have your blessing."

"When will you ask her?" Lee asked.

"Are you planning something wild and crazy?"

"Kay, Holly is not a wild and crazy person, and neither is Dan." Lee laughed.

"To answer your question, I don't know. Last night's experience of nearly losing Holly made everything clear to me, and I don't want to wait any longer. Probably very soon." He swallowed the last of his drink. "Thanks for this." He stood. "Wish me luck with your sister."

"You'll do fine, Dan. Keep us posted."

The women's giggles reached him through the closed door as he walked to his car. Holly had gone out to see clients at their offices since her house was still a mess. He'd pick up dinner from Central Market. She loved their salmon. He'd ask her tonight. Gosh, where would they live? Would she say yes?

Chapter Nineteen

Holly left her clients and drove toward the Grant Gardens development. She wanted to look at the suspected grave site of Barrett Armstrong's grandparents. She wanted to see for herself and make sure the builder had not disturbed the area. Of course, the whole idea may have been the rambling of a disturbed individual. She angled off to the side of the road, changed out of her heels into a pair of serviceable boots. No reason to look like an idiot traipsing around the rough ground in heels, not to mention running the risk of turning an ankle.

She crossed to the group of men gathered off to the left side of the area. One man glanced up, and she waved. Sam Ramirez nodded and crossed the bare ground to meet her.

"I'm surprised to see you today, Holly. How are you holding up?" He shook hands with her.

"I'm okay, given a rough night. But I wanted to check on something. Walk with me over to the large oak tree, please."

"Sure. Are you worried about the tree? We've never planned to take out this one."

"I know and I'm glad about that. Last night Barrett Armstrong told me he'd buried his grandparents under this tree." Holly's gaze traveled up through the thick branches and back down to the ground. "Yep. Barrett mentioned flowers. Could he have buried his grandparents here?"

"I don't know. What do you want us to do? Stop work?"

"No. You don't have to do that just yet. This is in the area that we planned to leave as a green space. We wouldn't need to do anything to finish it up until near the end of the project."

"Maybe you need to get the police involved to see if bodies are buried here or not."

"You're right. If his grandparents are buried here, we have to treat the area with a certain respect we won't have to if this was the raving of a confused brain. Thanks for your input. These flowers are planted. Some may have sprung up on their own, but all of them didn't. I'll call Detective Vela and see what he says. Thanks, Sam. Keep up the good work." Holly trudged through the dirt to her SUV. She opened the door and leaned against the seat while she yanked off the dirty boots, tossing them in the back, and slipped on her heels. Time to head home.

Home. Well, not exactly. At least not her home which still had tape across the front as a crime scene. No, she headed toward Dan's home. She felt comfortable there in his Craftsman house. She loved the arches and all the built-ins. He'd done a beautiful job remodeling. He took down a few walls to give a more open feeling but kept the Craftsman details including the dark woodwork. The fireplace, with shelves on each side, gave the house physical as well as emotional warmth.

Ecstatic was the word that came to mind to describe how she felt about how Dan had helped her re-discover her sexuality. Not something she'd ever given a thought to. She'd buried any ideas of sexuality and sensuousness in the deep recesses of her mind with any and everything connected to her ex-husband. Joe had done a total number on her self-esteem. She'd been lucky to get out with her life even if that meant taking his. A shudder shook her body despite the heat of the late afternoon. The temps still hit a hundred plus when normal would've been around ninety. The summer had been crazy, dragging into fall. Cooler temperatures couldn't come too soon.

BAM!

She jerked forward and back. Someone bumped into the back end of her SUV. Apparently, she'd slowed down while wool-gathering, and the person behind hadn't been paying attention either.

BAM!

Her glance in the rearview mirror showed a large black pickup right on her tail. What the heck? Holly tightened her fingers on the steering wheel and accelerated to get away from the road menace, but the vehicle increased speed and rammed her a third time.

Time to do something else. Call Dan. Yes. She should've done that already. Swerving into the middle of the right lane, she used the voice activation and called him.

"Hey, Dan."

"Hi. Where are you? I'm putting together a special sup—"

"I'm on the far south end of Bryant Irvin, and I've got a situation here. A truck is tailing me and has rammed me a couple of times."

"Holly, hang up and call 911 immediately. They'll be able to track your location. Call me as soon as you can. I'll head your direction."

Count on Dan to know what to do. She called 911 and explained about the truck tailing her and ramming her. Her breath came in gulps.

"Can you describe the truck, ma'am?"

"It's a black pickup, and I'm terrified. Please send police. I don't know how long I can keep going."

"Hang on. I've already sent patrol officers to meet up with you. Stay on the phone with me."

"Yeah. Thanks."

What a crazy driver! Holly slowed her speed and pulled toward the side of the road giving the jerk plenty of room to pass. The truck dropped back. What the heck? Her heart pounded in her chest like it would jump right out. Was the driver nuts? Drunk? This couldn't be intentional, could it? Her knuckles whitened on the steering wheel.

She kept to the far right of the road, even crossing off to the edge, praying he would drive by. The truck increased its speed and slammed into her left back bumper. The impact caused her to lose control and pushed her SUV off the side of the road and down an incline. She screamed as her SUV tumbled over and over.

H olly hurt. Why couldn't she open her eyes? She desperately wanted to open her eyes. But her eyelids wouldn't budge. Maybe she could use her fingers and give them a bit of assistance. But her hand didn't respond to the message from her brain to move. She succumbed to the pull of the darkness.

Holly hurt. Her whole body hurt. Her head pounded as if a small child sat inside banging symbols together. Each clang made her flinch. The flinch sent pain zinging through her middle. Her eyelids flickered open and then closed again. The next time they opened, she managed to keep them open, but then the spinning of the room snapped them closed again. Had she died?

Holly hurt. Her eyelids popped open. Thank God the spinning had stopped. A moan escaped.

"You're okay. Or at least you will be. You're in the hospital. Your sisters are outside. We're all waiting for you to rejoin the world of the living."

She squeezed the hand holding hers. Guess she was lucky to be alive, but man did her body hurt.

"Rest, Holly. We've got you. You'll feel better."

Hey eyelids fluttered and then closed. Dan's low tones comforted her, and she drifted back into nowhere land.

Dan and Holly's sisters took turns pacing the waiting area. The elevator door slid open, and a man stepped out.

"Detective Vela." Dan held out his hand and Vela met his grip.

"Hello, Mr. Morgan, ladies." He nodded at Lee and Kay, his eyes lingering on Kay for a bit longer, Dan noticed. "How is Ms. Grant doing?"

"Holly finally regained consciousness for a moment while Dan was with her." Lee shifted her gaze between her sister and Vela. Kay's face had a soft pink tint.

"That's good news. How soon will I be able to speak with her?"

"Do you have any news about who tried to kill her?" His words chilled Dan's heart. How could this one woman have this much bad stuff happen to her? Wasn't the damage Joe had done enough?

"We've arrested the woman who drove the truck that ran Ms. Grant off the road."

"Wow! That's fast, Detective," Kay spoke for them all.

Vela faced Kay. "When she hit Ms. Grant the last time, the woman lost control of her truck and ended up in the ditch on the other side of the road, and the impact knocked her unconscious. When the police officers arrived, they found her still in the car. Even if Ms. Grant can't identify the truck, the recording of the 911 call and the woman's ramblings when she regained consciousness made her intentions clear."

"And what were those, Detective? Other than killing my sister?" Lee demanded, her fists firmly planted at her waist.

Vela glanced back and forth among the three. "Her name is Maxine Krause, and she lives across the street from the development you and your sisters are working on to provide houses for the homeless. She didn't want your project to go forward."

Dan let out a long breath and gazed at the women he hoped soon to call sisters-in-law. "No accounting for what amounts to brains in folks. You all wanted to do something good and kind, and two crazy people try to kill Holly. At least with Armstrong, his thoughts were all messed up with his grandparents, but this person is just plain mean-spirited."

"Lots of folks out there like that, Mr. Morgan. But then there's lots of folks like you and you." He nodded at Lee and Kay. "I'll check back tomorrow to talk with Ms. Grant."

"Thanks, Detective Vela," Kay extended her hand and shook his. "We appreciate your good work and thank you for keeping us informed."

"Ditto, Detective." Lee nodded.

"Oh, and I know Holly intended to ask you if you can determine if Armstrong's grandparents are buried on the site." Kay's eyes welled up, and she blinked to keep a tear from falling. "If I remember correctly, she said they were supposed to be under the large oak tree on the south side of the property. If they are buried there, we plan to make sure to treat the area with dignity."

"Thanks for the heads-up on that. We can bring in a forensic team, and we'll let you know what we find."

"Thanks. That will be one worry off Holly's mind." Kay's gaze connected with her sister and Dan's.

Holly's eyelids quivered then opened. "Wa-wat..."

"The doctor said when you woke up you could have ice chips. Hold on a minute." Dan leaned over her holding a cup with something.

Oh, ice chips. She attempted a smile. She must've succeeded because Dan's face crinkled into a relieved smile in return. The ice melted in her mouth and trickled down her parched throat.

"Day?"

"You've been pretty much out for four days and have worried the life out of all of us. The doctor kept saying you'd be okay, and they performed a successful surgery, but you stayed out a long time. More ice?"

Holly tipped her head a bit. Oh yes, her head, which didn't throb even after the small movement. Thank goodness.

"Would you like to see Lee and Kay?"

Holly nodded and smiled.

"Good because they are chomping at the bit to see you. Let me get them." Dan stepped away from her sightline and in a few moments returned with her sisters.

Kay moved to her right and patted her arm. Lee stepped to her left and touched Holly's fingers where they extended from what looked like a cast.

"What?" She couldn't push out more words. Would they understand? Her gaze found Dan at the end of the bed.

"Do you want to know what happened?"

Again, Holly managed the small nod. Kay wiped a tear before it trickled down her face. Her lips trembled. Soft-hearted Kay.

"You were in a wreck." Dan's voice brought her gaze to his face. His face looked haggard. Like he'd aged. "A truck ran your SUV off the road, and you rolled several times."

Holly sucked in a sharp breath, which sent a pain through her middle. The truck that had followed her. A shiver shook her body. Lee pulled up the light blanket. Holly sent a small smile in her sister's direction. The cold was on the inside, and the blanket wouldn't help.

"Ah, I heard my patient had awakened." A tall, slender, silver-haired woman entered. "And there are entirely too many people in here with you. One at a time. You know the rules."

"Sorry, Dr. Levine. As soon as Holly woke, I brought in her sisters. They've—we've all been worried." Dan's wonderful deep voice surely soothed the doctor's ruffled feathers as they did everyone's.

"But I told you she'd be okay and needed to sleep. She had quite a concussion and a broken arm and rib. She needed sleep more than anything. Now, get out and let me check on my patient."

Her sisters blew her kisses and scurried out in front of Dan. His smile made her feel cherished. The doctor checked the machines hooked up to her by various tubes and then shined a bright light in her eyes. Holly jerked her head away.

"Yes, that won't feel great for a while, but you've definitely improved. Would you like another ice chip?"

"Yes." The melting ice soothed her aching throat. "Thanks."

"Tell me about your pain level on a scale of one to ten, ten being the worst."

Holly wiggled her toes, and thankfully they worked just fine. When she tried to lift her knees, her middle screamed, like she'd done too many sit-ups at the gym. Her right hand settled on her middle. "An eight or nine."

"Yeah, that's the broken rib and the strained muscles from the seat belt. All will heal in time. You'll need to be patient. Do you have access to a hot tub or a sauna?"

Holly nodded again, relieved not to feel dizzy.

"How's your arm?"

Holly glanced down and shrugged. "No pain there. My middle hurt badly when I moved my legs."

"You are making progress. Two whole sentences. If you continue to improve, I'll send you home late tomorrow. We'll set you up for rehab to follow up. How does that sound?"

"Good. Thank you. Can I see my family?"

"Not any more tonight. They can return in the morning. For you, rest is the most important thing you can do. I'll let your family know."

Holly nodded and her eyelids closed.

Holly regaining consciousness brought Dan and her sisters much relief, but still, they were eager to hear when she would be well enough to go home. He glanced up to see the doctor leaving Holly's room. All three stopped in front of her.

"Dr. Levine, will Holly be okay?" Lee asked as soon at the woman entered the waiting room.

"When can she go home?" Kay asked.

"Will she have any lasting effects from the wreck?" Dan asked at the same time as the sisters.

"Yes, tomorrow, and probably not." Her gaze directed at each in turn as she answered their questions.

"To your concern about lasting effects, being consistent with her physical therapy will be the most important. She'll be sore for quite some time. I'll send her home with pain meds. Now, you go home and rest. You've been up here almost constantly. You can come see her in the morning. I believe she'll go home late tomorrow."

"Thank you, Doctor." They all spoke together.

"You three have this choral speaking thing down, don't you?" Dr. Levine laughed. "I'm sure I'll see you tomorrow sometime." She hurried down the hall to her next patient.

"What do we do now?" Kay looked at Lee and Dan.

"We do what the doctor said and go home. Holly will need us all being strong and rested when she comes home and begins therapy." Dan ushered Holly's sisters toward the elevator and shook his head as he thought about the determination of the *antis* to have their own way. Fortunately, they weren't as determined as Lee, Kay, and Holly.

Chapter Twenty

One Friday afternoon in early November, Holly walked around her complex working on getting her ten thousand steps. The last two months had been busy and difficult with all the rehab, and her patience had worn thin with the slowness of her body healing. She'd followed Dr. Lanier's recommendation about regular use of the hot tub and sauna, getting to the gym at least three times a week. One week, work kept her tied up, and she only got in twice and paid the price. Ever since then she'd been faithful. Now she also walked on the treadmill and did a few hand weights while remembering to be gentle with herself. She was determined to get back to Pilates, too.

And thank heavens, the heat had finally broken. Summer had dragged through the entire month of September and part of October making everyone a bit nuts. Fall decorations came out earlier than usual. Holly figured people wanted to claim that fall would indeed come. Her sweater felt good against the crisp breeze. Leaves had finally begun to change unlike in the Northeast when they started in September. Fall in North Texas arrived late, but the leaves did change, not as spectacularly as in the Northeast, but they changed. Inhaling the lovely smell of new-mown grass, probably one of the last of the season, she settled on a bench to soak in the feel of the cooler weather.

Progress at Grant Gardens was on pace, and they expected a ribbon cutting in January. Before that, Holly, her sisters, and Dan had to get through two trials. One for Barrett Armstrong and one for Marilyn Chambers, the woman from the homeowner's association they'd never able to bring around about the project. How could one person harbor such hatred of people who'd been homeless?

Holly dreaded the trials and having the stories dredged up, but if she could use the time to increase awareness about the issue of homelessness, that would be worth the agony of the legal proceedings. She rose and began walking again to make three more trips winding through the complex's gardens. The pathways led in and out around trees and over small ponds. The trick was to keep moving and not get stopped by the beauty surrounding her.

She and Dan had a good relationship. She spent many nights at his place, and he at hers. Would moving in together make sense? Did she want to?

Yeah, she did. She loved waking up next to him and seeing his toothbrush in the bathroom next to hers. She'd come a long way after the heartache with Joe. Therapy helped, and Dan helped to give her back a sense of herself as a sensual person.

But where would they live? She loved her home here in The Oaks partly because of how much she loved all the old oak trees. But she and Dan wouldn't have anywhere near enough room for both of them living there, especially with her using one of the bedrooms as an office. Did he want things to continue the way they were with only spending nights together when it fit their schedules?

As if her meandering mind had conjured the man, he appeared around the next curve in the walkway.

"Hey, Beautiful." Dan stepped close and kissed her. "I've missed you. Too many meetings and the trip to Austin cut into my time with you."

"Hey, yourself. I've missed you, too. Glad I gave you the code to the gate. Makes coming and going easier for you and makes for nice surprises like this one for me." Holly took his hand. "Want to walk with me? I've got another loop to make to get to my ten thousand."

His fingers clasped hers. "Don't mind if I do. How are you feeling?"

"I'm doing well, thank you. I'm back to getting my ten K every day, and I go to the gym three times a week. Their hot tub and sauna have been good for me. I seldom have more than a twinge when I lean over or twist around. Not a hundred percent, but close enough."

"That's good news. I worried about you while I couldn't be here with you, but then I pretty much worry about you all the time." He brought their clasped hands up and kissed the back of hers.

Holly enjoyed how her stomach took that little nosedive of excitement and anticipation any time Dan came around. She'd missed him, too. How much she'd come to depend on him, and in a good way, surprised her. Apparently, absence did make the heart grow fonder. She looped her arm through his and rested her head on his shoulder as they continued to stroll through The Oaks in a companionable silence. Content to be together.

Their path took them back to Holly's house. "I've got a special new bottle of Merlot. Come in and we'll try it."

"Sounds like a good idea."

After Holly opened the bottle, she filled two glasses. They carried them to the patio and settled on the love seat.

"To you." Holly raised her glass.

"To us." Dan clinked her glass and then sipped. "Mmm. Yes. This is excellent." He set down his glass and cleared his throat. "You know I've been trying to find the right time to do this. And what with everything that's been going on, there never seemed to be the right time."

"The right time for what?"

"To ask you to marry me. Will you, Holly? I love you with my whole heart, but I'm not whole without you. When you were almost killed this last time, I determined not to miss out on us blending our lives. I gave you time after Joe, and then we fell into this comfortable friendship, and I didn't want to rush you. I wanted to give you time to heal, but I've loved you a very long time."

"Oh, my goodness, Dan." Holly's breath came in gulps, and her heart kicked into overdrive. Could this be happening? Was she ready to take this next step with this wonderful man?

"Say something, Holly. I'm dying here." He clasped her hand in his.

She set down her glass and threw her arms around Dan. "Yes! Yes! I say *yes*!"

He swung her around to sit on his lap. "Oh, thank God. I was afraid you weren't ready, or I'd misread the signs. You've made me the happiest man."

"I'm determined to make you as happy as you've made me. Thank you for being incredibly patient with me. Not many men would've been willing to wait."

"Well, that's because you're worth waiting for."

Holly rose and held out her hand. "Come with me, and I'll show you how determined I am to make you happy."

"Are you sure you're up for this? I don't want to hurt you."

"Oh, we can be slow and careful, but thorough." She smiled mischievously at her wonderful man.

On Monday after spending a lovely romantic weekend with Dan, Holly invited her sisters to come over in the afternoon. Eagerness to share the good news with them bubbled up in her middle. They would be happy for her. Promptly at four p.m., her sisters walked in. "Hey, sis." Lee closed the door behind her and Kay. They set their purses on the entry bench. "What's up? You seemed eager for us to come by."

"Talk, girl. What's going on? Have you heard something about the upcoming trials?"

"It's about this." Holly held out her left hand where a ruby and diamond ring sparkled on her ring finger."

Both sisters squealed. No other way to describe their reaction. Their words tumbled over each other, while they hugged Holly.

"Congratulations!"

"Tell us all about it?"

"When did this happen?"

"When are you getting married?"

"Hold on. Let me get you your iced tea." Holly placed three glasses with a lemon slice on the edge on a tray and set it on the coffee table. "Sit down and I'll tell you." They settled in the living room, one on each side of Holly. "When Dan returned from his trip to Austin Friday night, he asked me to marry him. I, of course, said yes."

Lee huffed a chuckle. "Maybe of course seemed obvious to you. To us not that much. We weren't sure you'd ever come around."

"He's the most patient man, but I did worry he'd give up on you," Kay teased. "And this ring is gorgeous! Where did you get this beauty, and how did you get it so fast?" Kay lifted Holly's hand again to study and appreciate the artistic beauty of the setting.

"And why did you wait to tell us?" Lee added.

Holly retrieved her hand from Kay and studied the ring. "The ring belonged to Dan's grandmother, and we were fortunate the size worked. We kept the news to ourselves over the weekend. This is the first opportunity to share the announcement with you."

"Have you decided when to get married? And where will you live?" Lee pushed for more details.

"We decided to wait until we've had the opening for Grant Gardens, which means we're looking at some time after the first of the year. And I don't know where we'll live. We've been floating between our two homes, and we love them both, but we'll probably get a new place that is all our own."

"That sounds like a great idea. I'm bubbling up with happiness for you, sis." Kay patted Holly's leg.

Lee leaned in and slid an arm around Holly's shoulder. "We need to have a party to celebrate your engagement. We can have a get-together at the country club in their garden room. Gosh I hope they have an open date. They get busy in the fall."

"Lee, we don't need to do that. At least, let me talk with Dan first."

Her sister laughed. "Of course, but he has to know we'll want to celebrate. We've been pulling for him for a long time and couldn't be happier."

"What? What are you talking about?"

Kay smiled. "Honey, we've seen how he looks at you. We've encouraged him to give you space. But we worried we were setting him up for disappointment and that you might never come around. He asked for our blessing right before the truck ran you off the road. A blessing we by-the-way gave."

"He did? You didn't say anything." Holly looked at both of her sisters.

"Well, no, we didn't." Lee leaned forward. "After the wreck, we all focused on getting you well. Kay and I figured he wanted to wait to ask you until you were back on your feet. We're relieved and pleased you said yes. You are both such great people, and you deserved to be happy."

Chapter Twenty-One

I n early December, Holly sat in the hallway of the courtroom for Barrett Armstrong's trial. Dan sat on her right and her sisters on her left on the long pew-like bench. The district attorney planned to call Holly sometime that morning. Her stomach bunched into knots. She hated the idea of testifying. Memories of when she had to testify against her ex-husband flooded her mind. Her testimony sent him away for fifteen years.

Oh, yes, Armstrong had done bad stuff. Good grief, he'd shot Lee! But Holly did feel sorry for the man. She completely understood his clinging to land that had once belonged to his family. In a way, Holly and her sisters were doing the same thing with their efforts to build Grant Gardens for the homeless. They were honoring their family.

But he'd shot Lee. And he'd nearly killed Dan. She couldn't ignore those actions. And what she and her sisters wanted to do was important. Standing up for the homeless. Helping them find homes. If testifying helped shine a light on this important subject, then she'd do the best she could. The DA had promised her she wouldn't be on the stand long. Still, she dreaded the whole ordeal.

The courtroom door opened, and the bailiff stepped out. "Ms. Grant. We're ready for you."

Holly's eyes cut to her sisters then at Dan. He stood, took her hand, and kissed her on the cheek. "You'll be fine. Remember to breathe. And I love you."

Holly nodded, straightened her shoulders and followed the bailiff into the courtroom. The DA spoke. "Your honor, I call Holly Grant to the stand."

Holly walked toward the witness stand and turned to face the DA. The bailiff stepped in front of her. "Please raise your right hand." Holly did.

"Please state your name."

"Hollister Grant."

"Do you promise to tell the truth and the whole truth, so help you God?"

"I do."

"Please be seated."

Holly drew in a deep breath, sat and folded her hands in her lap covered by a brown leather A-line skirt. She'd worn her high black boots and a brown sweater topped with a black blazer. She'd had an aunt, not the one who became homeless, but her father's sister who often dressed in black and brown. The sharp contrast made for a show of strength. Holly felt the need for family connections today to get her through this. She wore her smartwatch, her beautiful ruby and diamond engagement ring, and her mother's gold hoop earrings, all chosen to bring her comfort and strength.

The bailiff stepped away, and the DA moved to her side.

"What do you do for a living, Ms. Grant?"

"I'm a developer. I buy and sell land for people to put their businesses on."

"Are you familiar with the property at 7700 Bryant Irvin?"

"Yes, my sisters and I purchased the land to build a community for people who were without a home."

"I'd like to show the witness a picture of the property." The DA handed a photo to Holly.

"Yes, that's the property."

"When did you purchase the property?"

"Back in the early spring of this year."

"And did you begin work on the project immediately?"

"Not immediately."

"Why not?"

"We needed a variance to put tiny homes on the property. After talking with the neighborhood association, we went before the board of adjustment. They granted our request, and the proposal went to the city council."

"What happened at city council?"

"They granted our request, and we moved forward with the project."

"What happened next?"

"Samuel Ramirez, the construction manager, called to tell me the equipment wouldn't work. He suspected water had gotten in the fuel tank. Arranging for new equipment delayed work for a week, and then they got started again."

"Did anything else happen?"

"The equipment was damaged again in the same way. We reported to the police again and hired a private security person to stay on the grounds at night."

"Did anything else happen on the property after that?"

"No."

"Do you know Barrett Armstrong?"

"Yes, I do."

"How do you know him?"

"He's the president of the homeowner's association for the neighborhood across from Grant Gardens."

"How did you meet him?

"He presided at the neighborhood association meeting when Dan Morgan and I talked about our proposal to put Grant Gardens across from their property."

"How did that meeting go?"

"We understood that the association voted not to oppose our project. That was a relief because the board of adjustment listens to neighborhood associations."

"When did you next see Barrett Armstrong?"

He appeared and spoke at both the board of adjustment and city council meetings when our property was on the agenda. He spoke against our plan."

"And after the meetings, when did you see him next?"

Holly's breath hitched, and her hands clenched in her lap as the terror of that evening swept through her.

"He came into my house in the middle of the night."

"Did he have a weapon?"

"Yes. He had a gun."

"Tell me what happened."

Holly recounted what took place, including hitting Armstrong on the head with the wooden mallet, and the blood going everywhere. All the while she testified, the actions took place in her mind as if she watched the flickering images of a movie.

"At one point he said he'd hit the wrong woman. I assumed he referred to the evening someone shot my sister when we gathered on my patio."

"Objection. Not relevant." Armstrong's attorney said.

"Sustained. Go on, Ms. Grant," the judge said, urging Holly.

She nodded and concluded with the arrival of Detective Vela. Her eyes filled with tears as she thought of how close she'd come to losing Dan that night.

"Thank you, Ms. Grant. I have no further questions."

"Your witness," the judge said to Anderson's attorney.

"Did Mr. Armstrong break into your house, Ms. Grant?"

"Well, he wasn't invited in if that's what you mean." Holly had trouble swallowing. She could guess where this was going.

"Ms. Grant, I'm asking if you had locked your house or put on a security alarm?"

Holly, swallowed before answering. "No, I had not."

"Thank you, Ms. Grant. That's all I have, your honor."

The judge nodded. "You may step down, Ms. Grant."

Holly pulled herself up, using the railing in front of the witness stand and carefully stepped down. The shakiness of her legs didn't give her much confidence they'd carry her outside the court. She glanced at Barrett Armstrong as she passed. He sat with his head down, and Holly couldn't help herself, she felt sorry for the man.

A guard opened the back door of the courtroom, and she hurried out and straight into Dan's open arms.

"Thank God that is over."

"Breathe, Holly. You're fine." Dan rubbed a hand up and down her back.

She drew in a deep breath and let it out. "Boy, I hate courtrooms. I don't know how you deal with them all the time." She pulled back and studied her fiancé.

"Well, I'm a good enough lawyer, and I mostly avoid getting into a trial setting."

"Are you okay, Holly?" Lee rested a hand on Holly's shoulder.

"Yes, thank you for being here, Lee." She turned to Kay and hugged her younger sister. "You, too."

"I'm glad I didn't have to testify." Kay sent a rueful smile in her sisters' direction.

"You know, Holly, you'll have to do this one more time for the Maxine Krause trial." Dan squeezed her hand.

"Don't remind me."

"Well, sorry to do that, but that trial will be in early January. You'll have gotten it behind you before you have the ribbon cutting on Grant Gardens."

"What a relief I will feel to put the whole mess behind me. I'm determined there should be nothing to mar that happy occasion."

The door to the courtroom opened, and the bailiff said. "Mr. Morgan, the DA is ready for you."

Dan turned to Holly. "You stay with your sisters. I'll be out soon, and we'll all eat lunch together."

Holly smiled and nodded. "I'm okay. You go on." And Dan walked into the courtroom to give his testimony about the night Armstrong entered Holly's house.

The jury took a full day to deliberate, but in the end, they found Barrett Armstrong guilty of entering with a weapon with intent to do bodily harm and attempted murder. The judge sentenced him to five years in prison. Holly testified after the verdict asking the judge for leniency. She felt so sorry for the man. And yes, he'd tried to harm them and stop the Grant Gardens project, but still....

In early January, the trial for Maxine Krause took place. Holly testified about how she'd met Maxine at the neighborhood association meeting and then heard her speak at both the board of adjustment and city council meetings. Other than those times, she had no dealings with the woman. Holly assumed the woman tried to ram her car because of her opposition to the Grant Gardens project.

After a short deliberation, the jury found the 911 recording of Holly's call and Maxine's own comments at the accident site enough evidence to convict her of attempted murder. She had no other arrests or charges against her, not even a speeding ticket. She was a misguided, seventy-year-old grandma. Holly's injuries hadn't been life threatening, and just as she had for Barrett Armstrong, she asked the judge for leniency. Ultimately, the judge sentenced Maxine to two years in prison. Relief swept through Holly at the conclusion of the trials. She breathed easier. If she never saw the inside of a courtroom again, she'd be happy.

Chapter Twenty-Two

The beautiful day in March had begun with brilliant sun, warm temps, and a slight breeze. Excitement ran through Holly's blood like a rushing river, bubbling and tumbling over rocks making that wonderful babbling sound. Finally, the day had come. She and her sisters were about to hold the ribbon cutting ceremony for Grant Gardens. Now they all waited for the mayor to arrive. Holly appreciated that she took such an interest in the issue of homelessness.

Her sisters moved from person to person, making sure everyone found a place to be comfortable while they waited for the event to begin.

A familiar, tall man approached Holly and held out his hand. "Holly, I don't know which of us is more excited for today to come. Me or you."

Holly laughed. "I couldn't be happier that you could be here, Ben. Your support and that of the members of the Homeless Coalition have been essential."

"Well, having Dan on our board has been invaluable. He convinced me you were the kind of determined woman that if you set your mind on something, then we could count on you being successful."

Holly laughed. "Some people call that stubbornness and not determination."

Ben glanced toward the road. "Oh, look. That must be the mayor's car."

"That's great. We can get this show on the road. Can you go stand on the other side of the ribbon with Dan and the other board members and my sisters? I'll go meet the mayor." Ben nodded and moved toward the group gathering behind the ribbon while Holly made her way toward Mayor Jennifer Jones, a blond woman in her forties who everyone considered was doing a great job as mayor of Fort Worth.

"Mayor Jones. Thank you for coming." Holly held out her hand, and the mayor, dressed in a black pants suit with low heels, clasped Holly's hand with a strong grip.

"It's Jennifer, Holly. Sorry to keep you waiting. Unexpected call from the governor. But I didn't want to miss this. I hope your project will inspire others to build similar communities."

"Thank you. We're right over here." Holly led the mayor to the front of the community building. Holly glanced around the property. Pride in what they had accomplished made her smile. Lots of green spaces, with the tiny homes spread out in spokes. People had already claimed about half of them, and three of the residents would take part in the ceremony.

Before Holly stepped forward, she took a minute to squeeze Dan's hand. He winked at her, and her heart swelled with love.

She stepped up to the portable mic. "Good morning. Good morning," she repeated when people didn't immediately get quiet. "Thank you for being here to celebrate the ribbon cutting and grand opening of Grant Gardens. Many of you have played an integral part in making this dream come to fruition. First, let me say welcome and thank you to Mayor Jones for her support along the way." The mayor nodded and waved a hand at the gathered group who applauded. She joined Holly at the mic.

"Homelessness is a problem for all of us, and solutions will have to come from all of us. I've been happy to support Holly and her sisters in the creation of Grant Gardens and hope this will be the first of many such communities." Applause followed the mayor's words.

"Thank you, Mayor. Ben Stevenson—" Holly urged Ben to come forward. "—has been working in this arena for many years with the Homeless Coalition, and we appreciate your belief in Grant Gardens. You and the members of your board have been invaluable in helping us work through all the intricacies of getting this project off the ground." Ben waved as he acknowledged the applause and then stepped back.

"Of course, none of this would've happened without the great work of our architect, Juan Lopez, and the project manager, Samuel Ramirez, with his hard-working crew." Both men stepped forward, and the crowd again applauded.

"So, it's time." She looked over her shoulder. "Lee and Kay, please join me." Her sisters came forward. "The last people we'd like to thank are our parents, Bradford Grant and Sarah Leeland Grant for their wise handling of their finances and investments which gave us the wherewithal to take on this project, but also for modeling concern for those who are hurting and the determination to do something about it." She smiled at her sisters, and they each gathered up a pair of scissors. "I hereby declare that Grant Gardens is officially open." And they snipped the wide blue ribbon in three places to the cheers of those standing on the grounds.

"Please join us inside for refreshments, and you can meet our new residents."

People moved into the main meeting room to enjoy the refreshments Holly had provided. The serving of which were overseen by the volunteer group from the neighborhood across from Grant Gardens. Holly took pride that she and her sisters were able to bring that group along.

"Ms. Grant."

Holly turned at her name. "Oh, hey, Maddy." The woman appeared to be in her sixties but was only in her late forties. She'd had a hard life, and her difficulties showed in her gray hair and lined face. "This is pretty exciting, isn't it?"

The smile on the woman's face couldn't be wider. "I want to thank you for what you and your sisters done. Some of us—" She gestured to the two women and three men behind her. "—well, we're grateful to be the first ones here."

Holly smiled at each of the residents.

"And we promise to take extra special care of the place," continued Maddy. "Gladys, our director, told us she'd help us set up a kind of leadership team. If someone messes up, we'll deal with them. And we'll help each other." The other residents all nodded.

"That's great to hear. But I never doubted it. We know because you've lost a home, that doesn't make you a bad person. Any of you. For those of you who are able to work, we'll help you find jobs and provide transportation until you're able to manage on your own."

Holly shook hands with each of the residents and thanked the ones who were letting people take a tour of their tiny house, their home.

After a time, Holly asked for everyone's attention. "Tours will begin in five minutes if you'd like to see the inside of our tiny homes. You can go into any of the vacant units, and a few of our residents have offered to let you see their digs. Others are not settled enough for visitors."

People moved outside to take advantage of the opportunity to see in person the tiny homes.

"How are you feeling?" Dan strolled up and slid an arm around her waist.

She leaned into him. "So happy. I can't tell you. For the longest time, this seemed like a dream we'd never be able to pull off. All the setbacks we hit along the way. And some of them were scary." Holly shuddered, remembering when Barrett shot Lee, Holly and Dan's run-in with Barrett Armstrong, and then Maxine crashing her truck into Holly, and both trials. "After Vela confirmed that indeed human remains were under the tree, the authorities excavated and determined Barrett's grandparents had indeed been buried there. They removed the remains to a cemetery. But once we got past those issues—well, it's amazing. I can hardly believe we're here."

"I'm proud of what you and your sisters have done. You should be proud of yourself, too."

"I am. It's been fun for Lee and Kay and me to work on this project together. Made us feel good to be honoring our parents this way. And you've been invaluable as you always are, but especially with all of this." Holly spread her arms wide. "Not to mention keeping me safe." She slid her hand into Dan's.

"You can count on me to do that. You're the most important person in the world to me."

And with that, Holly threw her arms around Dan and hugged him right there in front of God and everyone.

Epilogue

On a beautiful April day, Holly stared at herself in the full-length mirror in the bedroom of the house she and Dan had bought. They'd dithered about where to live but decided they both needed a new beginning. A new beginning together. While Holly hated to leave what she saw as the safety of The Oaks where she'd lived for over ten years, she'd accepted that no place could promise absolute safety. Lee had been shot when they were on the patio of that house, and Barrett had gotten into her home. So stone walls and gates didn't necessarily make you safer.

She and Dan found the perfect place—a modern, sprawling ranch style in Westover Hills all on one level. Past the pool, the wide grass lawn overlooked a hill that went down to a small creek. Very private and very green.

Holly's gaze met Lee's in the mirror and slid to Kay's. Her sisters' dresses were a floral peachy-pink silky material. Kay's dress was full and frilly. Lee wore a soft A-line. Each to her own taste.

"You look amazing, Holly." Kay slid an arm around Holly's waist.

"And you look radiantly happy. Happier than I can ever remember seeing you except the morning we cut the ribbon on Grant Gardens." Lee moved to Holly's other side.

"I love you both so much. Thank you for always being there for me." Holly pulled them in for a group hug, which they returned.

"Now, wait a minute. We can't be messing up the beautiful bride." Kay backed out of their clasp and rearranged the material of Holly's palest peach wedding gown, a silky ankle-length concoction with a scooped-neck top. "We searched a long time to find this amazing dress, which is simply perfect, and we're not messing it up before Dan sees you and before pictures are taken."

Dan. Holly fought to keep tears from forming when she thought of how much she loved that man. He'd been incredibly patient waiting for her to wake up to what they had and what she felt for him. But he had waited, and she had come awake. And she was profoundly grateful.

Holly saluted. "Yes, ma'am. Anything you say, ma'am."

"In this instance, Kay is right." Lee glanced at her watch. "And it's about time to get the show on the road. We'll see you in there in front of the fireplace."

"Don't be late." Kay hugged Holly one more time.

Holly chuckled. "I can promise you I won't be late. I'll follow right after you." A last hug for Lee, and her sisters slid from the bedroom.

Holly glance up. "Well, Mom and Dad. Sorry you're not here to see this day. I know how much you liked Dan. I took way longer than I probably should have to realize what I felt for him. I'm grateful to y'all for standing by Lee, Kay and me and supporting us in all we've attempted. We've tried to make you proud with Grant Gardens. We are determined to make Grant Gardens a place that makes a difference in a lot of people's lives."

One last look in the mirror and Holly followed her sisters into a long hallway that led to the main living room of the house. A fireplace stood in front of her, and to the right, sliding doors led out to the large patio and the pool. The home was made for entertainment. Holly expected they would do that a lot.

Her sisters stood to the left of the fireplace. Jenny Hayes, a minister friend of hers, stood in front of the fireplace. Dan's best friend and partner, Jon Baxter, stood with him on the right side. The cousins, Brad, Leeann, and Sarah, sat on the front row of the bride's side. Guitar music led her toward her future husband. Dan looked handsome in his tuxedo. The look in his eyes when he first saw her made Holly's breath catch. Her love for the man had grown every day since she'd allowed herself to recognize what she felt for him. And she'd nearly lost him through her own stupidity and fear. Fortunately, he'd been determined to get her to come around.

The beautiful service was short and before she could imagine it, Jenny said, "You may kiss the bride." And Dan did, to laughs and whistles of their friends.

Holding her hand tightly in his, Dan turned to their guests. "Thank you all for being here to help us celebrate this special day in our lives. The buffet and wine bar are set up on the patio. Please enjoy while we get a few pictures to memorialize this occasion."

He slid both arms around Holly's waist and pulled her closer, resting his forehead on hers. "Gosh, I love you."

"Me too, you."

The photographer caught the embrace. "That's a good one. Unplanned and perfect. Now let's get the formal shots done." He arranged Holly and Dan with her sisters and Jon and the minister, then he took separate ones of the three sisters together and one with Dan and Jon.

"Can I have one with the whole family?"

"Of course."

Holly waved to the cousins who joined her, Dan and her sisters. Lots of laughter and hugs all around.

"Okay, the rest of them will be like that first one, spontaneous. You go and enjoy your friends."

"Good job getting that done so quickly. And I can't wait to sample the buffet. The shrimp look divine. And then we can get to the most important part—the cake."

Everyone laughed at Kay's comment and followed her out to the large patio and the pool surrounded by level green grass, an outdoor area spacious enough to comfortably handle the twenty-eight people gathered for the celebration.

All the guests and caterers finally departed after eleven that evening leaving Holly and Dan alone.

He closed the door for the last time. "I didn't think they'd ever leave."

Holly smiled and looped her arm through his and led him back to the patio. "I've found a bit of Champagne left in this bottle." She lifted the bottle and filled two glasses half full. "Just enough for a last sip." And she handed Dan a glass and tipped her glass to his. "Happy wedding, my love."

"Happy rest of our lives."

They sipped and settled down on the plush outdoor sofa. Dan let out a long sigh, pulling off his bow tie. "A great day, don't you think?"

"No arguments from me. We couldn't have been luckier with the weather."

"That's for sure. This time of year, we could've been having tornadoes."

"In my opinion, we've had our share of tornadoes." Holly sipped her Champagne.

"I'm glad you were determined to overcome and even flourish after all the bad stuff you've endured."

"Well, if I did, the reason was because of the aid I received from a wonderful family and wonderful friends like you. You've been important to me for years and years. When I contemplated not having you in my life, I woke up to the idea I couldn't live without you. Thank you for not giving up on me."

"I'll never give up on you, Holly. Frankly, I thought about it, but then I couldn't imagine my life without you, so I just hung on. I'd say we are two very determined people. There will be no stopping us."

Holly rested her head against Dan's shoulder. Yes, they were two determined individuals. Determined to make a good life and determined to help others.

The End

ACKNOWLEDGEMENTS

N o book ever gets published by the efforts of the author alone. In one way writing a book is a lonely activity, but it takes a village to publish a book, and this one is no exception.

First, I want to recognize my husband Bob West for his untiring support of my work as an author. For answering questions, for cheering me on, and talking with me about story ideas.

Four Beta Readers made this a better book. Thanks so much for your time and ideas: Olivia Alexander, Teresa Cromer, Janet Hallum, and Julie Miers. They gave input into the book and helped pick out the book cover. Thanks, gals.

I worked with 100 Covers, and I'm so pleased with the results for Determined.

Thanks to my editor Susan Vaughan, a wonderful author in her own right. Check out her website for her romantic suspense books. Susan Vaughan—Author of Romance...Adventure...Suspense[1]

And please remember, any mistakes are my own. ☺ Marsha

---

1.   https://www.susanvaughan.com/

OTHER BOOKS BY MARSHA R. WEST

The Second Chances Series

Second Act, Book 1

Addison Jones Greer, divorced mother of two teens, is the executive director of Cowtown Theatre. When someone murders a member of the board in the costume room, suspicion rests on everyone involved with the theatre, including Addie. She has angered some board members because she wants to fire the artistic director. Although she's warned him several times, he continues to go over budget for productions.

Mike Riley, Fort Worth homicide detective, hates that he caught this case. His sister-in-law dragged him to a theatre fundraiser where he met Addison, the first woman he's wanted to pursue a relationship within a long time. Not about to happen now.

Act of Trust, Book 2

A widow since 9/11 and a mother of a grown daughter, **Kate Thompson** wants to keep her and her daughter safe, but an unexpected inheritance of land in Maine pushes her out of her comfort zone in Texas and into the arms of a Maine lawyer.

Maine lawyer and environmentalist, **Jim Donovan** wants to protect Aunt Liddy's land and keep it from falling into the hands of developers, but first he must convince Kate Thompson she should hold on to the family land when she doesn't even want to go look at it. However, he's unprepared for the attraction each feels for the other but denies exist. Will they be able to settle the land deal before anyone else is murdered or they break each other's hearts?

Act of Betrayal, Book 3

A cosmetics company owner in Dallas, **Devon Moore**, wants to save her company from bankruptcy, but her ex-husband's embezzlement sends her into dangerous waters trying to pay back his clients, replace the money he stole from her company, and keep her and her daughter and her parents safe.

Private Investigator, **Brett Townsend**, wants to find who is threatening his new client and locate the missing money. He suspects the beautiful Devon hasn't been completely honest with him. A wife, even an ex-wife, has to know, doesn't she? When she is attacked twice and her daughter is kidnapped, he adjusts his thinking.

A**ct of Survival, Book 4**

Encouraged by her friends to protect herself, **Kim Mason Dennison** is determined to divorce her abusive husband. **Cooper Wray**, an attorney, assures Kim that her husband, Hunter, can't keep the proceedings from moving forward because Texas is a no-fault divorce state. But why is Hunter doing everything he can to stop the divorce? And will that even include murder?

Stand-Alone Books

V**ermont Escape**

Jill Barlow has lost everyone she cared about except her grown children. Caught in her father's fight to keep casino gambling out of Texas, her husband and dad are murdered. She'll do what it takes to ensure her kids safety even if it means leaving Texas and moving to Vermont.

Jerrod Phillips has come a long way in the twenty-odd years since his wife abandoned him and their two children. With no room in his heart for love, he'll do anything to keep his family from being hurt again, especially when the threats come packaged in the form of the attractive Jill Barlow who he suspects is involved in murder.

Forced to trust each other when trouble follows her, they'll battle, not only killers intent on ending her life, but the attraction drawing them together.

T ruth Be Told

Looking forward to a peaceful Christmas visit with her Fort Worth family, **Meg Bourland** is shocked to discover someone is blackmailing her father. When he rebuffs her offer to help, the Atlanta SWAT team member enlists her LA police officer brother and his former partner to uncover the truth. She fights her attraction for **Scott McClaine** and the immediate tug to her heart caused by his sacrifice. Her life is in Atlanta, and his is in California.

Scott McClaine, a medically retired homicide detective, came to Fort Worth to recuperate from life-threatening bullet wounds he received saving the life of Meg's brother. Hard enough to accept his new physical limitations, but they make him unacceptable for strong Meg. Regardless, he commits himself to helping her stop the blackmailer. Working closely with her, a bond forms. Could she feel the same?

In the search for truth, they uncover pieces of the puzzle, which threaten to ruin her father's career as mayor and destroy the family she holds dear. Will Meg and Scott find their way through the maze of family secrets? Will they find the strength to make the sacrifices required for real love before the blackmailer makes good on threats to kill?

T he Theatre

Forty-year-old, never been married stage and TV actress **Kelly Lawson** returns to her Texas home to choreograph and star in the Glenview Theatre summer season. Kelly's mother has made a hobby of trailing out every new man in town for Kelly's inspection, hoping she'll fall in love and use Glenview as her home base, especially now that Kelly's father has entered the beginning stages of Alzheimer's. Two years ago, Kelly broke off an engagement shortly before she discovered her former fiancé dead, a gun in his hand and a hole in his head. Reason enough to guard her heart.

When Kelly accuses a Glenview police officer of harassing two of the theatre's gay actors, Police Chief **Josh Kincaid**, her mother's candidate for this trip, becomes involved in the investigation. Incidents pile up, making it clear someone has it in, not only for the theatre, but for Kelly as well. Josh searches for clues to the person behind the attacks and the reason for them, all the while trying to ignore his developing feelings. How could he trust his heart to a New York actress?

Tainted

Socialite and philanthropist **Elizabeth Hartman** needs to start a new life after divorcing her husband Gerry Richardson who's in federal prison for money laundering, a crime the Feds suspected her of being involved in. Her mother's family vacation home in Red River, New Mexico offers just the respite she needs. Or does it?

One too many deaths sends retired Dallas homicide detective and now **Marshall Matt Thornton** to Red River to seek a less dangerous place to serve. The New Mexico mountains promise to be that refuge until his high school sweetheart Liz Hartman arrives, bringing with her danger to his town and his heart.

Compromise

Widowed, shop keeper, and transplanted Texan **Jessica Allen** fights to protect the Green in the New Hampshire town of Tidbury, settled by her late husband's family. New Hampshire of the beautiful fall leaves and sometimes brutal winters. She's angry to learn developers plan to use Worley Construction, a company she holds responsible for her husband's death. When a member of the board of selectmen is murdered, family and friends encourage Jessica to run for the seat. Will threats force her to compromise her principles?

Developer **Jeff Hudson** wants to build a retirement center on the Tidbury Green. Despite Jessica's opposition, he believes he can convince her of the need for the center and that its place on the Green will leave plenty of room for all of the town's activities. But has he partnered with an unsafe builder? How much money will he lose if he breaks the contract to please Jessica? Her position on the board of selectmen may cause a conflict of interest and force them apart. Will more people have to die to save the Green?

Will Jessica be forced to compromise to find her second chance at love?

Vulnerable

Interior designer and junior college professor **Maddy Crawford Crain** wants to stand on her own after the loss of her husband two years ago but being sexually harassed makes her feel vulnerable and forces her to seek help.

Former LA Homicide Detective and now security expert **David Bourland** wants to protect his heart & protect his clients after seeing his wife gunned down, but Maddy's problems draw on all his protective instincts to keep her safe.

Will David's fear of falling in love with someone who could die violently and Maddy's determination to stand on her own keep them from finding each other?

Don't miss out!

Visit the website below and you can sign up to receive emails whenever Marsha R West publishes a new book. There's no charge and no obligation.

https://books2read.com/r/B-A-HZRF-RCKXE

BOOKS 2 READ

Connecting independent readers to independent writers.

About the Author

I'm a retired elementary school principal, a former school board member, and theatre arts teacher, and write Romance, Suspense, and Second Chances. Experience Required. I live in Texas with my supportive lawyer husband and Charley, a deaf, Chihuahua/Jack Russell Terrier. Our two daughters presented us with three delightful grandchildren all who live nearby.

The theme of my eleven books is always second chances. I even named my four-part series The Second Chances Series. I believe in Happily Ever Afters. My husband picked up a plaque for me on one of our several trips to Maine that states my philosophy exactly. *Everything will be all right in the end. If it's not all right, it's not the end.* The Heroines and Heroes in my books range in age from 40 to late 50s and their parents and children often playing supporting roles.

I am a member of North Texas Romance Writers, Texas Authors Institute, and the WORD BY WORD Blog. I send out a monthly newsletter and give away an e-book to some lucky commenter. I enjoy making presentations to groups, and I've twice taught a Silver Frogs class on Indie Publishing for Texas Christian University.

Blurbs for each of my books with links can be found on my website www.marsharwest.com Where you can also sign up for my NEWSLETTER MRW Press LLC (list-manage.com)

Contact me at marsha@marsharwest.com and follow me on... https://www.facebook.com/?ref=tn_tnmn

https://www.twitter.com/Marsharwest @Marsharwest

Word By Word Blog found at https://sisterhoodofsuspense.wordpress.com/home/

https://www.pinterest.com/marsharwest/

https://www.instagram.com/marsharwest

Marsha R. West (Author of Vermont Escape) | Goodreads

I love hearing from readers and hope you'll leave a review for this book. ☺ Marsha

Read more at https://www.marsharwest.com.